"Life, in today's society, [obscured by sticker]
ing that sometimes pleasure reading gets put on the back burner. I even listen to CDs of the Scriptures on the road to get my 'Bible reading' in every day. This book, *Air of Truth*, is a refreshing, suspenseful, and captivating book. I did not want to put it down at all. It was also refreshing to know that a Christian writer could write a book, incorporating the truth of the gospel and the real biblical plan of salvation—and make it a book that keeps your interest all the way to the end. I loved the twists and turns and how the plots unfold. This book was certainly worth the time spent to read it."

David & Sharon Jones, Ministry,
Northampton Church of Christ, Hampton, VA

"Deftly plotted and skillfully executed, *Heir of Deception* offers a tantalizing tale of tangled relationships and tangled emotions. Joanne Liggan's outstanding debut novel definitely demands an encore, and *Air of Truth* delivers."

John Conley, author of *The Dragon Stone* and
other tales of Arthur, Merlin, and Cabal

"Liggan is a fine storyteller with a vivid imagination. She excels in taking the reader on a satisfying trip."

Karen Jones, writing coach and author of *Up the Bestsellers List!* and *Kingdom of Hearts*

"A story of love and passion mingled with intrigue, *Air of Truth* continues the family saga begun in Joanne Liggan's first novel, *Heir of Deception*. The second in a series of three, *Air of Truth* leaves the reader eager for the sequel."

Sonja Lauren, author of *The Covered Smile*

"The twists and turns in this novel will keep you engrossed right into its surprising conclusion. *Air of Truth* is well-titled, as Liggan drives home the adage that things are seldom what they seem..."

Connie Lapallo, author of *Dark Enough to See the Stars in a Jamestown Sky*

"Joanne has done it again with *Air of Truth*! This is a page-turner for those that love a little romance and mystery to keep you thinking. Bree Chavis is an awesome character!"

Loretta R. Walls, Author of *Spices of Life*

To Jack –
I hope you enjoy the journey!

Air of Truth

Love is not elusive, as some believe;
it is the truth that is obscure

Love,
Joanne Liggan

Air of Truth

Love is not elusive, as some believe;
it is the truth that is obscure

A Novel by

Joanne Liggan

Tate Publishing & *Enterprises*

This title is also available as a Tate Out Loud product. Visit www.tatepublishing.com for more information.

Published by Tate Publishing & Enterprises, LLC
127 E. Trade Center Terrace | Mustang, Oklahoma 73064 USA
1.888.361.9473 | www.tatepublishing.com

Tate Publishing is committed to excellence in the publishing industry. The company reflects the philosophy established by the founders, based on Psalms 68:11,
"The Lord gave the word and great was the company of those who published it."

Cover design by Jennifer Redden
Interior design by Janae J. Glass

Published in the United States of America

ISBN: 978-1-60247-518-2

07.05.02

Dedication

To my parents, Charles and Mary Anne Dunkley. It is my greatest fortune to have been raised by Christian parents who tried to instill in me Christian values and love of family. "Train up a child in the way he should go: and when he is old, he will not depart from it" (Proverbs 22:6 KJV). Thank you, Mom & Dad.

To the wonderful doctors at the Medical College of Virginia, Dr. Harold Young, and Dr. Vincent Calabrese. Thank you for being there and getting me through a very dark time in my life.

And to the dedicated workers at the National MS Society for giving hope to millions.

Acknowledgements

To my husband, Jerry, for being patient with me and my passion for writing;

To my support system, The Hanover Writers Club, for helping me stay focused and for your kind critiques;

To all who purchased my first book, *Heir of Deception*, for encouraging me to continue writing;

To my daughter and my greatest fan, Angel Dawson, for her love and support;

To Aimée West, for being my dear friend and editor:

May God continue to richly bless you all.

Chapter 1

Wednesday, May 26—El Paso, TX—

Mitchell hurried through the airport corridors toward the passenger greeting area. Glancing at his watch, he took a deep breath, mumbling to himself, "Why am I rushing? I'm an hour early, and rushing isn't going to make the plane get here any faster." He looked up at the Flight View Monitor at the map of El Paso showing all departing and incoming planes in the air. He found MW247. *That's her flight number.* Below it was ATL ELP. *Atlanta to El Paso.* And below that was 13:39 15:05. *So she left Atlanta on time at* 1:39, *and they are on schedule to arrive here at* 3:05. *Good.* He looked around the meet/greet area and headed for an empty seat. Too nervous to sit still, he was soon back on his feet, pacing and looking through the window at the white puffy clouds. "God, am I doing the right thing?" *No, I can't second guess myself. This is the right thing for Brianna. I'm only helping destiny along a little bit.* He glanced up at the monitor again in time to see the arrival time change from 15:05 to a flashing——:——.

Over the New Mexico/Texas border—

I frowned at the passenger beside me. The annoying clicking of his laptop keyboard had been torturing me since the long layover in Atlanta three hours ago. I leaned my head back on the headrest of the seat, closing my eyes.

"Irresponsible." My mother's voice echoed in my mind. I knew she was right. I was being irresponsible. *But I'm young. Can't the realities of life wait for a couple of weeks? I'm going to have to be responsible for the rest of my life.*

"Good afternoon, ladies and gentlemen," came the calm, friendly male voice from the intercom. "I'm Captain Welford, and I hope you've had a relaxing flight. If you look to the left side of the plane, you will see the Rio Grande, also known as the Rio Bravo."

I leaned over to view one of the most beautiful sights I'd ever seen. It wasn't the river that caught my interest, but the patchwork quilt around the river that was so captivating—the farmers' fields had been tilled and planted, so perfectly divided into squares.

The disembodied voice continued. "It is among the longest rivers in North America stretching—*what the...*" The intercom clicked off.

The plane quivered, lurched, then evened out again. A man in a blue shirt rushed to the front of the plane. Wide-eyed passengers gasped. Flight attendants, regaining their balance, calmly helped to wipe up spills and attempted to reassure nervous travelers. The FASTEN SEATBELT sign lit up, and one of the attendants grabbed the intercom microphone. "Please remain calm. A little turbulence is perfectly normal at this altitude. There is no cause for alarm."

I watched for the man who had rushed to the front of the plane, hoping he was an air marshal and not a hijacker.

Another click and the captain's voice continued. "Sorry about that, ladies and gentlemen. As your flight attendant said, there is no cause for alarm. Everything is under control." The seatbelt sign blinked off, and the man in the blue shirt walked calmly back to his seat. "As I was saying, the Rio Grande stretches 1900 miles through New Mexico, forming the boundary between Texas and Mexico for about 1300 miles. It empties into the Gulf of Mexico at Brownsville, Texas. I want to take this opportunity to thank you for flying Midwest Airlines. Please relax and enjoy the rest of your flight."

I noticed the pilot's tone wasn't as composed as before.

The passenger next to me who had been working feverishly on his computer, so absorbed in his work that he hadn't acknowledged my existence, now put his laptop away.

Finally!

He grabbed a magazine and began to flip the pages. Ironically, a picture of my mother and a few of her designs was the center fold-out of the publication. I smiled, pride swelling within me when I saw my mother's photo; the dark eyes, high cheekbones, and long, straight raven hair portraying her Shawnee heritage. But my smile faded when I thought of all the hours of hard work she'd put into her career. Her entire life was work. She seemed happy, but there's got to be more to life than a job.

The keyboard demon cut his eyes at me and smirked, "First flight, huh?"

"Why would you think that?"

"You looked a little panicked by the turbulence."

"It was a bit unusual, don't you think? I've been on a lot of flights, but never experienced anything quite like that."

"Oh, a world traveler!" he scoffed.

His surly attitude irritated me. "Excuse me." I pointed to the magazine that was still opened to the page about my mother. "Have you heard of that lady, Rachel Chavis of Brittain Designs?"

He looked down at the magazine. "You mean this fashion designer?"

"She's my mother. And, yes, I have been around the world a few times, thank you very much." Why did I do that? I sounded like a spoiled brat. Why should I care if this stranger believes me or not? I realized it wasn't the man who had riled me, but his earlier incessant tapping of his keyboard, and I knew I was being unreasonable. He had every right to work on his computer. Great! So now I'm irresponsible and unreasonable.

"I'm sorry. I didn't mean to offend you." The male voice broke into my thoughts, and I focused on the face of the man next to me. He was muscular, in his late twenties or early thirties, with sandy hair and icy blue eyes that seemed to look right through me. "Can we start over?" He held out his hand. "I'm Paul Kellerman."

I shook his hand. "Brianna Chavis."

"So what brings you to this part of the world, Miss Chavis?"

Still feeling embarrassed about my immature behavior, I found it difficult to look him in the eye. "Visiting a friend stationed at Holloman Air Force Base. And you?"

"Medical conference in Phoenix."

"Oh, a doctor." I tried to act impressed. "What's your specialty?"

"I'm a family practitioner, but the conference is about auto-immune diseases."

"Where's your practice?"

"At the moment, I'm in Chicago, but I'd prefer to relocate to a small town. I'd like to bring back the family physician that actually makes house calls."

Now I was impressed. "Maybe you should try Eastridge. We could use another doctor. Old Doc Wilson is probably going to retire soon."

The FASTEN SEATBELT sign flashed and the plane began the descent into El Paso. The doctor busied himself, shuffling papers and storing them into his briefcase with the laptop, while I used the time to freshen my makeup and brush my hair. Being shoulder-length, it could look stringy when not brushed, especially since I'd added the highlights to brighten up the drab auburn color, which had only dried it out and turned it bright red. At least it isn't drab anymore.

As we exited the plane and were herded by the horde of rushing travelers through a narrow hallway, the doctor leaned toward me so I could hear him over the noise. "I've got to run to catch my connecting flight. It was nice to meet you. I hope you enjoy your visit with your friend."

"Thanks. Enjoy your conference."

We spilled into the vast waiting area. Mitchell stood in front of the waiting throng with open arms and a big smile. He was an inch taller than me with brown hair and brown eyes behind metal-rimmed glasses.

After giving him a big bear-hug, I looked around for the doctor, but he'd disappeared into the crowd.

Turning back to Mitchell, I was glad to see he hadn't changed. Although a bit of a nerd, he'd always managed to wear the most stylish fashions. Here he stood impeccably clothed in his plaid western shirt with tan corduroy slacks hugging his slim hips. Probably not the most fashionable thing to wear anywhere else, but perfectly appropriate for here. All he needed was a cowboy hat. "So how's my favorite cowboy?"

"Terrific, now that you're finally here. How was the flight?" Placing his arm around my waist, he led me through the terminal to baggage claim.

"It was a little scary toward the end. They claimed it was only a little turbulence, but it was unlike any I've ever experienced."

"The flight monitor acted a little strange. At one point it didn't show an arrival time at all, which made me a bit nervous. But that only lasted a few seconds."

"All I know is I quickly realized that this girl is nowhere near ready to meet her maker."

"Of course not. You've still got a lot of living to do."

"That's right. I haven't even found the love of my life yet." I was half joking, but noticed a gleam in his eye as he grinned at me. "And what is that look all about?"

"Sometimes we don't recognize what's so clear to others."

"What is that supposed to mean?"

"You've met the love of your life. You just didn't know it."

I stopped walking and stared at him, hoping he wasn't talking about himself. I loved him as my best friend, like a brother, and wouldn't want to hurt him. I worried that I might have given him the wrong idea by coming to visit. "And who would that be?"

"Never mind. You'll figure it out soon enough. Come on." Our arms full of luggage, he led me through the parking lot to an antiquated white Chevrolet station wagon with a broken windshield. I smiled when I noticed the cowboy hat sitting on the dashboard. A blue uniform, covered with plastic from the dry cleaners, hung on a hook over the rear door. I noticed the insignia, four wing-shaped bars with a star in the center. On the backseat sat a blue hat with black rim and band.

He cranked the starter several times before the engine coughed and sputtered, then jerked forward, rattling and squeaking along the way. Mitchell saw me cringe and laughed. "Sorry about the wheels, but it's all I need to get me to work and back." He switched on the radio and static filled the air. "Oh, come on now," he muttered, jiggling the knob until the station finally broke through, bits and pieces of music interrupted every few seconds by buzzing and scraping sounds.

I cast him an inquiring look, but he stared straight ahead. I groaned. "Are you really enjoying that noise?"

"No, but it's time for the news, and I haven't had a chance to read the paper today. I like to keep abreast of things that might affect my job." He reached over and turned up the volume as the reporter began his newscast.

The first report related to threats against United States' allies. It was difficult to decipher much through the crackling noises. The correspondent's voice changed from serious to light-hearted, a note of skepticism evident. "In other news, another unidenti*krkrkrk*ing object was *krkrkrk* early this morning *krkrkrk* 3:00 a.m., Mr. and Mrs. David E. March of Galveston spotted *krkrkrk* lights *krkrkrk* took a ninety-degree turn, straight upw*krkrkrk* disappeared. This makes the fourth UFO reported this month off the coast *krkrkrk*."

Mitchell clicked off the radio. "The stupid media! Always stirring things up."

His irritation took me by surprise. I'd known Mitchell for eight years and had never seen him angry about anything. "You can't blame them; they're simply trying to keep the public informed. That situation in the Middle East worries me."

"We can handle the Mid-East. It's those blasted flying saucer reports that get people thinking crazy."

"Oh, those prank reports have been going on for years. Most people don't even listen to them anymore. People who claim they've seen them must be desperate for attention, or maybe the increase of drug use has something to do with it. These so-called sightings are probably drug-induced hallucinations."

Mitchell glanced at me but didn't bother to comment. I peered into the sky, silently speculating about the possibility of life on other planets. "By the way, how far is Roswell from here?"

With an eye roll and a deep breath, Mitchell smiled. "Far enough. That's a two-and-a-half-hour drive we will *not* be taking while you're here."

"Did I say I wanted to go there? I was just wondering."

We both fell quiet, my thoughts turning to all the reports I'd heard through the years concerning UFOs. My Grandpa Raymond had told stories about the 1940s and 50s, and how the first UFO was found in Roswell. The government had squelched the conjectures by informing the media that it had been a huge six-hundred-foot weather balloon experiment.

"So tell me what's been going on with you." His voice brought me back down to earth.

"I don't know where to start. Getting fired from the bank has created problems I've never had to deal with before." I'd written to him soon after losing my job, and he'd responded by sending me the airline ticket.

"You mean, like being poor?"

"Exactly! I don't want to go back to depending on Momma and Daddy, but I'm going to have to do something soon. Bills are piling up. I shouldn't even be taking the time to come here, but I figured one or two weeks out of my life can't make that much difference. And I really needed to see my best friend. You always know how to make me feel better about things."

"You never told me why you were fired. What happened?"

I'd left out the details in my letter because of my embarrassment over the circumstances. I hesitated, then decided Mitchell was the perfect confidant. He was a gentle soul who never judged anyone. In fact, he was so benevolent, I was having trouble picturing him in a military uniform. "I told my boss 'no.'"

"No what?"

"No, I wouldn't go out with him. No, I wouldn't have sex with him. No, I wouldn't lie to his wife for him. Little things like that."

"How can he fire you for that?"

"Well, obviously that's not what he told personnel. He told them that I was fired because I'd missed too much time from work."

"Had you?"

"I'd been out with the flu, which turned into a horrible cold. I almost wound up in the hospital with pneumonia, so I missed two weeks of work. The day I went back, he approached me with this little idea of me going out with him. He'd hinted at it before, but I never took him seriously. This time, he was straightforward. When I asked him how his wife would feel about it, he told me to leave his wife out of it."

"Let me get this straight. This guy is asking you out, and you respond by asking him how his wife would feel?"

"Well, I thought that was kind of an important detail. Anyway, I told him that I don't go out with married men, and that's when he threatened me. He said if I didn't do things his way, he'd fire me. I went straight to personnel and filed a report about it, but they said they didn't want any controversy within the company. They told me to go back to work and keep my mouth shut, and they'd talk to him. But at the end of the day, he told me I was fired. When I went back to personnel, they said there was nothing they could do because it was my word against his, and I had missed too many days."

"If that happened anywhere except the backwoods city

of Eastridge, they'd never let that slide. But even in Eastridge, it sounds like a lawsuit to me."

"It's like they said, my word against his. Being a respected member of the community, no one would ever believe he would do such a thing. I couldn't believe it myself! I'm still in shock."

"But you're from a highly respected family yourself! Your Aunt Marty used to be the mayor. Do you really think people would believe him over you?"

"Don't forget, my daddy was from the most respected family in town, but that didn't stop everyone from believing he killed his mother. He was convicted and put in prison, remember?" Although that had all happened before I was born, it was a well-known and much-talked-about event in Eastridge. "Everyone in town knows me as Rachel Chavis's daughter, and people love nothing more than a good scandal when it comes to famous people. I can see the headlines now: 'Rachel Chavis's daughter slanders bank official.' I couldn't do that to my mother and her career. It's better to let it drop."

"So what are you going to do now?"

"Look for another job, I guess. I brought along a list of places to look into. Maybe I could use your computer?"

"Sure."

I didn't want to think about job hunting right now. I only wanted to enjoy my vacation and forget about my problems. "So enough about me, what's happening with you?"

"Work keeps me busy."

"So what is it you do at the base?"

"Mostly paperwork. Everyone thinks if you're in the

Air Force, you must be a pilot. But there are other jobs to be done. I'm actually an accountant. Not very exciting, huh?"

"There's nothing wrong with being an accountant." An accountant? What kind of news report would he be concerned about affecting his job? Tax or stock issues maybe. But he'd switched off the radio before they reported on financial news. Why did he get so riled about that UFO report? My mind was wandering. I tried to focus back on the conversation. "Before you came here, you were working for a law firm. I thought you would become a lawyer. What happened?"

"That was only a part-time job. I never wanted to be a lawyer. I've always liked working with numbers and someone else's money."

"You never told me that. I had no idea you wanted to be an accountant."

"Being an accountant doesn't exactly make for titillating conversation."

"So, why the Air Force? Why not go into private practice?"

"I probably will eventually. By joining up, the government paid for my education. I chose the Air Force because I'm fascinated by jets and other aircraft."

I looked ahead at the endless straight road. "How much farther?"

"You might as well sit back and enjoy the ride. Alamogordo is at least eighty miles from the airport, and we've only gone about thirty so far."

I gazed through the dirty, cracked windows at the desert sand and cacti. There were miles and miles of nothing—no trees, no grass, nothing but dirt and the occasional cactus, hut, or brown shrub—not even another vehicle. The road was a black line drawn in the sand and stretching straight ahead as far as I could see. In the distance was the brown outline of mountains. Not even the mountains were green.

Mitchell began to beat his fingers nervously against the steering wheel. "So are you dating anyone? I know you were seeing that guy, Mark. Are you still?"

My love life was the last thing I wanted to talk about. "No. He wanted to get married, but I turned him down. He wasn't the right guy for me."

"I could have told you that."

"How would you know? You never met him."

"I could tell from your letters that you weren't that crazy over him." We rode along in silence for a few minutes before he continued, smiling, "Hey, do you remember when we met?"

"Of course. It was in that garage where your band was practicing and Troy brought me along to meet all of you."

"Yeah, the band. I really miss those guys. Ol' Rusty on the drums and Bobby on the bass. But Troy, now he was one talented musician. He could play the guitar, keyboards, sax, whatever we needed. Do you ever think about him?"

"Sometimes." I shrugged and tried to sound indifferent. I didn't want Mitchell to know how often I thought of Troy. I hadn't seen or heard from him in seven years, but time hadn't cured the void he'd left in my heart. "Do you still play the guitar?"

"Yeah. I have a regular gig here in a little restaurant a few nights a week."

"That's great! I might get to hear you play then." I yawned. "Sorry, I guess I'm a little tired from the flight."

"Why don't you sit back and rest? I'll wake you when we get to town."

Closing my eyes, I saw Troy; the proverbial tall, dark, and handsome. Why did Mitch have to mention him? I forced myself to think about Mitchell rather than Troy. Mitchell was there for me so many times. Ever since Troy discarded me, Mitchell had been like a big brother, always looking out for me. And here he was again, coming to my rescue. When everyone else thought I should be doing the sensible and "responsible" thing, looking for another job so I can pay bills, Mitch understood my frustration and offered me the opportunity to get away from it all.

I must have dozed off, but the next thing I knew, the car slowed down and I opened my eyes.

"Welcome to Alamogordo." Mitchell maneuvered the car to merge with the other slow traffic and rolled down his window. A parade of smiling pedestrians and motorists waved and yelled greetings to one another.

Cranking down my window, I smiled and waved. "Everyone is so relaxed and happy."

"That's the beauty of living here. No one worries about the time. Everyone takes life slow and simple so they can enjoy as much of it as possible."

The majority of the townspeople were Mexican, and I caught bits of Spanish conversation as we rode along. Adobe huts scattered among modern shops and hamburger stands created the illusion of a double-exposed photograph of the Old West and modern day.

We soon left the main part of town, continuing down another straight, flat highway. There was still nothing green in sight and the lack of color was disturbing. Back home, flowers were in full bloom, and there was the freshness of spring green everywhere. Here everything blended together with dull browns and grays. In the pale light of dusk, it was a dismal place—*eerie* in fact. Although the evening temperature was in the mid eighties, a sudden chill ran through me.

Mitchell steered the rattletrap onto a dirt road that led into a mobile-home park, and we bounced along until we came to a dusty halt in front of a long, tan trailer. "Here we are. Home sweet home. My roommate is out of town for a few weeks and said it's okay for you to stay here while he's gone."

My father's warning echoed in my head. When I'd told my parents about this trip, he'd said, "Bree, honey, a man doesn't usually pay for a woman to come see him unless he expects something in return. You might think he's only a friend, but Mitch might be thinking it's more than that." I froze beside the car scrutinizing the unappealing accommodations while Mitchell began unloading my luggage. Okay, maybe this wasn't such a good idea.

The door of the trailer opened and a woman about five years older than me came bounding down the salt-treated wood steps. "I see ya'll made it jest fine. I'm Gina, and I guess you're Bree."

I nodded. Gina was shorter than my five-foot-six frame, with a slightly chubby figure, short black hair, and cherubic face, accented by round-rimmed glasses and a joyful disposition.

Mitchell handed us the smaller pieces of luggage. "Gina will be staying with us, and I'll be sleeping in a room at the other end of the trailer. I figured you might be more comfortable if you had another female around." He winked.

I followed Gina and Mitchell into the trailer. I should have known better than to doubt Mitch. He's got to be the most considerate man I've ever met. It's really too bad there's no chemistry between us. He'll make someone a terrific husband.

I unpacked my things while Gina fixed sandwiches.

After eating my sandwich, I retreated to my room. It had been a long, tiring day, and I was soon sound asleep.

Thursday, May 27—Alamogordo—

I awoke before dawn to the braying of an automobile engine and jumped up, peeking through the window curtains in time to see the departing taillights of Mitchell's car. Reaching for my robe, I followed the aroma of freshly perked coffee to the kitchen where Gina was washing their breakfast dishes.

She turned with a smile. "I hope we didn't wake you. We tried to be quiet as possible. There's some eggs and toast in the oven keepin' warm for ya if ya want 'em." Her southern drawl was as cheerful on this extremely early morning as it had been the night before.

I wasn't hungry, but since Gina had gone to so much trouble to fix and keep my breakfast warm, it would be rude not to eat. I pretended to be starved and thanked Gina for all her trouble.

"Twern't no trouble. I had to cook Mitch's and mine, so I jest threw on another couple of eggs for you."

"Well, thanks anyway. Do you always get up so early down here?"

"Mitch usually has to be at the office by seven and it's a long drive from here." Gina's eyes sparkled with excitement. "How would you like to go into town with me? I've been dyin' to get me some new jeans. I saw a picture of some your mom designed. Of course, I can't afford those, but I thought I'd try to find something similar."

"Sounds great! I'll go get dressed."

The air was nippy, so I chose to wear jeans and a sweatshirt. Wandering outside to wait for Gina, I gazed across the wide-open spaces. The ground was completely flat with a few bushes and a tree or two scattered around. Jagged mountains outlined the horizon where the sun rose over the distant hills, changing the barren ground and mountains into shimmering gold. In the light of day, it was no longer gloomy, but friendly and peaceful.

The sun's blazing rays quickly turned the morning chill to steam. It was obviously going to be too hot for jeans and long sleeves. I retreated back inside to change into more appropriate apparel.

Dressed in shorts and a halter top, Gina gave me a knowing smile. "I figured ya might change your mind about those long sleeves. That's the way it is here. The nights are cool, but when the sun's up, it can get hot as blue blazes."

Gina's aqua Volkswagen buzzed toward town. I rode along quietly taking in the scenery until Gina broke the silence. "I've been wanting a pair of them jeans for so long, but I really don't need 'em. Mitch knew how bad I wanted 'em though, so being the sweet guy he is, he gave me some money so I could go buy some today."

Why would Mitch be giving Gina money? I wondered if he was paying Gina to stay at the trailer with me. "Have you known Mitch very long?" I pried.

"Almost a year. He came into my restaurant in answer to an ad I ran in the newspaper for a musician to entertain in the evenin's. I was having a hard time decidin' between him and this other guy, but they teamed up and formed a duet and have been workin' for me ever since."

Mitchell playing guitar brought back memories of the old band, and I found myself thinking of Troy again. I recalled the night my daddy finally allowed me to attend a school dance where Troy's band was performing. I arrived as the band stopped for a break and saw Troy with another girl. At the tender age of fifteen, it shattered my world. Now, eight years later, I could still feel the sting. And that was only the first time he'd hurt me. I actually let him back into my life after that and was disillusioned again a year later.

I tried to shake thoughts of Troy from my mind. "Why did Mitch have to be at work so early?"

"That's not early for servicemen. Mitch doesn't work regular hours. He more or less goes in whenever he's needed. Sometimes he works sixteen-hour days and other days he only works four or five hours. All depends on what's going on."

"But he's an accountant. I would expect fairly consistent hours for that type of job."

Gina shrugged and raised her eyebrow. "You would

think so, huh? But I guess it must be different when you're working for the government, because they are always calling him in on weekends and for special meetings."

I looked at Gina, deciding if I should explore the subject further. I had a nagging feeling that there was more to Mitchell's job than we knew. I decided to drop it until I could learn more.

The little shopping center was a series of quaint shops with papier-mâché animals, macramé items, and kites hanging outside the entrances. We browsed these items until the stores opened, then purchased Gina's jeans. I tagged along as Gina proceeded to a music shop where she purchased guitar strings for Mitchell. I didn't want to leave empty-handed, so I bought an inexpensive necklace with a delicate chain and hand-painted locket.

In no rush to go back to the trailer, we stopped to eat lunch at a charming little diner, sitting and talking well into the afternoon. Mitchell was waiting for us when we finally arrived back at the trailer.

Gina looked surprised. "What are you doing here?"

"I took off a couple of hours early. No big shots were around, so I snuck away." He threw his arms around Gina and gave her a long, tender kiss. I tried to conceal my surprise. Feeling like an intruder, I wanted to slither from the room. Obviously, my father was wrong about Mitchell's motives for giving me this vacation.

Breaking away from the embrace, Mitchell turned to me. "I wish I could take you sightseeing today, but I really need to rehearse for tonight's gig. I hope you don't mind. I'll take a day of vacation tomorrow to make up for it."

Veiling my discomfort, I shrugged. "I don't expect you to entertain me while I'm here. I'm fine."

Mitchell settled himself on the sofa with his guitar and began playing a mixture of folk, rock, pop, and Salsa tunes. Before I realized it, I was singing along. He stopped playing and looked at me.

Embarrassed, I tucked my head and smiled up at him. "Sorry."

"Hey, you're not bad. I had no idea you could sing. With a little practice, maybe we can do something together before you leave."

My pulse quickened at the thought of singing on stage. I looked at Gina. "What are you trying to do, lose Gina's customers for her?"

Gina giggled. "I think Mitch is right. The two of you should sing something together."

We practiced a couple of songs, enough to discover that our voices blended well. At least I thought so, but Mitch didn't seem too excited about it. "We'll practice more later, but right now I'd better worry about tonight." He continued practicing alone.

I slipped into the bedroom to call home. I debated between Momma's office phone, her home phone, or her cell phone. Not that it mattered. I guess one voicemail is as good as another, but I knew she'd be more likely to check her cell phone before the home phone, and if I called her at work, I'd have to talk to her nosy assistant, Milly. So I dialed her cell phone and waited for the beep.

"Hi, Momma. I just wanted to wish you and Daddy a Happy Anniversary. I love you."

Meanwhile, back in Eastridge…

It had been a long day of meetings and conference calls. Rachel Chavis hung up the phone and gazed through the tinted windows of her top-floor office. She didn't see the birds in flight or the sun setting over the picturesque little city of Eastridge tucked into the Appalachian foothills. Instead, she was recalling the day she and Collin had stood before Aunt Marty and said their wedding vows. *I can't believe that was twenty-four years ago.* She smiled. *They've been good years. Collin's a wonderful husband and has been so supportive of my career.* She pulled her thoughts back into her office and looked around at the pictures and award plaques lining the walls. Her eyes focused on the photograph of their children. *Ahh, Bree, searching so desperately for your place in this world. But you're smart and sassy. You'll no doubt be a success one day. And dear Jesse. You've needed a lot of prodding, but hopefully you'll get your act together soon.*

Her intercom popped. "Excuse me, Rachel. I'm ready to head home, but I have a few messages for you."

"That's fine, Milly. Come on in."

Her office door opened. She smiled at the little woman with the short salt-and-pepper hair and hazel eyes. Milly had been her first friend in the town of Eastridge over a quarter of a century ago. As soon as Rachel's rise in the fashion industry afforded her the luxury of an assistant, she'd insisted that Milly take the position. Rachel attributed much of her success to Milly's efficiency.

Milly hurried to Rachel's desk. "I didn't want to bother you, but Heather called. She needs me to watch Caleb tonight, so I need to go." She sorted through the pink message slips in her hand. "Let's see. The Paris office called. They needed more organza for gown 452. Their supplier can't get anymore for two weeks, so I had Brent ship some of ours to them since we have plenty in stock." She flipped to the next message. "Monroe called from Venice. He needs you to call him about, quote, the situation you discussed last week, end quote. He sounded rather mysterious. What is that all about?"

"He wants to retire and have me buy out his half of the business."

Milly's eyes widened. "Wow, I had no idea he was thinking of retiring."

"He's been running this company for over fifty years, and now he's ready to benefit from the fruits of his labors while he and Enrique are still young enough to travel and enjoy themselves." Monroe and Enrique had been lovers for many years, but had remained quiet about their relationship for most of them. Now they spent nearly all of their time in Europe where people were more accepting of the gay lifestyle than they were in Eastridge.

Milly's attention shifted back to the messages in her hand. "There's also a call here from Dr. Vernelli at Eastridge Medical. He wants you to call him. Are you okay?"

"I had some routine tests done. I'm sure there's nothing to worry about. I'll give him a call tomorrow."

Milly hesitated, but decided she shouldn't push. "There are a couple of other minor calls here that you can take care of tomorrow. And last, but most important, your husband called and said he's running late, so he'll meet you at the country club restaurant at 6:30."

Rachel glanced at her watch—5:05—enough time to go home and freshen up and change. "So you're babysitting your grandson tonight, huh?"

Milly beamed. "Yes, it's so much fun being a grandma! I never thought I would enjoy it so much."

"Well, Grandma, I guess you better get out of here."

"You're right. I'll see you tomorrow." She handed the messages to Rachel and scurried back to her office.

"Good evening, Mrs. Chavis. Your husband is waiting. I'll show you to your table." The maître d' led her through the elegant restaurant to a private dining room.

Soft music played, and Collin stood when she entered. "There's my lovely bride, still as beautiful as you were twenty-four years ago."

"Oh my, aren't you being gallant tonight." She smiled, looking into his clear blue eyes. "And you, my dear husband, are more handsome than ever." She truly felt that he was. His graying temples gave him an air of confidence. *There is nothing sexier than self-confidence*, she thought as she took her seat. "I'm glad we're having a quiet dinner for our anniversary this year, but what about next year? It'll be our silver anniversary. Should we plan a big party?"

"Let's not even think about next year. Tonight is just for us. No kids, no business, only you and me. In fact, where is your cell phone?"

She reached into her purse and pulled out the phone. He took it from her and turned it off.

The meal began with a delicious crab bisque soup. They were finishing their salads when her favorite song began to play. *At Last* by Celine Dion. She looked at her husband and smiled, realizing that he'd remembered and requested it be played during their meal. He held out his hand and they danced.

After the hectic lives they led day in and day out, tonight was like a mini-vacation.

They returned to their table as the main course arrived. Rachel tasted her lobster. "I got a message from Bree. She called to wish us a Happy Anniversary. Collin, do you think we should have stopped her from going to New Mexico?"

"Come on, Rae, do you really think we could stop her? She's twenty-three years old with a mind of her own. You raised her to be independent. You can't change that now."

"I know, but I still worry about her."

"She'll be okay. Let's not worry about her tonight. This night is about you and me."

"But this *is* about us. She and Jesse are the best part of us. When they turned eighteen, I thought I could stop worrying about them, but I worry about them now more than ever."

He looked into her dark brown eyes and shook his head. "We have to let them make their own mistakes and establish their own lives. We can't do that for them." He stood up, holding out his hand. "Let's dance."

Trying to ignore the pain surging through her right arm, Rachel smiled, took a slow and silent breath in an attempt to breathe through the pain, and took her husband's hand.

Alamogordo, New Mexico—

I sat at a corner table watching Mitchell adjust his equipment on the small platform. Gina disappeared into the kitchen. The restaurant was cozy with its wooden beams across the ceiling and columns supporting the roof. Rustic wooden chandeliers hung from the ceiling with electric candles throwing a soft glow through the room. Mouth-watering aromas filled the air each time the kitchen door swung open.

Finishing my steak dinner, I glanced around the room and spotted Gina greeting a man at the door. He was short, blond, and carried a guitar case. Gina smiled as they looked my way, then started toward me.

"Bree, this is Jacques Borgman. He's Mitch's singin' partner."

Jacques caressed me with his eyes and gently lifted my hand, brushing it with his lips. "How very nice to meet you, Bree." He had a throaty French accent. "I look forward to getting to know you, but now I must get ready. Excuse me, please."

Watching them perform, I was amazed at how two men from completely different backgrounds and cultures could come together to create such perfect harmony in their music. Jacques was sophisticated and smooth, while Mitchell was plain and unpretentious. Jacques looked a little shifty, and there was something about him that made me think he could be hot-tempered, and Mitchell was honest to a fault and mild-mannered. But somehow these differences disappeared when they began playing.

I sat alone for most of the evening, observing the two men. During breaks, Mitchell mingled with the crowd, seeming to forget I was there. I watched Jacques go into the kitchen. When he reappeared, another man was talking to him. I was struck by the other man's appearance; olive skin, coal black wavy hair, prominent nose, possibly Italian or Greek.

Gina walked past my table, so I touched her arm. "Gina, who is that with Jacques?"

She gave me a wicked grin. "That's our cook. Isn't he gorgeous?" Then she continued working the room, checking on her patrons.

Jacques strolled over to my table. "How are you enjoying the music?"

I smiled. "It's beautiful. Do you and Mitch practice a lot together?"

"No, we only play here together. We never practice what we will do. We, what he calls, 'wing it.'" He turned to see Mitchell back on stage and excused himself, making his way back to the platform.

I couldn't help wondering why such a refined man would be living in this crude setting. He definitely seemed out of his element.

Friday, May 28–Eastridge—

Rachel and Collin sat in the frigid, claustrophobic examination room waiting for Dr. Vernelli. Rachel fidgeted with her bracelet. "I don't understand why we have to wait in this little room for a simple consultation about the results of the tests he took." She stood and began to pace, wringing her hands. "I've got so many things to do today at work. We've been waiting here for over forty-five minutes! Where on earth is this doctor?"

Collin stood and put his arms around her. "I'm sure he'll be here any minute. Work can wait. Your health comes first."

"Well, if he doesn't come soon, I'm going to send him a bill for my time. It's ridiculous for doctors to make you wait so long. Do they think no one has anything to do but sit around a doctor's office?"

The door opened and Dr. Vernelli emerged. Rachel broke away from Collin's embrace. Forgetting the prolonged wait, she searched the doctor's face for a hint of whether he brought good or bad news, but there was no clue other than the lack of eye contact. "I apologize for the wait. I was getting a second opinion on your tests before I gave you my diagnosis. Rachel, I'm afraid you might have multiple sclerosis. The MRI shows a few lesions in your brain, and the spinal tap results support the possibility of MS." He was being very clinical, showing no emotion or compassion.

Rachel looked at Collin, hoping she'd heard wrong, but the tears in his eyes doused those hopes. Her lungs deflated as if she'd been sucker-punched. Taking a deep breath, she tried to remain stoic as she turned to face the doctor, her voice weak. "So what do we do now?"

"I'm sorry, Rachel, but I can't help you. I suggest you find someone that specializes in that area."

"What do you mean? Can't you recommend someone?" Still reeling from the shock, she felt dazed, unable to muster enough energy to be angry.

"No. There's nothing we can do for MS. No one knows what causes it, and there is no cure. I'm very sorry." He opened the door and was gone before they could stop him.

Rachel and Collin stood in each other's arms staring at the door, tears streaming down their faces. Collin broke the silence as he held her next to his chest and stroked her hair. "He said you *might* have MS, not that you do. We'll get another opinion. Don't worry, honey, we'll find someone that can help. Let's go home."

Rachel agreed. Suddenly work didn't seem so important.

New Mexico—

The aroma of freshly perked coffee drew me from the depths of slumber. The smells of home warmed my inner being, filling me with tranquility and making me smile.

I expected Momma would soon be coming to awaken me. Opening my eyes to the strange surroundings, reality slowly edged in. I moseyed into the kitchen and found a note on the table: *Gone to the ranch. Mitch.*

What ranch? I thought he said he was going to take off from work to spend time with me.

Gina appeared in the doorway wearing a swimsuit and matching cover-up.

I held up the note. "What's this about a ranch?"

Gina poured two glasses of orange juice. "Mitch had a little errand to run for a friend and wanted to get it over with early so he can spend the rest of the day with you. He's gonna meet us at my folks' place later. They have a pool, so I thought we could go for a mornin' swim. Jacques might join us there later too." She seemed to be waiting for a reaction from me after the mention of Jacques's name. Could she actually believe I'd be interested in Jacques?

Gina's parents owned a Spanish-style stucco rancher with a cemented front yard. It was landscaped beautifully with cacti growing through holes formed in the concrete.

Gina noticed my puzzled expression. "What's wrong?"

"I've never seen anyone pave their entire yard before."

"It's hard to grow grass around here because of the dry weather, and if you don't cover the ground with something, it can get awfully dusty."

I looked at the surrounding lawns. One was covered with white stone, but two others had beautiful grass. "What about those? How did they get their grass to grow?"

Gina laughed. "Mr. Ayers across the street has an elaborate sprinkler system that's timed to come on every few hours. It's terrific if you can afford it, but I wouldn't want to pay his water and electric bills, not to mention what all the equipment cost him. And Cheryl, next door, cheated." She walked over to the other yard, motioning for me to follow. "Look closer at her so-called 'grass.'"

I bent down and tried to pull a blade of the short-cropped greenery. "It's plastic!"

"That's right." Gina giggled. "I guess there's nothing the plastic industry can't replace with their versatile product."

Gina led the way through the house and into a modern kitchen and great room. Sliding glass doors opened onto the cement patio that surrounded the Olympic-sized pool.

The two of us stretched out on our towels in the sun before going for a swim. Mitchell arrived at eleven thirty, and Jacques joined us ten minutes later. Jacques's hungry eyes watched as I swam across the pool, making me self-conscious in my bathing suit. My towel hung on a chair at the opposite end of the patio. Collecting my nerve, I emerged from the pool, the warm water tugging gently at the bit of material that made up the bottom half of my suit. As I went to retrieve my towel, the water steadily streamed down my legs, splattering onto the cement. Refusing to look up, I could feel Jacques's gaze following me.

Gina yelled from the kitchen doorway, "Mitch and I are going to pick up a pizza. Jacques, you and Bree enjoy the pool. We won't be gone long. It's just around the corner."

Snuggled in my towel, I sat at the edge of the pool

with my feet dangling into the water watching Jacques swim laps. Feeling less intimidated and wanting an even tan, I spread the towel behind me and lay back to gaze into the clear blue sky. The heat of the sun was intense, making it difficult to lie there more than a few minutes. I sat up and stared into the pool, mesmerized by the bright, glittering water, and tried to figure out what I was doing there. I knew I should be home finding a job. Mitch and Gina didn't need me hanging around, and I certainly didn't want to be matched up with Jacques for the sake of not being in their way like an extra appendage.

By the time I realized Jacques was headed toward me, it was too late to escape. He jumped from the water, showering me with its refreshing coolness, and plopped down next to me. "You look unhappy. Is there anything I can do to cheer you up?" He sounded genuinely concerned.

"Maybe so. Do you get the feeling that Gina and Mitch might be doing a little matchmaking?"

"You mean between you and me?" He looked shocked.

I tried to dismiss the idea. "I'm probably being silly." Wishing I hadn't blurted out my thoughts, I attempted to change the subject. "So what do you do, other than play music at the restaurant?"

"I work for the government."

"Oh? Doing what?"

"Acquisitions."

Whatever that means. He was obviously not interested in talking about his job, and I wasn't overly enthralled, so I gave up on the conversation and reached for my towel.

Jacques changed the subject. "Tell me something. What's the deal with you and Mitch?"

I shrugged. "We're friends. He's like a big brother to me."

"I watched last night. He was very rude to leave you alone. He ignored you most of the evening."

"I didn't mind. Like I said, we're only friends."

Jacques leaned closer to me in an attempt to put his arm around my bare waist. "So you think maybe he is trying to do some matchmaking between you and me?"

Jacques was cute, in a little boy sort of way, and the choppy way he spoke made him even more charming; but there was something unnerving about him. I slipped into the water and swam to the other side of the pool to avoid his advances. When I turned to swim back, I bumped into him. He reached out, grabbed me around the waist, and pulled me toward him, claiming my lips before I could react. Stunned, I jerked away in time to see Mitchell in the doorway. Looking as shocked as I felt, he quickly retreated into the house. I turned back to see Jacques smiling.

"We will know now by his reaction how he feels about you." Jacques pulled himself out of the water and onto the pool's edge, then reached for my hand to help me exit the pool. "Let's go eat some pizza." Rather than take his hand, I swam to the ladder.

The four of us sat soberly eating our pizza, a heavy silence hovering in the air. Mitchell glared at Jacques, but said nothing. Without warning, he jumped up, knocking his chair over, and schlepped away to the other side of the pool.

With one look between us and no words necessary, Gina and I decided to leave the guys alone to settle their differences. Gina grabbed her keys. "We're going back to the trailer for a nice, quiet siesta. If you two decide to join us later, please leave your bickering behind."

Jacques shrugged and was the epitome of innocence. "I don't know what is going on. I am not the one who is angry." He glanced at Mitchell, who glared back at him.

Gina continued. "Well, when you two can agree that there's nothing wrong, then maybe we can all have a good time together. But right now, I don't feel like standing here in the line of fire. We'll see you later."

When we reached the car, we could hear Mitchell's voice explode as he released the resentment he'd been suppressing.

"Thar she blows!" Gina laughed as she and I slammed the car doors simultaneously and she started the engine.

I was stunned. "I've never seen Mitch angry before. What is his problem?"

Gina shook her head. "I've never seen this side of him either, but he sure didn't like seeing you with Jacques."

"He's not the only one. It happened so fast, I couldn't respond. I was too shocked."

"So Jacques isn't your type?"

"Not at all."

Gina smiled. "Good."

She'd said the word so low, I wasn't sure I'd heard correctly. "What?"

"Nothin.' I didn't say a thing."

We spent a peaceful afternoon relaxing and chatting, waiting to see if the raging battle would follow us. Time rolled past until it was time for Gina to leave for the restaurant, and we still had not seen or heard from the two men.

"Would you like to go to the restaurant with me?" Gina offered.

Knowing that Mitchell and Jacques would be there to perform and unsure of the mood they might be in, I declined the invitation. "I wish I had my computer so I could look for a job. Mitch said I could use his, but…"

"My laptop is in the bedroom, under the bed. Help yourself."

I surfed the net until almost midnight, looking for jobs that might be available back home in Eastridge, but with little luck. There was always the fashion business, but I didn't want to depend on my mother for a job. That would be a last resort.

Giving up on the job search, I settled comfortably into the soft bed. Seconds later, there was a knock on my door. "Come in."

Mitchell inched in like an ashamed little boy. He sat on the bed, staring at his hands fidgeting nervously in his lap. "I'm really sorry I haven't had much time to spend with you."

"That's okay." I wriggled from under the covers, wearing a tee shirt and plaid pajama pants, and sat on the edge of the bed beside him. "I don't expect you to babysit me."

"I have to go into work in the morning, but we could do something in the afternoon if you'd like."

"Tomorrow is Saturday. Do you work seven days a week?" I wasn't trying to make him feel guilty, but was curious to know more about his job.

Standing, eyes cast downward, he explained, "No, but since I took off today, I have a couple of things I need to take care of. Some big wheels from D.C. were down here all week, and I've been so busy running errands for them I didn't get all of my regular duties completed." He looked at me, his expression both apologetic and hopeful. "You can go with me to the office, if you don't mind sitting around there while I finish some paperwork. Then we can go on from there. Do you like beaches?"

I was confused. If my geography wasn't failing me, I was sure that New Mexico was nowhere near the ocean. "Beaches? Around here?"

He chuckled. "Yep. You'll see what I mean tomorrow. Be sure to wear your bathing suit under your clothes, and take some suntan lotion."

"Great!" I jumped to my feet and gave him a quick hug in my excitement. He backed away, holding me at arm's length and looking serious. "Bree, what's going on with you and Jacques?" His voice was calm and caring.

"Nothing."

"It didn't look like nothing when I saw him kissing you. You need to stay away from him."

"It was only a kiss. Besides, I thought that's what you wanted. It seemed like you were trying to pair us up."

He shook his head. "No way. If I had any idea that you would get involved with him, I never would have invited you here."

"I don't understand. Not that I even like him, but why should you care one way or the other?"

"Look, you just don't belong with him." Lowering his

voice and his head, he muttered to himself, "That's not why I brought you here."

Not why he brought me here? What could he mean by that? But before I could respond to his strange remark, he looked back at me and shrugged. "Seeing you with Jacques like that made me a little crazy."

"To be honest, the whole thing took me by surprise too. But I still don't understand why you got so upset."

"I guess I'm a little overprotective. You're like my little sister, and Jacques is a jerk. So just stay away from him, okay?" He sounded frustrated.

I shrugged. "No problem. He's not my type. Frankly, I find him a little creepy. But if he's such a jerk, why do you hang around with him?"

"He's a good musician, so we work together at the restaurant. That doesn't mean we're best friends."

"So why did you invite him to the pool?"

"That was Gina's idea, not mine. But that's enough about Jacques." He smiled. "I'm glad you're here. When I sent you that ticket, I wasn't sure if you would use it. I've really missed talking to you. Letters aren't the same. It's hard to tell how a person is feeling by reading words on a piece of paper."

"I know. I've missed you too. So tell me about you and Gina. Is it serious?" We both sat back down on the bed.

"I guess so. She's pretty terrific."

"From what I can see, she's perfect for you. I like her."

"So tell me about everyone back home."

We talked for over an hour. During a lull in the conversation, he became pensive, then gave me a curious look.

"What is it?" I asked.

"I'm not sure if I should bring it up."

"Well, you're gonna have to now, or I'll stay awake all night wondering what 'it' is."

"Well…" he stalled.

"Come on. Out with it."

"Okay, but remember, you asked," he surrendered. "Have you heard from Troy?"

Emptiness swelled in my chest at the mention of Troy's name, and my palms became hot and sweaty. I looked down at my hands. "No, I haven't," I answered in a terse tone.

"I'm sorry. I told you I probably shouldn't bring it up."

I'd been enjoying our conversation up to this point and didn't want the evening to end on a sour note, so I choked back my discomfort. "No, it's okay. I wasn't expecting to hear his name, and it caught me off guard."

"How do you feel about him these days?"

"Nothing's changed. The feelings are still there, but they're well hidden most of the time."

His voice was quiet and sympathetic, "You still love him, don't you?"

"Yes, but the last I heard, he was about to get married. That was almost a year ago, so I'm sure he's married by now. I can only pray that he's found happiness." My words sounded false even to my own ears.

Mitchell began to say something else, but changed his mind. "It's late. We'd better say goodnight and get some sleep." He gave me a quick kiss on the forehead and left the room.

I attempted to go to sleep, but once again Mitchell had forced me to think about Troy. Would I ever be able to escape those memories? The most painful day of my life to date replayed in my head. It had been seven years, but the wound was as fresh as if it were only seven days.

Seven years earlier–Eastridge—

"Bree, have you heard from Troy yet?" Chloe asked as we peddled our bicycles through the streets of Eastridge. It had become a ritual for us to ride bikes after school each day, weather permitting.

"No, he still hasn't called. I've only gotten one phone call and one letter from him since he left for Coast Guard training, and that was months ago. I keep telling myself he's probably too busy with boot camp, or maybe he's not allowed to call. But there was something in his voice during that one phone call that nags at me."

"Like what?"

"He didn't sound angry or anything, but more like he had something else on his mind."

Chloe shrugged. "Something, or someone? Troy's in the service. He's probably met someone else by now. Even if he's not allowed to make phone calls, I'm sure they allow letters. So if you haven't heard from him, I'd say it's a pretty good bet it's over between you two."

"Ouch! That was cold." That was Chloe's way, always practical and straight-to-the-point. She wasn't one to sugarcoat things, but that's what I liked about her. Everyone knew where they stood with her and could always depend on her to be upfront and honest.

"I'm sorry, but you might as well face it. Troy has always been a playboy, and that's probably not going to change."

"Do you really think he's found someone else?"

Chloe pulled to the side of the road and stopped her bike. She twisted around to face me as I parked behind her.

Chloe sighed. "I didn't want to tell you this, but I think you need to know."

"What?"

"Troy has been calling and writing to me."

"Why?"

"Because he wants to break up with you. In fact, he's been asking me to go out with him."

I studied my friend's face, hoping it was a joke, but it was obvious by her concerned expression that it was no joke. "I don't understand. Why would he do that?"

"Bree, you're too nice. He wants someone he can have fun with. You're only sixteen, and at nineteen, he's not a boy anymore. You need to learn how to make a man happy." Chloe was almost two years older than me.

"So you're saying he's only interested in sex? And because I won't put out, he's turning to you? What does that say about you?"

"That he sees me as a woman, and not a goody-two-shoes little girl."

I fought to keep my temper under control. "So, Miss Sex-queen, have you gone out with him?"

Chloe looked shocked. "Of course not! You're my best friend. I wouldn't do that to you."

Tears made it difficult to see. I blinked in an attempt to dissuade the waterworks and turned my bike around. Why do I always cry when I'm angry? "I'm going home now. I have a letter to write."

I remained in my bedroom all evening, avoiding my family by pretending to be submerged in homework. Avoidance was easy in our household since family dinners were almost non-existent due to my parents' active business and social calendars.

After wringing myself of all the tears my eyes could muster, I decided to stop feeling sorry for myself and allowed anger to take over. "What a jerk! Going after my best friend like that. Who needs him?" Again the tears threatened to spill over. "No! I won't cry over him anymore. Ever!"

I looked at my ceiling. "And I'm through being a goody-two-shoes. God, your way isn't working for me."

2:30 *a.m.–New Mexico—*

I'd tried desperately over the past seven years to forget Troy and Chloe, but each time I came close to having a relationship with anyone, male or female, alarms in my head warned me of the impending pain that lurked in the shadows. I lived with that ghost every day. I suppose that's why Mitchell had become so important in my life. Being a male friend, he wasn't going to steal my boyfriends, and since we were only friends, he couldn't hurt me the way Troy had.

I tossed and turned all night wondering about things Mitchell had said. The remark about me having already met the love of my life—who was he talking about? And he'd been insistent about hearing the news because it might affect his job, yet had clicked off the radio right after the first two reports, one of which was about UFOs. Why was he so unnerved about that report? He also insisted on talking about Troy, knowing how painful it was for me. And his anger over a simple kiss from Jacques. What was that remark about not being why he brought me here?

This was not turning out to be the relaxing vacation I'd hoped for.

Chapter 4

Saturday, May 29—Alamogordo—

Jeans and tee-shirt worn over my bathing suit, I joined Mitchell at the car bright and early. The air was peculiar; cloudy, yet arid. At home it's usually humid in May. "Do you think it's going to rain?"

Mitchell studied the sky. "No, those clouds are full of wind, not rain." He didn't bother to explain further, his mind apparently already at the office.

Entering the back door of one of the plain one-story office buildings, we dodged boxes and barrels to get through the small supply room. The next room wasn't any more welcoming, with its cold tile floor and drab beige walls. It was a large room filled with heavy metal desks and chairs, computers, and other normal office equipment. The musky smell of mothballs assaulted my nostrils.

Mitchell motioned around the room. "Have a seat anywhere. I have to take inventory to see what we need to order. I'll be right back." At a desk bearing his name plate, he pulled some papers from his briefcase and headed toward the back room.

I glanced through the window. The clouds were even more ominous than before. So much for a suntan.

Twenty minutes passed. Bored, I walked around the office, then wandered into a small conference room in the back of the building. On the wall hung a large sheet of white paper with drawings. I inched closer. It appeared to be schematic drawings of flying saucers, with scribbles of equations and technical jargon, none of which made sense to me. After studying it and realizing I could stand there all day and still not understand any of it, I walked back toward the front of the building and was standing beside Mitchell's desk when he returned.

He stormed, "Bree, what are you doing? Were you going through my briefcase?"

Surprised at his outburst, I whirled around. "Of course not. It was sitting there open, and I was simply walking past it. Why? Is there something in there you don't want me to see?"

He was flustered. "Um, no, of course not. It's just that I've been working on some stuff that's kind of top secret. I guess I should be more careful about leaving it open, huh?"

"Ooh, top secret, huh?" I teased. "Well, don't worry. I didn't see a thing."

He grinned sheepishly. "I'm sorry. Are you ready to get out of here?"

A door slammed and the windows rattled. Dust and rocks struck the windows. Mitchell sighed and shrugged. "Doesn't look like we can go just yet. We'll have to wait for this storm to blow over."

He led me to the back of the building, away from the windows, where we stood watching the dust storm. The dust was thick as if dirt were being dumped over the entire building. Mitchell yelled above the howling winds,

"This is why my windshield is broken. You'll notice a lot of broken windows around here that nobody bothers to get fixed. That's why I keep my old car. I can't see buying a new one to get beat up in this stuff."

We stood in front of the little conference room. My curiosity about the drawings nagged at me. "What are those drawings in that room all about?"

He looked around at the door of the room and swore. "That door is supposed to be locked. What were you doing snooping back here?"

"I wasn't snooping. I was bored, so I walked around. Why, is that 'top secret' too?" I was being sarcastic, but the look on his face made me wonder if I had stumbled onto something important. It was a quick flash of something in his eyes, but he recovered quickly.

"Of course not. Some guys were back there doodling, that's all."

Doodling? Why waste such a huge sheet of paper on doodling? Our tax dollars at work.

The storm was short-lived. We waited until there was only a light dust blowing, then ventured to the car. Having left the windows down, Mitchell proceeded to clean the accumulated dirt and debris from the seats and examined the sky. "The sun will probably be out in about thirty minutes. Are you hungry?"

We stopped at a small diner for a sandwich. As he'd foretold, the sun was shining bright and hot by the time we'd eaten lunch.

"Okay, to the beach we go." He drove along another straight, flat road. "I'm taking you to a place called White

Sands. It's miles of nothing but white sand, two hundred and nineteen square miles of it. It's bigger than any beach I've ever seen, and a great place for picnics and sunbathing. A lot of movies are made around here. Especially chase scenes and desert scenes."

We were soon weaving through pathways around sand dunes. There were people throwing frisbees and sunbathing everywhere, reminding me of ants among the ant hills. Mitch found a relatively secluded area and helped me spread a blanket.

"So, Bree, what do you think of this place?"

"It's great! Like being at the beach. All I need is a book to curl up with, and I wouldn't even miss the ocean."

"You're so predictable. Look what I brought." He pulled out a couple of paperbacks from a small duffle bag. "I know how you love to read, so I came prepared. I have books, magazines, snacks, bottles of water, and a frisbee. We're all set for a relaxing day at the beach."

We each chose something to read and settled down to enjoy the serenity of the warm sunshine. After only one paragraph, I sensed I was being watched. Shifting my focus above my book, my gaze met Mitchell's. "I thought you were going to read."

"I am. I was trying to read your mind."

"Oh? And did you learn anything?"

"I don't know." His gaze lingered on my face for a moment before he returned to reading his book.

I stared at him until he looked up again.

"So why are you staring at me?"

"Just trying to read your mind."

"And could you?"

I sighed as if bored. "Yes, but it was a very short story."

We both laughed until the smile faded from Mitchell's face. "How would you feel if you were to see Troy again?"

Shocked by the unexpected change of subject and mood and by the bluntness of his question, I erupted. "What is this about Troy? Why do you insist on talking about him? It's over! He's married and out of my life for good, so would you please let me forget him!"

Mitchell wasn't bothered by my outburst but appeared pleased with himself for setting me off. He continued to study my face and remarked, "But can you?"

I grabbed my book and turned my back to him. "Would you just read your book?" I reread the same paragraph for the third time, only to be interrupted by a frisbee sliding to a halt beside me, sprinkling sand over me and the book. Startled, my mouth fell open, collecting a mouthful of sand. The tasteless grit ground between my teeth. Shading the brilliance of the sun from my eyes, I looked up to see Mitchell bending over to retrieve the disc.

"Care to join me in a little frisbee throwing?"

I filtered the grains of sand from my mouth. "I might as well. I'm not getting very far with this book. Besides, it sure beats eating sand." Jerking the frisbee from him, I giggled and ran across the sand, scaling one of the tallest dunes. Reaching the top, I turned expecting to find him at my heels, but he was nowhere to be seen. I called for him, but there was no answer. I stood atop the dune observing the horizon.

A large, bright light streaked across the sky and disappeared behind a distant dune. Spellbound, I barely noticed when Mitchell grabbed me from behind. "Got ya!"

"Did you see that?"

"What?"

"A light, or something shiny. It came from nowhere and went behind one of those dunes out there."

"It was probably nothing. Maybe a plane went over and the sun reflected off it."

"No, this was some sort of large, glowing projectile. Maybe it was a comet or something."

"Probably not. It was most likely an optical illusion of some kind. With all this sand and sun, your eyes can play tricks on you."

I continued to stare at the spot where I'd last seen the object. "Maybe," I said, but I was sure there was something there.

No longer in the mood to toss the frisbee, we returned to our blanket. I sat with my eyes closed, drinking in the delicious warmth of the sun.

Suddenly, with concerned urgency, Mitchell whispered, "Don't move!"

Motionless, I asked through clenched teeth, "What is it?"

"A scorpion. Just don't move." He eased himself to his knees, then slowly to his feet. He held the frisbee ready to scoop and heave it as far as possible, but a raspy voice halted him.

"Don't! I'll get him." A gray-haired, bearded man appeared within my view, stalking toward me. In one hand, he carried a large can with a lid that opened and shut at the touch of a lever. In the other was a large pair of forceps.

I couldn't see the scorpion without turning my head,

which I didn't dare try. Judging from the man's eyes, intent on his prey and staring at the ground next to me, I knew it must be close. I shut my eyes and held my breath, hoping this guy knew what he was doing. I heard a rush of scampering feet, a determined grunt, and then a loud clank as the lid blinked open to devour its victim.

"You can move now. He got it." Mitchell helped me to my feet and showed me how close it had been. Less than twenty inches of sand had separated me from the poisonous sting of the scorpion.

I tried to stand, but my knees buckled when I realized how close I'd come—had come to what? "Will they kill you?"

The old man tilted his head. "Some can, but most will jest make ya so sick, ya'd wish it'd killed ya. I've been lookin' for one 'round here for a long time." He walked back to where he'd dropped his other buckets and tools. "Today I was out here lookin' for other kinds of critters. Scorpions hide durin' the day, so I usually look for 'em at night. This one must've been tryin' to hide under your blanket. They won't attack ya unless they think they're bein' threatened. Even if they don't get ya with their stinger, those pinchers of theirs can be pretty painful."

"What other creatures are you looking for around here?" Mitchell asked.

"All kinds of insects, beetles, and mice. Ya see, all the critters 'round here are either white or a near-white shade of color. So they'd add a lot to my collection of unusual plants and animals I've found 'round the U.S." He gathered his paraphernalia and wandered off, searching the ground as he walked.

Mitchell and I cautiously checked the blanket for more scorpions and sat back down. Unable to free my thoughts from scorpions and other creepy, crawly things, I began to walk around snapping pictures of the dunes, Yucca plants, and people throwing frisbees and flying kites. I stood on top of a large dune staring over the endless miles of sand, my mind pondering the question Mitchell had raised earlier. *How would I feel if I saw Troy again? How would I react? And why does Mitch continue harping on the idea and filling my head with these depressing thoughts?*

A tender voice behind me broke through my reverie. "Bree, are you okay?"

I tried to shake myself out of my doldrums and put on a fake smile. "Sure, I'm fine."

"It's getting kind of late. I think we should be heading back. I need to get ready for the show tonight."

Somehow I needed to get Troy out of my head and move on with my life. I stepped back from the hole I'd made in the sand with my foot and stooped over to fill it back in.

"What are you doing?"

"Burying the past," I murmured.

Chapter 5

Sunday, May 30–New Mexico—

Mitch sat at the kitchen table drinking his morning coffee, pondering what he should do about Brianna. She was becoming too curious. The last thing he needed was her asking a bunch of questions. If his superiors thought she knew anything about their project, he wasn't sure what might happen. To save her from herself, he needed to remove her from things. She was too smart and too inquisitive for her own good. *I guess I'd better speed up my plans.*

When I walked into the kitchen the next morning, I was surprised to find Mitchell sitting at the table. "You mean you're not off to work this morning?"

"It's Sunday."

"I know that, but you seem to work strange hours."

"Not today, it's Memorial Day. How would you like to see some mountain scenery?" Mitchell asked while I poured my morning coffee.

"I'd love to."

"I need to pick up a package for my roommate at his uncle's tavern in the mountains, and I thought you might want to ride along."

"Is Gina going with us?"

"No, she's sleeping late, and then she's going to have dinner with her family. It's just you and me, kid."

The mountains weren't at all what I was used to. Instead of the lush, thick greenery, these mountains were brown and rough with tall and sparse trees. Mostly pine, I was intrigued with how perfectly straight they'd grown. Each time I was poised to snap a photo, the car rounded another curve and the opportunity was lost.

The tavern was a log building snuggled beside the road among the rocky cliffs.

Mitchell parked the car. "You wait here. I shouldn't be long."

I watched him enter the back door. True to his word, a few minutes later he returned carrying a package the size of a brick wrapped in brown paper.

"We've got one more stop to make. A friend of mine is expecting me to drop by today, so we may as well do that now. Do you like horses?"

"Yes, I love horses. I don't ride well, but I like trying."

His eyes twinkled and he suddenly seemed very eager. "Great! My friend lives on a ranch. Maybe we can go for a ride before we leave."

"Is this the same ranch you visited Friday morning?"

"It sure is. It's a beautiful place. You're going to love it."

The further we twisted our way through the mountain roads, the more narrow the road became. A wall of rock closed in on us on both sides, allowing only a limited amount of sunlight to filter through from above. The constant squeaking of the car and clattering of the engine echoed off the stone barriers. As if passing through a golden gateway, the walls ended, and before us was a valley of lovely rolling grasslands and large trees with beautiful, thick foliage.

"Stop the car!" I exclaimed.

"What for?"

"Just stop!"

Making sure no other cars were around, he pulled onto the road's shoulder. Camera in hand, I sprang from the car and clicked toward every angle possible. "This is the most beautiful place I've ever seen. I can't wait until we get a little farther down the road so I can get a contrast shot of the green fields with the barren mountains in the background." Anxious to continue on the journey in search of the perfect photo, I scurried back into the car.

Mitchell chuckled and shook his head. "You're quite the shutterbug, aren't you? I'll stop one more time for snapshots, but no more."

"Why are you in such a hurry?"

He looked surprised that I would question him, then shrugged his shoulders. "No reason."

I studied his face; his eyes focused on the road, his expression revealing nothing. He was acting strange, almost secretive. That's not like Mitch.

A few miles down the road, I spotted the perfect setting for the contrast I wanted. Rolling his eyes and sighing, Mitch stopped the car again while I pretended to be Miss *National Geographic*, then we continued on our way. A warm breeze whispered through the branches that hung over the road forming a tunnel.

We eventually turned down a dirt road that led through a white gateway and up to an old, but stately, two-story house. Climbing from the car, we were stretching our legs when a man emerged from the house. I closed my eyes, shook my head, and did a double take to be sure I'd seen correctly the first time. He was well over six feet tall, very slim, with bronzed skin, coal black hair, and looked as stunned as I felt.

"Troy!" I ran toward him, and he picked me up in a bear hug. The sensuous scent of his aftershave was the same as I remembered from years past.

"Bree, oh, how I've missed you." His voice quivered. I averted my eyes to prevent him from seeing my tears and saw Mitchell standing aside looking very proud of himself.

"So this is what you've been up to. Why didn't you tell me Troy was here?" The second I finished my question, I realized I'd forgotten about the new Mrs. Troy Garrison. Backing away, I glanced toward the house expecting to see his wife materialize. "Aren't you married now?"

"No, I didn't go through with it."

Mitchell turned to leave us, talking as he walked away. "I'll leave you two alone now. I think you have a lot to talk about. I'll be inside visiting Uncle Jake if, for some strange reason, you happen to need me." He disappeared into the house.

Troy placed his arm around my waist and we started to walk. His touch sent a warmth through me that brought back memories of the first time we'd kissed. I'd been kissed by other men, but none had caused the fiery response of his kisses. It felt good to be with him again, but I didn't dare look at him. Staring at the ground as he led me down the path toward the stables, I knew if I were to look up, his warm brown eyes would melt and consume me like a flame with wax.

I needed to break the silence before the desire crying out within me became obvious. It had always been that way between us. If we weren't talking, the electricity became unbearable. "Why didn't you go through with it?"

Troy's answer was matter-of-fact. "I didn't love her." The muscles in his arm tensed to draw me closer. "I guess I cared too much for someone else."

I wanted to believe him and believe that he meant me, but I was afraid. He'd hurt and disappointed me too often in the past. "When I didn't hear from you, I assumed you had taken the final step."

"I was afraid to call you. I'd messed up your life long enough, and I heard you were dating someone else, so I decided to leave you alone and move out here."

"When did Mitch find out you were here?"

"It was his idea from the beginning. Mitch knew I had an uncle living in New Mexico, so he looked him up when he first came here and they became good friends. Uncle Jake needed someone to help him run the ranch, and Mitch felt I was the logical person to turn to."

"He never even mentioned you in any of his letters. How long have you been here?"

"About six months. I really love it here too. Being with my uncle is almost like having my father back again. He's a lot like him." His father had passed away nine years ago, and although Troy rarely talked about his parents, I knew they'd been close.

Troy's mood brightened, casting me his disarming smile with a twinkle in his warm, dark eyes. "So you had no idea I was here?"

"Not until you came out the front door. Mitch told me we were going to visit a friend of his, but he never mentioned any names. Now I know why."

"That sneaky son-of-a-gun," he muttered. "Now I understand why he kept asking me all those questions about how I felt about you. And I thought he was asking because he was interested in you himself."

"He must have planned this for a long time." God bless him. I couldn't believe I was really standing there with Troy.

I was feeling giddy when we arrived back at the house. Mitchell was on the front porch ending a phone conversation. He snapped his flip phone shut. "Well, should I go get her things and bring them here?"

I stood gaping as Troy agreed that was the only logical thing to do.

"Hold it!" I exclaimed. "Don't I have a vote in this?"

Troy held me firmly at his side. "Now you don't think I'm going to let you stay with him, do you?"

"But all my things are back at the trailer, and it's too far for Mitch to bring them all the way back here," I argued, turning to Mitchell for support. The thought of staying under the same roof with Troy caused a flood of emotions within me, both exciting and frightening. Yes, I wanted to be with him, but could I survive the inevitable pain when it was over again?

Mitchell looked into my pleading eyes, then lowered his head, looking contrite and helpless. "I'm sorry, Bree. I never planned to leave you here without consulting you first, but Gina just called and it really would be safer for you to stay here. She already has all your things packed."

Troy and I looked at him with blank faces. "What's happened?" Troy asked.

"It's Sal. He's been arrested. He was coming home and had barely crossed the border when they caught him. I'm sure it will only be a matter of hours before they get a warrant and search his trailer. I don't want Bree mixed up in this."

"Of course not! She's staying right here. Was it drugs?"

"It looks that way."

I stood back watching and listening to their discussion and thought about the package Mitch had picked up for Sal. *Could he be getting himself involved in Sal's illegal activities?*

"What are you going to do? You know you can always come back here to live," Troy suggested.

"It's too far to commute from here to the base. I'll stay at the trailer."

"But you can't be associating with drug dealers."

"It's not my place to judge Sal. I'm only his roommate."

"But this is something that could get you into trouble too."

"I know, but I keep hoping I can help Sal straighten out. He's a good person deep down."

"You think everyone is a good person, Mitch. But not everyone is."

Mitchell started toward the car. "There's good in everyone. In some, we have to look a little harder, but it's there. Bree, I'm going to get your bags now. I'll be back as soon as I can."

"Wait!" I ran after him and whispered so Troy wouldn't overhear. "You need to be careful. What was that package you picked up from Sal's uncle?"

"I don't know, and I don't want to know. I was only doing a friend a favor."

"But what if it's drugs and you get caught with them?"

"His uncle wouldn't be involved in that. Don't worry. Now I gotta go."

"Why are you doing this to me? You can't leave me here with him. You know how he always ends up hurting me."

He placed a comforting hand on my shoulder. "Look, it's obvious to me that you are in love with him. Your letters clearly spelled it out. Then you confirmed it the other night during our talk, and you happen to be all he has talked about for the past six months. So relax and enjoy the happiness you two were always meant to have." With that, he got into his car and drove away.

Left with no other option, I accompanied Troy inside to meet Uncle Jake. Walking through the foyer and kitchen, through a wrought-iron archway, and into a large study, we were greeted by the pungent odor of a cigar. Bookcases full of books lined the walls on three sides. Against the other wall was a television, an old record player, and a roll-top desk. Uncle Jake was resting in a green recliner watching the television. Although elderly and unable to get around the ranch the way he had at one time, he jumped up to greet me, demonstrating that he still possessed plenty of spunk. Indicating the overstuffed chairs arranged in the center of the room, he coaxed, "Come on in and have a seat, young lady." An old dog, that appeared to be a shepherd-retriever mix, raised his head to make sure Uncle Jake wasn't leaving him, then settled back down.

"Thank you."

"My, my, Troy, where'd you find this fine little filly?"

"Uncle Jake, this is Brianna. I've told you about her."

"You mean the young lady you've been wanting to call but was so scared to? Boy, what's wrong with you? You can't let someone like this get away from ya. Young lady, you remind me a lot of my Elissa, God rest her soul. She was a good woman, a wonderful wife."

"How do I remind you of her?"

"You are beautiful like she was. And I can see the same spark in your eyes that she possessed. I'm a good judge of character, boy, and I'm telling you to hang onto this one."

Feeling a tad uneasy, I attempted to turn the conversation back to Elissa. "How long were you married?"

"Not long enough. She passed away while still very young. We'd only been married a few years when she fell ill. We were planning a family, but it never happened."

"I'm sorry."

"Don't be. The short time I had with Elissa was worth everything to me. I'm a fortunate man to have known such love and devotion. Many a person goes through this life and never experiences a love like that. I was beginning to think this one was going to be one of them," he added, pointing at Troy.

Troy simply smiled and shook his head.

Uncle Jake reached down to stroke his dog's head. "This here is my constant companion. No one has ever had a better friend than old Rufus here. He listens good and never gives me no back talk or bad advice." Muttering to himself, he added, "And he's always here when I need him." Rufus lifted his head to look up at him, then yawned and settled back down for another nap.

Troy stood and stretched. "Bree and I are going for a ride."

"Sure, you kids run along. It's about time for my afternoon nap anyhow."

"We'll be back before dinner."

Mitch drove away from the ranch with mixed emotions, talking to himself as he drove. "I'm sorry, Bree. I hated to lie to you, but you were getting too nosy. I wanted to get you and Troy back together, but I'd hoped to do it more gently. This is going to work out best for everyone. You are right where you belong." He took the package he had picked up from the tavern and unwrapped it. There was the most delicious rum fruitcake he'd ever eaten. *Sorry, Sal. As far as Troy and Brianna are concerned, you are now a drug dealer.*

After escorting me to the stables, Troy grabbed one of the saddles. My nostrils flared from the muskiness of the horses, the leather, and the hay, among the more unpleasant odors. Within minutes, he had a beautiful black stallion saddled and was mounting it. He held out his hand. "Climb on up. I'll slide back and you sit in the saddle."

Intimidated by the size of the horse, I took a deep

breath, conjuring all of my strength and courage. I told myself, *You can do this. Legs, don't fail me now.* I placed my foot in the stirrup and, with his help, managed to get myself into the saddle.

"Hang on," he called as he started the horse into a fast trot and then a run.

"What's your hurry?" I yelled back over my shoulder, but there was no answer. We soon came upon a creek and stopped. He helped me down and led me into a small sandy area beside the water.

"I've waited way too long for this." He gently pulled me to him and kissed me, first tenderly, then more savagely, pulling me closer and pressing himself firmly against me. I grew weak, the passion I'd held inside for so long surfacing. I allowed myself to drown in his rugged embrace, the pounding of my pulse ringing in my ears. My legs melted from beneath me as he slowly lowered me to the ground. Our lips never parted until his fingers began to fumble with my blouse buttons, bringing me back to my senses. I pulled away. To my surprise, he sighed with understanding, smiled, and said, "You haven't changed a bit."

I giggled and snuggled into his arms, the sweet sensation of contentment washing over me. With closed eyes, listening to the water rippling over the pebbles and the birds twittering, I had the sensation of floating, held only by his strong caress. I'd never felt more secure.

His fingers gripped my ribs, causing me to jump. "I see you're still ticklish."

"Yes," but when I tried to get him back, I added with disappointment, "and I see you're not."

"Nobody's perfect." He sat up and stared into the sky.

I watched him, and then my gaze also reached into the heavens and my thoughts turned to the UFO reports and the strange object I'd seen at White Sands. "Troy, do you believe in flying saucers?" I asked.

He looked at me and laughed. "Where did that come from?"

"I was thinking about those people who claim to have seen them and wondering if it could be possible."

He looked back toward the sky and smiled. "I've seen one."

"Really?"

"Yeah, not long ago. It was the most incredible sight I think I've ever seen. The light that shone from it was amazing!" He stared in front of him, awe in his voice. He remembered every detail, reliving the experience as he spoke. "I can't really describe it. It wasn't a beam of light, but a kind of wavy, brilliant, and yet soft glow. It had a calming effect. It moved slowly, then hovered, turned a ninety-degree angle and shot away like a bullet." He turned to me, bringing himself back to the present. "You're only the second person I've told about it." The wonderment was gone from his voice.

"How can you be so matter-of-fact about this? Are you pulling my leg?"

"No, I really did see it," he confirmed casually.

"Well, what do you think it was?" I was astounded at his attitude. I'd never met anyone who had actually seen a UFO before, and he was acting as if it happened to everyone.

"A UFO. If I knew what it was, it wouldn't be an

'unidentified flying object,' right?" He stood up and held out his arms to help me up. "We'd better get back. Sheila will be setting the table soon."

"Who's Sheila?"

"She's the lady that keeps Uncle Jake's household from falling apart." He helped brush the dirt from my clothes. "She and her husband, Joe, are Hopi Indian. He works on the ranch while she keeps the house straight and cooks Uncle Jake's meals. They live in a cottage on a plot of land on the edge of the ranchlands. Uncle Jake gave the property to them and helped them build their home when they got married about seven years ago."

As we walked along the path toward the house, I asked, "You said I was the second person you've told about the UFO. Who was the first?"

"Mitch, but I'm not sure he believed me."

Maybe that could explain why he was so upset about that news report about UFOs.

Anxious to know everything about Troy, I changed the subject. "So fill me in on what you've been up to since I saw you last."

He thought for a moment. "I was in the Coast Guard for two years. Then I went to school, majoring in architectural drawing. I enjoyed that for a few years, but decided I hated working at a drawing board day-in and day-out and began searching for a new career. Then Mitch called and told me how Uncle Jake needed someone to help him out. Being a cowboy sounded like fun, so here I am."

Arriving back at the house, the smell of onions, peppers, and spices filled the air. We sat down to a pleasant meal served by Sheila, a quiet woman in her early thirties.

After dinner, Troy and Uncle Jake went out to be sure everything on the ranch was secured for the night. I helped Sheila clean up the kitchen until Mitchell rapped on the door, carrying my suitcases and overnight bag.

"I think I got everything. If I find anything at the trailer that we missed, I'll bring it over later," he said while I held the door open for him to enter. Sheila led us to an upstairs room she'd prepared, and I began to unpack a few things I would need that night. Mitchell stood in the bedroom doorway watching me.

"So, Mitch, did you know your roommate was into drugs?"

"Yes. I knew he'd get caught with drugs one day, but he insisted on dealing with the stuff. I guess some people have to learn the hard way."

"Have you learned any more about his situation since you left here?"

"Yeah. He's being held at the police station. They came and searched the trailer, but luckily he didn't have any hidden there. I wasn't sure if he did or not."

"If he's dealing in drugs, you shouldn't be associating with him."

Mitch shrugged. "It's none of my business what he does with his life. He's got no family here, or anyone else to help him out. But don't worry about me. How is everything going here since I left?"

I gave him my most mischievous smile. "Everything is perfect—so far."

"I must say, you look happy. And, I might add, it's about time. You two have both been miserable when it was obvious that all you needed was each other."

"Well, Cupid, how can I ever thank you?"

"By being happy. I'd better get going. Gina is waiting in the car."

"Why don't you ask her to come in?"

"No, she wouldn't. I promised her we would go to a movie tonight, and she's not about to let me off the hook." He took my hand and gave it a little squeeze. "Goodnight."

Mitchell left, and I grabbed my robe and slippers and went down the hall to shower.

Returning to my room with a towel around my head, I found Troy waiting in my doorway. He grinned. "Aren't you cute in your little fuzzy robe. I could have come in and scrubbed your back for you, if you'd asked."

"Oh, I'm sure you would have liked that." He was blocking my way into the room. "Excuse me, may I come into my room?"

"Only if I can stay."

"Sure, you can stay for a little while."

He moved aside and followed me into the room, watching as I towel-dried my hair and combed it out. He walked across the room and took my comb. "Here, let me help you." He stood behind me, combed a few strokes, then reached his arms around me and held me close. "You smell good." He stood holding me until I relaxed in his caress and leaned on him. He began kissing my neck, causing my pulse to race.

I leaned into him, enjoying my body's heightened awareness of my own sensuality. No one else had ever been able to make my body melt the way Troy did, and he knew it. With that thought, I pulled away from him. "I'm really tired. Maybe you should leave now."

He pulled me back close to him and whispered into my ear, "Are you sure?"

"Positive."

He stood still for a moment, holding me. "Okay. If that's what you want." His hands moved down both of my arms as he released me and slowly backed from the room. I turned and smiled. "Goodnight."

I crawled into the canopied bed and surveyed the room that Sheila had chosen for me. It was decorated with pale blue carpet, blue flowered wallpaper and bedspread, and the bed had a velvet, royal blue headboard. I turned off the small lamp on the nightstand, pulled the covers over me, and heard the old grandfather clock down the hall strike eleven.

Monday, May 31–Eastridge—

It had been a long and tearful weekend without much sleep. Rachel had spent a lot of time on the Internet researching MS. It was frightening not knowing what to expect. There were no hard facts about what causes it or how to treat it. There were several types of drugs that might help, but no guarantees. During her web search, she located several support groups and foundations that could give her more information.

But for now, she was relieved to get back to work and attempt to recapture some kind of normalcy in her life. She hoped to lose herself in her work the way she'd always done during tough times, but when she entered the office, Milly was waiting for her. "Okay, Rae, tell me what the doctor had to say."

The flood of tears started all over again. Angry at not being able to control herself better, she cried even harder.

"Oh no, Rae. What is it?"

After pouring herself a glass of water and getting control of her emotions, Rachel looked at her dear friend with sad eyes. "The doctor said I have MS and there's nothing he can do for me."

Milly froze. "What do you mean, there's nothing he can do?"

"That's all he said, but I'm going to find another doctor and get a second opinion, even if I have to fly to Europe to do it."

Milly walked around her desk and gave Rachel a hug. "Of course you will! And you know I'll do anything I can to help."

"I've already called the only neurologists in this sleepy little town, and there's a four-month waiting list. I've been doing research all weekend about Multiple Sclerosis, but I'm still not sure I understand any of it. I'm really scared, Milly."

New Mexico—

Most of Monday morning was spent carrying my camera around the ranch shooting anything that caught my eye. Troy was helping groom the horses in preparation for a few prospective buyers that were coming later that afternoon. About to go inside to see if Sheila could use some help, I spotted a small, dark-headed boy running across the field toward me. A black puppy barked joyously at his heels as the boy laughed and played. They came closer and I thought I'd never seen such an adorable child. His face was round and chubby with big, dark brown eyes and solid black hair. Cheeks rosy and eyes sparkling, he smiled up at me while I snapped his picture.

"Hi," he said cheerfully. "I know who you are. You're Brianna. Uncle Troy told me about you."

I knelt down to talk on his level. "And what did Uncle Troy say about me?"

"Not much. Just that you're his girl, and that I would like you."

My heart fluttered at the words "his girl." I'd wanted to hear him say that for so long; and now, though it excited me, it was also a little frightening. There had been countless times in the past that I'd thought he felt that way, only to be wounded by the truth later. He'd never said he loved me, and I wasn't going to fool myself into believing he did this time around. I shifted my attention back to the little boy. "Okay, so you know who I am. It's only fair that you tell me your name."

"I'm Manuel. Can I touch your hair? I've never seen red hair before. It's pretty."

"Sure."

He reached out and felt my hair. "Mama's hair is long too, but hers is black like mine."

Sheila stood in the doorway. "Manuel, leave her hair alone. I'm sorry, Brianna. I hope he wasn't bothering you."

"No! He's delightful. We've been having a nice little chat."

"Manuel, why aren't you helping your father?" Sheila scolded.

"But Papa said I should go play some before dinner." He looked confused.

"Sheila, would it be okay if Manuel took a walk with me? I'd love the company."

The child's eyes pleaded with his mother. She smiled. "Okay, go ahead, young man, but you behave yourself."

We walked down the lane to the creek, the puppy close behind. I bent down to pet his soft fur. "Who is this little guy?"

"His name is Shadow. I just got him. I think he likes me because he follows me everywhere."

Manuel was overjoyed to have someone spend time with him. It didn't take long for me to realize how lonely and difficult it was for him to have both parents working at the ranch. When he tried to help his father, he was in the way, and his mother was too busy to spend much time with him. There were no other children to play with, but he talked proudly of his Uncle Troy and called him his "best friend in the whole world." Manuel showed a love and respect for him rarely seen in a child his age.

Obviously, Troy was marvelous with children. I loved kids and yearned to have a family of my own one day, but whenever thinking about having children, I could imagine nobody else as the father except Troy, and I refused to allow myself to think along those lines.

In a few days, I would be returning home to Eastridge to the real world, leaving this dream world behind. A sudden ache coursed through me when I thought of leaving Troy.

After lunch, Manuel and I sat outside together in the slight shade of a small tree. It was a comfortable afternoon and we sat quietly, Manuel coloring in the new coloring book Troy had bought him, and me looking over pages of job listings I'd printed from the Internet.

There was nothing that interested me. Watching Manuel color in his book reminded me how much I wanted to work with children, but I didn't have the education to be a teacher or counselor. My parents had encouraged me to continue my education after my two years of undergraduate studies, but I was so tired of school I chose to quit.

Taking a deep breath, I went back to searching the list of jobs, only finding one possibility. It was a position at the hospital. At least if I worked there, I might feel somewhat useful.

Manuel jumped up. "Uncle Troy!" He ran into Troy's arms and Troy lifted him to ride on his shoulders.

"You two getting along okay?"

Manuel beamed as he told of our walk to the creek and showed him the pictures he'd colored. After amusing him a while, Troy told him to go see if his father needed him to help put the horses away. After he ran off, Troy took my hand. "Looks like I may have a little competition."

I smiled. "Yes, he is the cutest guy I believe I've ever seen. We really had a terrific time today."

Troy looked proud, as if the child were his own. "Manuel is quite a boy. His parents work too hard to be able to take the time with him that they'd like. It will be good for him when he finally goes to school."

"Any luck selling the horses?"

"We sold a few, but not as many as we'd hoped. A couple of men said they might be back tomorrow. They had another ranch to visit before making a final decision. So what have you been doing here?" He indicated the papers I'd carefully laid aside under a rock to keep them from blowing away.

"Job possibilities."

"Anything interesting?"

"Maybe one at the hospital."

"Hospital? You mean Eastridge Medical?"

"Maybe. I don't know if I'm qualified for anything, but it's worth a try. I really want to work with children. I'm also going to apply at the school. Maybe they'll need someone to help out in the office."

"I'm sure you'll find something. If you need a personal reference, you can put me down. I'll let them know how lucky they would be to have you as an employee," he teased. I wondered if he was making fun of me. He didn't seem to take my job hunt seriously, and for me, this was very serious business. I had bills to pay, and my small savings wasn't going to last forever. Suddenly, my mood changed, and I began to worry about being on vacation when I should be home finding a job.

The heat of the day was at its peak. Everyone retreated inside, pulled the drapes to keep as cool as possible, and turned on the television. Most decided to take a siesta, and Troy resolved to do the same. Stretched out on the sofa, his head in my lap as I played with a curl that fell across his forehead, he was asleep almost instantly. I tried to sneak away, but when I attempted to lift his head in order to slide my legs from under it, he grabbed my wrist and said sleepily, "Don't go. Please don't leave me." I settled myself back where I'd been and rested my head on the back of the sofa. I was close to dozing when I heard a tease from the news, "Midwest Airline pilot sees UFO. Details tonight at five." I glanced at the small clock sitting on top of the TV—2:50.

An hour passed before everyone began to get back to their chores. I watched the clock all afternoon, not wanting to miss the evening news. Sheila began preparing dinner. The men, with Manuel in tow, were out checking on the horses. I slipped back into the den and switched on the television, watching commercial after commercial. I let out a deep breath of frustration. *Come on with the report already!* Finally, the news reports began. Ten minutes later, there was another tease, "When we come back, an airline pilot sees a UFO." Then more commercials. *Now I remember why I don't watch much TV.*

Finally, the anchor reporter was back on. "Last week, Midwest Airline pilot Dan Welford was flying over the Rio Grande when he saw what he says was a UFO. We go now to Maija Avery, reporting live from the airport."

I sat on the edge of the chair remembering that I'd flown into El Paso last Wednesday on a Midwest Airline flight, and the pilot had been startled by something while talking about the Rio Grande.

A young, attractive reporter stood on the tarmac at the airport, the wind from the planes blowing her hair and the noise causing her to yell at the camera. "I'm here with Captain Dan Welford, a Midwest Airline pilot, who claims he's seen a UFO." Turning to the pilot, she began her interview. "Captain Welford, what exactly did you see?"

The captain blinked nervously, his eyes darting back and forth, seemingly uncomfortable with the interview. "At first I noticed a reflection out of the corner of my eye. Then as it approached, I could see that it was some kind of aircraft. I thought we were going to hit it, so I had to take evasive action. In my effort to avoid whatever it was, I lost eye contact, and when I tried to find it on my radar screen, it wasn't there."

"So what did it look like?"

"It's difficult to describe since I only saw it for a few seconds. It was a bright metal like none I've ever seen before. It had about six glowing orbs across it."

"Glowing orbs? You mean like headlights?"

"I wouldn't even call them lights. They had a soft, pulsating glow about them."

"How large was this aircraft?"

"Not as large as I would expect a UFO to be. I guess it was two, maybe three hundred feet long and cigar-shaped."

"You seem pretty sure it was a UFO. Is there a possibility that it was another airplane, and the fact that it appeared in your view so unexpectedly made you jump to conclusions?"

"It wasn't like any aircraft I've ever seen before. There was something ominous about the way it hovered near us. My co-pilot saw it too, but he's not talking about it, afraid of losing his job. But I know what I saw, and I don't believe it was from this world."

The reporter looked skeptical, raising her eyebrows and stifling a snigger. "From this world or not, it's apparent that Captain Welford is a believer. This is Maija Avery, reporting live from El Paso."

I sat back, clicking off the TV, and staring into the blank screen. I thought about the event on the airplane, then the streak of bright light at White Sands, and the "doodling" paper at Mitchell's offices. I couldn't wait to talk to Troy about it all.

I watched from the window and ran to meet Troy when I saw him walking from the stables. "You aren't going to believe what was on the news!"

"Hey, slow down and take a breath."

I giggled and took a breath. "The pilot that was flying

the plane that I took into El Paso last Wednesday was on the news. He saw a UFO when we were flying over the Rio Grande. Do you believe that?"

"Sure, why not? I told you I've seen one."

"I know, but this is getting more strange all the time. Everyone is seeing them. I even think I might have seen one, but I'm not sure."

"Really? You didn't tell me about that. What exactly did you see?"

"Not much. It was a streak, or flash, of something in White Sands. It happened so fast I didn't have time to process it. I thought maybe it was a meteor or comet, but now I'm not so sure."

"Well, you know they use White Sands as a missile-testing range, so that might be what you saw. I wouldn't concern yourself about it too much. These so-called 'sightings' have been going on for decades, and life goes on as usual. The earth is still here and there are no little aliens wreaking havoc." Placing his arm around my shoulders, he changed the subject. "Come on, let's go eat. I'm starving."

Mitch rushed from the stage of the restaurant to find Gina in the kitchen. "I've got to go. There's an emergency meeting at the base. Tell Jacques to take over here for me. I'll see you later." He gave her a quick peck on the lips and dashed to the parking lot.

Gina shook her head, remembering Brianna's words, *"But he's an accountant. I would expect fairly consistent hours for that type of job." What is going on with you, Mitch?*

Although it worried her that there were strange things going on, she knew Mitchell was an honest and devoted man. If he was involved in anything, it was because it was his duty. She had to believe in him.

Although the house was dark and quiet, and my bed warm and cozy, sleep eluded me. I could feel Troy's presence down the hall, so dangerously close, and couldn't suppress my longing to be with him. My heart ached for his love, yet my mind remained terrified of the agony I would experience if he discarded me again. I'd loved him for a long time, and it had hurt to have him not return it, but my suffering so far could not compare to the torture of having his love and then losing it. *Should I dare hope he's changed?*

There was a gentle tap on my door. In the pale moonlight, I saw it open slowly, and my heart skipped a beat. I switched on the lamp, the dim light filling the room, illuminating Troy's face as he peeked around the door.

"Good, you're awake," he whispered. "I couldn't sleep."

I sat up. "Me either. Are you okay?"

He sat beside me. "No, I keep thinking of you in here, and me in there, and it doesn't seem right. I want to be with you. I didn't get to see you much today because we were so busy with the horses, but tomorrow should be better." He reached to put his arm around me. "Hey, come here," he said, and he drew me closer and started to kiss me. I tensed and turned away, knowing I would be unable to control my need for him.

"What's wrong?" He looked bewildered. I'd never been this cold toward him in the past.

"I think you should go back to your own room. Your uncle might not like finding you in here."

"Don't worry about him. He'll understand." He began to kiss me again, and again I withdrew, stiff and cool. "You act like you're afraid of me. What's wrong?"

I tried to be apologetic, not accusatory. "It's been years since I last saw you. A lot has happened. We need time to get to know each other again. I mean, the last I heard you were about to marry another woman, and now you expect us to pick up as if nothing ever happened?" It must have sounded more convincing than I'd expected. He backed off seemingly satisfied with the explanation.

"Yeah, it has been a long time, but we're still the same people, and the electricity is still there. I could feel it even when I was in my room. No one else could ever make me feel the way I do when you touch me." His arm moved stealthily around my shoulders and his fingers stroked my forearm, sending the current through me as he'd done so often in the past. My body ached to be closer to him. I allowed him to pull me firmly against him, and he pressed his lips to mine. Relaxing and responding, my body screamed out for more.

He pulled back, looking at me, a warm understanding in his now lustful eyes. "I'd better say goodnight now." His lips swept mine once more with a lightness that made me shiver with desire. When he left the room, I sat staring in disbelief at how he could make my head spin. Whenever he caressed me, he took complete control of me. How could I fight him when his touch was all he needed to make me melt?

Chapter 7

Tuesday, June 1—Eastridge—

Rachel sat at her desk staring at the papers in front of her, unable to concentrate on the words printed on the pages. Her life was suddenly taken over by this disease. She'd tried to ignore the pains in her right arm and the weakness in her right leg, but now her arm was becoming numb, and she was losing the use of her fingers. Picking up her pen to make a note, her fingers cramped and she dropped the pen. She wanted to cry, but there were no more tears, only emptiness. *God, I need your help. You've blessed me with so much in my life, but I still have so much I want to do. Please, dear God, help me get through this.*

New Mexico—

I tossed and turned until dawn, finally relinquishing to a deep slumber. I awoke well past ten o'clock. Ashamed of staying in bed so late when I was a guest in someone else's home, I jumped up, took a quick shower, and dressed. On the vanity, a piece of paper was stuck in the bristles of my hairbrush.

> Good morning, Brianna.
>
> Sheila is making us a picnic lunch. Please bring it and meet me at noon on top of the hill that overlooks the ranch. Bring Manuel and he can show you where. It's his second favorite spot.
>
> Troy

Joy and anticipation flooded through me. A picnic with Troy and Manuel. What a perfect day!

Sheila had the picnic basket packed, and Manuel was animated with excitement. We set out walking down the dirt trail, Manuel leading the way with confidence. He obviously knew exactly where Troy had meant. We started up a steep incline. "Troy said this is your second favorite spot. Where is your first favorite?"

The boy's smile broadened as he pointed through the woods. "The creek down there. That's where Uncle Troy and me always come fishing. Ain't much in that old stream, but we always have lots of fun floating sticks in it. We pretend they are enemy boats, and we try to bomb them with rocks and dirt clogs." He began to run. "Come on, let's hurry. I'm hungry." I laughed and ran to catch up with him. At the top of the hill, I dropped to the ground panting. Manuel grabbed my hand and tried to pull me back up. "Come on. It's right over there, not much further." I picked myself up, and we walked over to where three trees shaded a small area of the grass-covered hill. From there you could see the complete ranch; the pastures for grazing, the stables, the house, and even the cute little cottage where Manuel and his parents lived. The cottage was attractive and inviting, painted white with pale blue trim, surrounded by flowers and a white picket fence. It would make a beautiful photograph, and I had the urge to go back to the house to retrieve my camera but decided to wait and come back another time to take pictures.

At the sound of horses' hooves, I turned to see Troy riding up the hill. I'd never seen a more splendid sight. He was more handsome than ever with his black, wavy hair matching the shining black horse.

With the horse grazing nearby, we spread the blanket and emptied the basket of food to see what Sheila had prepared. I poured lemonade and Manuel grabbed a sandwich.

"Oh boy! Mama fixed me my favorite sandwich, peanut butter and jelly." He tore into it and finished eating before Troy and I had barely begun. He went to climb one of the trees with low branches while we finished our lunch. A rope hung from one of the higher branches.

Troy smiled. "I'm glad I put that rope in that tree. He sure enjoys it."

I sat quietly thinking about Mitchell. "Do you know what's going on with Mitch?"

"What do you mean?" Troy inquired, keeping his eyes on Manuel.

"Well, first of all, Mitch paid for me to come out here, yet he doesn't get any benefit from it. You and I both know that Mitch is not a fighter, yet he joins the military? He says he's an accountant, yet he's working strange hours and meeting with big wheels from D.C."

"Hold it. Let's take one of these concerns at a time. First, he's a great friend. He knew we were both miserable, and he knew the cure."

"Yeah, but those plane tickets had to have cost him a few hundred dollars!"

Troy nodded. "But he is one of those rare people that believes everyone is good and everyone should be happy. He never judges anyone and does anything and everything in his power to cause peace and harmony. That's what he lives for. I wouldn't go so far as to say he's perfect. He still has his desires, and I've seen him be very selfish at times, but I've never seen him kill anything, not even a bug."

I was bewildered. "Unselfishness is one thing. Giving away hundreds of dollars is something else."

"Not to Mitch. His religion teaches that money in excess is evil. They recognize it as a necessity of life, but believe any excess is to be used toward helping others. They teach that when someone is upset, it affects the whole universe because we are all a part of the same spiritual existence. So whenever they see someone unhappy, they do all they can to help. It's really a beautiful idea, albeit misleading."

"How do you mean?"

"Well, Satan has this way of using beautiful ideas such as this and drawing the attention away from Christ. It worries me that his religion doesn't believe in Jesus as the Son of God, but rather as *a* son of God in the same way that all of us are sons of God."

I couldn't believe those words were coming out of Troy's mouth. "So when did you become so religious?"

His eyes sparkled when he smiled. "That's probably the biggest change in my life since I saw you last. About four years ago, a good friend of mine passed away. At the funeral I came to realize how fragile life is. He was only twenty-four and died of a heart attack! It made me think a lot about what happens after we die. I started going to this little country church and studying the Bible. It's really amazing how much is in that two-thousand-year-old book that still pertains to us today. The more I studied it, the hungrier I became. I needed to know more. It wasn't long before I accepted Christ as my Savior and was baptized. Since then, my life makes a lot more sense."

I'd been raised in a church, so none of what he said was news to me, but I suddenly felt very uncomfortable. Maybe this guy wasn't the same Troy I'd known all those years ago. "Getting back to Mitch, we both know he's a passivist. Like you said, he won't even kill a bug, so why would he be in the service?"

"He's an accountant, not a fighter. He only went in the service to get the free education. If he had to actually go to war, he'd probably go AWOL."

"So what do you make of all of his strange hours?"

"As an accountant, he's dealing with the government's money. I'm sure that involves having meetings with higher-ups. You're making way too much out of this."

"Maybe, but I haven't told you about the UFO drawings."

Troy took a deep breath. "What UFO drawings?" He sounded bored with the conversation.

"Never mind." I turned my attention to Manuel and changed the subject. "Manuel brought his ball. Why don't you go play with him while I clean up."

Collecting the trash and stuffing it into a bag, I placed

the leftover food back in the basket while Troy and Manuel played pitch, then joined them in a short game of keep-away.

Starting back down the hill, Troy led the horse while Manuel rode, and I walked along beside him. I glanced up to see him staring at me with an impish grin that spread into his gleaming mocha eyes. "What? Why are you looking at me like that?"

Troy chuckled. "Do you remember our first date?"

"How could I forget?" I recalled the evening perfectly. Daddy had allowed me to go, but only if we double-dated. When Troy came to pick me up, instead of another couple, there were two other guys in the car. Since one of them had long hair, Daddy hadn't known the difference. All he could see from the house was two people in the car, one with short hair and one with long, blond hair. "I don't think Daddy knows to this day that there were two guys in the back of that car."

"What I remember most about that night is how you almost killed me with that bowling ball."

"I know, but I think the embarrassment was what almost killed you, not the ball."

Bowling had been a new experience for me. Troy had tried to show me how to hold the ball and then went to sit down. I took a couple of steps toward the pins, and as I let my arm drop for the swing, the ball rolled from my hand and headed straight for Troy. When I turned to see where the ball had gone, I saw Troy jumping over it to keep from being hit. I hadn't noticed until then that all the professional league players were standing behind us watching.

Like a scene from a cartoon, it was too hilarious for me to be embarrassed. I'd laughed until I could no longer stand, but Troy glared at me, his face flushed. At the time, I was convinced he would never ask me for another date, but he called the very next week to go bowling again, but only if I promised to aim at the pins instead of him.

Passing the stables, I noticed a gray horse grazing in the field. "I didn't notice that horse before."

"That's the new Arabian mare, Misty. We purchased her to breed with Stormy here." He indicated the black horse Manuel was sitting on, the same one we'd ridden to the creek the day I arrived. I wanted a closer look at the mare, so we went into the pasture, and Troy used a lump of sugar to coax Misty to us.

"She never turns down sugar," he said as Misty inched toward us. Once she was certain we weren't going to hurt or try to saddle her, she relaxed and allowed me to stroke her.

One of the ranch hands came from the stables. "She doesn't let many people pet her. Looks like you've made a friend." He sauntered over to meet me. "If you decide you want to ride her sometime, just let me know and I'll get her saddled up for you."

Troy introduced us, "Bree, this is Pete. He shoes the horses and helps keep them groomed. You can usually find him working in the stables if you need him."

I was glad to have the invitation to ride Misty. I'd already fallen in love with the horse and was dying to ride. "Thanks, Pete. I'll take you up on that sometime." I gave Misty one more sugar cube, and we continued our walk to the house.

After dinner, I went with Troy and Uncle Jake to secure the ranch for the night. It was the perfect opportunity to ride Misty. The mare had a lot more spirit than any horse I'd ridden before, and it was difficult keeping her at a walk. Misty wanted to run, so when we reached an open field, I let her gallop. Then we stopped to wait for the others. While sitting there, I looked around. This was paradise; to be with Troy and the others I'd met here and to be able to ride such a fine horse on this beautiful ranch. It was as if this fantasy world had been created just for me. Thank you, Mitchell! For the first time in my life, I felt I knew what the word *freedom* meant.

A voice interrupted my thoughts, and I realized Troy and Uncle Jake had caught up and were now waiting for me.

"Where were you? Your mind must have been miles away."

I didn't answer. I simply smiled and rode along. *No, I was right here in my own little heaven.*

Wednesday, June 2—

I awoke at dawn the next morning, early enough to have breakfast with Uncle Jake and Troy.

Uncle Jake looked surprised when I entered the kitchen at such an hour. "Well, good morning, Sunshine."

"Good morning, Uncle Jake. What's with the 'sunshine?'"

He chuckled. "You're the closest thing I've seen to sunshine today. 'Twas a cloudy day 'til you walked in all smiling."

After breakfast, the men left for their morning chores while I helped clean the kitchen. The telephone rang, but Sheila was up to her elbows in dishwater, so I went down the hall to answer it.

"Hello, Garrison residence."

"Sheila?" came a female voice.

"No, this is Brianna Chavis."

"Oh, Bree! How've ya been doing since Mitch dropped ya off there?"

"Gina?" I was relieved to hear a familiar voice.

"Yes, it's me. You doin' okay?"

I laughed. "Yes, thanks to Mitch's sneaky stunt. Were you in on the act too?"

"You might say that. Mitch told me how unhappy you two were, so I suggested we get you together again. We tried to be sure you would both want it before we interfered though."

"Well, you sure did a good job of keeping it all a secret. I had no idea what was happening until I saw Troy's face."

"I'd like to have seen both of your faces. Is Troy there?"

"No, he's out making his morning rounds. Do you want me to ask him to call you?"

"Please do. Mitch has some kind of big meeting tonight at work, and Jacques called to say he had something he had to do, so I need someone to entertain at the restaurant. Troy has been helping us some since he's been here, so I thought if he doesn't mind, he could fill in tonight. Ask him to let me know as soon as possible."

"Okay, I'll tell him."

It was an hour later before Troy came back and I gave him the message.

"Do you mind if we go to the restaurant tonight?" he asked as if expecting me to object.

"Of course not. I'd like to see Gina again. Besides, I want to hear you sing. It's been a long time."

After lunch, we sat down for a practice session. He practiced most of the afternoon with me singing along on the tunes I recognized. He incorporated a lot of the wonderful Appalachian tunes in his act, songs we'd both known growing up in Eastridge. I glanced around. "You don't happen to have an autoharp here, do you?"

"That's right, you do play, don't you?" He glanced around the room. "Well, let's see. There's bound to be one around here somewhere. I mean, doesn't everyone have one of those laying around their house?"

I laughed. "Yeah, I guess maybe back home in the hills, but not around here, huh?"

Soon, we had an audience. Uncle Jake, Sheila, and Manuel wandered into the room, clapping and swaying to the rhythm. Manuel beamed. "You guys are good!"

Mitchell sat alone in his car staring into the dunes of White Sands. *All I wanted to do is get Troy and Brianna back together where they belong, but I should have known better than bring Brianna here. She's too sharp to be snooping around while this stuff is going on. Why on earth did I get myself into this?*

Earlier that day, Mitchell had been informed of a

breach in security. Someone had leaked information that was getting into the hands of other countries. Then Troy had called and told him about Brianna asking more questions. *I know Brianna isn't involved, but if she continues to ask questions, she could get herself, and me, into trouble.*

He stepped from the car and began walking across the sand. He'd told Gina he couldn't play music at the restaurant tonight because he had an important meeting. *Now I'm lying to her too. I'm sorry, Gina. When I got myself involved in all these top military secrets, I didn't realize how it could put my friends at risk. I hate this!*

He continued walking, climbing and descending the dunes, searching—not for the vessel Brianna had seen, it had already been recovered. He was searching for the person he used to be—the person he felt slipping away into a dark, slimy hole.

When we arrived at the restaurant, Gina was busy keeping her customers happy and making sure everything ran smoothly in the kitchen. I sat alone, watching people come and go. Being a Wednesday night, the crowd was small. There was a young man sitting alone in the corner that captured my interest. He was built like a football player; not fat, but very muscular.

Gina made her way around the room, finally arriving at my table. "Are you okay? Can I get you anything?"

"No, I'm fine." I motioned toward the man in the corner. "Do you know him?"

"Sure, that's Sal, Mitch's roommate."

"That's Sal? I thought he was in jail."

Gina looked confused. "Um—no." Glancing toward the kitchen, she placed her hand on my arm. "Excuse me, hon; I've got to get back to the kitchen."

I looked back at Sal, who was watching me. He smiled and winked, flirting. I quickly turned my attention back to Troy on stage.

Every few minutes, Troy would look my way to let me know I wasn't forgotten. After singing a few songs, he made an announcement.

"Good evening, ladies and gentlemen. Tonight I want to sing a song dedicated to a very special lady. Bree, this is for you. I call it *Electric Breeze*."

All eyes turned to me as the audience figured out that I was his target. I felt the blood rush into my face and the heat caused my eyes to water. The song was one he'd sung to me years ago, claiming he'd composed it for me. At the time, I'd doubted him, believing he probably told all the girls he dated the same story.

The smooth, flowing rhythm caused listeners to sway:

> She softly swept into my heart, A calm whisper o'er rolling seas
> I felt her presence in the air, It was an electric breeze
> When her world was in turmoil, My heart could hear her pleas
> Unspoken was her anguish but I felt a restless breeze

> Everyone keeps telling me I'll only cause her strife
> That I should leave and let her be so she will have a better life.
> This passion deep within my heart that's driving me insane
> How do I simply let it go to live with emptiness and pain?

Listening to the words carefully, they expressed the feelings I'd never been able to explain. The pull between us had always been so strong; I could feel his presence before actually seeing him. All those times when I felt Troy's restlessness or pain even when he was miles away. Or those times I'd be thinking about him and he would call, asking if I was alright. There was an unexplained telepathy between us until he'd left for the Coast Guard and the connection had been broken.

The last time I'd heard it, the song had ended there. I looked up in surprise when he continued:

> Now she's gone from my world and there's nothing that can ease
> This pain within my empty soul, I miss that electric breeze
> A tear escapes my closed eyes as I fall upon my knees
> I ache, I want, I need, I pray to feel the electric breeze
> Then it happened again today, I felt the electric breeze
> She's back to sweep my pain away, I pray she'll never leave.

> A second chance has blown my way, and now
> I'm telling you
> This time I will not go away, we'll start our life anew.

If he'd cared so much, then why had he abandoned me? My heart had cried out, but there'd been no answer. I'd felt he was troubled but couldn't find him. For seven years, we'd both suffered, but for what? Why did he leave me?

His voice brought me back to the present. "Folks, I'm going to take a short break. I'll be back in about ten minutes." Leaving the stage, he joined me at the table. "Did you remember that song?"

I had the urge to reach out and kiss him. "How could I forget a song that was written for me? But you added more to it."

"Did you like it?"

"Of course."

A few people strolled by the table to tell him how much they enjoyed his music. When they left, he cocked his head and gave me a quizzical look. "That song we were singing together this afternoon. Do you know all the words to it?"

"Which one? We sang more than one song."

He hummed the beginning of one of the melodies I'd sung the harmony to earlier.

"I think I know all the words. Why, have you forgotten them?"

"I get stuck on the second verse."

We discussed the words until he was sure he had them straight, then it was time to go back onto the platform.

I glanced back into the corner. Sal was gone.

Troy leaned into one of the two microphones on stage. "Folks, I've got a little surprise for you tonight. I want you to welcome a friend of mine that's going to come up and help me sing this next song. Meet Miss Brianna Rae Chavis! Bree, come on up here."

Everyone began to applaud, and I could hear a few whistles filtering through the haze of my shock. I'd never confronted an audience before, and I didn't like being surprised. I moved toward the stage, feeling as if I had no other choice in front of all the people applauding. My heart pounded, not only from stage fright, but from anger. I climbed onto the platform, not knowing what to do with my hands. I was conscious of my clothes, my hair, even my shoes. I wasn't prepared to be on stage. He began to play and sing, and I sang along in a trance. After the first few measures, I started to relax, and we sang together as we had earlier that afternoon. The audience encouraged me to sing something by myself, so Troy picked out a familiar ballad from our youth, and the words came back as if it were yesterday.

After the second song, I returned to the table to find Jacques waiting for me.

"You're good," he complimented me as I sat down beside him.

"Thanks, but I was a bit unprepared," I stated through clinched teeth. "I had no idea he was going to ask me to sing tonight." I glared at Troy to let him know that I didn't appreciate what he'd done. Suddenly, the delayed reaction from being nervous hit me like an earthquake. My body began to tremble, and I became weak and flushed. I headed for the door for some fresh air, with Jacques at my heals. The night air was cold, but it helped to restore my composure.

I stood leaning against the brick building. "I can't believe he did that!"

"You did a good job. No one knew you were not prepared. You're a natural," Jacques reassured.

A chill ran through my body. Jacques didn't miss the shiver and removed his jacket, placing it around my shoulders. His eyes met mine, and he began to move his mouth toward my lips. I turned my head. "We'd better go back in before we catch cold out here."

Suddenly, a voice in the doorway spoke, "I think that would be an excellent idea." I whirled around to see a furious Troy. I wasn't sure what to say. Although I hadn't done anything, I felt like I'd been caught.

"Troy, time for another break already?" I tried to sound light, but instead it had come out flippant.

"I wanted to be sure you were all right, but I can see you don't need my help." He turned and stormed back inside.

Jacques stood by waiting for my reaction. I remained still, unsure of what to do. He reached out his hand to comfort me. "Hey, I'm sorry if I caused you any trouble."

Not wanting him to touch me, I sidestepped toward the door. "No, it's okay, but let's go in. Oh, and here's your coat." I gave him the jacket and went inside to watch the conclusion of the show.

On the way back to the ranch, Troy was silent and I could feel the tension growing with every mile traveled. I wanted to vanquish the barrier between us but was afraid anything I tried to say might make matters worse. I remained quiet and waited for him to speak first. The minutes and miles ticked by without a word. When we reached the house, he went inside ahead of me, and with his back still to me, mumbled goodnight as he walked toward his room.

I threw myself across my bed. When I closed my eyes, I could still see the fury on Troy's face, his eyes like a dark tempest brewing. I could even feel its fierceness consuming me as tears spilled down my cheeks. I rolled over and stared at the ceiling. "This is so stupid!" The events of the evening played over in my mind until I slipped into a restless sleep.

Chapter 8

Thursday, June 3—

Still wearing the clothes from the night before, I awakened feeling stripped of all emotion. I showered, redressed, then walked to the stables.

Pete looked up from brushing Misty. "Ready for a morning ride?"

I attempted to appear more pleasant than I felt. "Yes, it's a beautiful morning, so I brought my camera and thought I'd ride up the hill and take some shots of the ranch."

He reached for a saddle. "I'll get her saddled for you. Do you prefer this Western saddle, or would you rather use English?"

"The Western one for me, please. I've never cared for English. I like having the horn to grab onto."

Ten minutes later, I rode along the pathway leading to the hilltop. I reached down and stroked Misty's gray-speckled mane. "You know, Misty? You're about the only bright spot in my morning." I continued talking to the horse about Troy being angry with me as if it could understand. At one point it appeared that Misty was nodding in agreement.

I took a few snapshots of the little cottage and the horses in the pasture, then sat in the grass to watch Misty graze. The rumbling in my stomach reminded me of my lack of breakfast, so I climbed back into the saddle and started back down the hill. We hadn't journeyed far when Misty reared back, then bucked uncontrollably. I let out a feeble shriek while trying to hang on. The horse took one final wild leap and lunged forward into a full run. I tumbled to the ground catching a glimpse of a snake slithering into the weeds beside the path.

"Bree," a distant voice reached through the fog. Recognizing Troy's voice, I breathed his name. I opened my eyes but couldn't focus. The blue color of the room slowly became visible, and I felt Troy holding my hand as the grogginess faded. I tried to sit up, but the pain in my skull was so excruciating, I fell back to the pillow.

Troy leaned over me. "Don't try to move too much yet. You got quite a bump on the head when you fell. Take it easy for a while."

"How did I get here?" Disoriented and tired, I drifted back into a deep sleep, never hearing his answer.

Eastridge—

Milly was on the phone when Rachel arrived at her office. "She's walking in now, Mr. Milliken. Do you want to hold on for a moment, or should I have her call you back?" She smiled up at Rachel. "Yes, sir. I'll tell her." She hung up. "He's anxious to know your decision about taking over the business when he retires."

Rachel flopped into an easy chair. "I can't deal with this right now. Milly, how can I think of running this business with MS robbing me of the use of my arms and legs? What am I going to do?"

Although it was meant to be a rhetorical question, Milly refused to see it that way. "I'll tell you what you're going to do. You're going to find another doctor who can treat whatever this is. I've been doing some research, and although there is no cure, there are treatments that have shown some success in slowing down the progression. You might have to go somewhere besides Eastridge to get treated, but it's not like you don't have the resources. Just do it!"

"I've done research too, and I didn't find it to be comforting at all. In your research, have you found a specialist who might be able to help me?"

"As a matter of fact, there's a doctor in Richmond at the Medical College of Virginia who specializes in MS. Do you want me to call him and get an appointment for you?"

"Of course! I have to do something. I can't just sit around and wait for this disease to consume my entire life. Call him." Renewed hope gave Rachel the boost she needed to make it into her office and begin work. *Monroe, you will have to wait a little longer for my answer. You've waited fifty years to retire, you can certainly wait a few more days.*

Her intercom buzzed. She picked up the phone. "What is it, Milly?"

"Mitchell Sibley is calling from New Mexico about Bree."

Rachel punched the button on her phone. "Hello?"

"Mrs. Chavis?"

Obviously there was something wrong or Brianna would have called, not Mitchell. "Yes, Mitchell. What's wrong?"

"Brianna had a little accident. She was horseback riding and fell off the horse. She's sleeping right now. I think she'll be okay, but I thought you should know."

"Are you sure she's alright?"

"A slight concussion, but she's responding okay. I'll get her to call you when she wakes up."

"Please do. And Mitch…"

"Yes, Mrs. Chavis?"

"Thank you for calling."

New Mexico—

Mitchell crept into the bedroom and saw Troy kneeling by the bed, praying. Brianna rested peacefully, a small bandage on her forehead. "Troy?" he whispered.

Troy looked up, stood, and moved quickly across the room. "Thanks for coming, buddy."

"How's she doing?"

"She's been asleep since I called you. I think she'll be okay. She hit her head when she fell, so she may have a bit of a headache for awhile."

"Shouldn't you call a doctor?"

"Uncle Jake looked at her. He's had a lot of experience with people falling from horses, and he didn't think it was necessary to call the doctor. If she doesn't wake up in a few hours, I will overrule my uncle and call the doctor anyway."

"I called Mrs. Chavis and told her about the accident. I didn't mention you. Only that Bree had fallen from a horse, and I tried to reassure her that Bree was okay. She wants Bree to call her when she wakes up."

"Of course. I'll make sure she does."

"I'm going downstairs to talk to Uncle Jake. Let me know if she wakes up."

"Sure thing. I'm sure she'll want to see you."

Mitchell slipped back out of the door, leaving Troy to his prayers.

Awaking again, I felt more like my old self. It was dusk and I was starving. Scanning the room, I saw Troy sitting in a rocker by the window reading a magazine.

"You should turn on a light," I spoke in a feeble voice.

He looked up and quickly crossed the room. "How are you feeling?"

"Better, but I could eat a cow right now." I struggled to sit up, and he helped me prop myself with the pillow. Then he went down the hall calling Sheila. A few minutes later, I was sipping soup and nibbling on crackers.

Troy sat by the bed and stared at me with a happy glow on his previously worried face. "Mitch came by earlier, but left just before you woke up. I should call and let him know you're awake."

Uncle Jake walked in. "I'll call Mitch for ya. You take care of this little lady. How are ya feelin,' darlin'?"

There was something about Uncle Jake, an aura or warmth that emitted from him that made one feel better whenever he was in the room. I smiled. "I'm feeling a lot better now that I've eaten some soup."

"Good. I'll go make that phone call to Mitch. Troy, you take care of our girl." Uncle Jake hobbled from the room.

Troy placed the dishes and tray on the vanity. "You had me scared to death. When Misty came back to the pasture without you, I imagined all kinds of terrible things. Then when I found you sprawled out on the trail unconscious, I…I was afraid I might never get the chance to…" his voice cracked and he stopped to clear his throat.

"I don't know what happened. One minute Misty was walking calmly and the next she went wild."

Troy nodded. "Something must have spooked her."

Then I remembered. "The snake! There was a snake going into the brush when I fell. I only got a quick look at it, but that must have been what scared her."

Troy stood up and began to scold me. "You had better promise me one thing, young lady; that you'll never go riding again by yourself, at least not until you either learn to stay on or learn to fall off a bucking horse."

"You wouldn't have gone with me even if I'd asked you to, you were so mad at me. If you hadn't been so mule-headed, I wouldn't have gone to begin with," I defended myself.

He chuckled, sat on the edge of the bed, and leaned back on the headboard, placing his arm around my shoulders and hugging me tenderly. "Okay, I'll take the blame. I just thank God you're okay."

Uncle Jake peeked into the door. "I called Mitch and he said to remind you to call your mother. She's worried about you."

I looked at Troy. "My mother? Did you call her?"

"No, Mitch did. He thought she should know about your accident."

"Does she know I'm here with you?"

"No, he didn't mention me at all. Only that you'd fallen from a horse."

"Okay. Give me my cell phone so I can call and ease her mind. I wish he hadn't called her."

Friday, June 4—

I remained around the house the entire next day trying to get my strength back and shake my dull headache. While Troy was busy helping Uncle Jake mend fences and other chores around the ranch, Manuel kept me company. We played quiet games, and I read him simple storybooks.

By late afternoon, I was feeling exhausted. I grabbed a quick sandwich for my dinner and slept through the family meal. When nightfall came, I was wide-awake and feeling restless.

Standing at the back door, I stared into the speckled sky. It was a crisp, clear night and the winking stars beckoned me to join them in the calm, velvety darkness.

I felt the warmth of Troy's presence behind me and welcomed his gentle embrace as I leaned back and enjoyed the security and tenderness of being in his arms. I was at peace with myself except for one small matter tugging at my mind. I knew I had to go back home in three days.

Troy sighed. "It sure is a beautiful night. The air is so refreshing and crisp, yet it's not quite cool enough to cause a chill."

"Yes, it's so peaceful here," I agreed. He turned me around to face him.

"Then why are you so solemn?"

I hadn't realized my sadness had shown. "I was thinking about how close Tuesday is getting."

"So, what's Tuesday?"

"The end of my vacation and time to go home." I hoped he might ask me to stay longer. I needed to get back home to look for a job, and I'd told my parents I would be back by Tuesday evening. Also my rent was due, but even with so many reasons for going back home, I knew I would find a way to stretch my money and my vacation for a day or two if he would ask me to stay.

After a long silence, all he said was, "We'll simply have to make the most of the time that's left. It's such a beautiful night; let's go for a midnight stroll around the grounds tonight."

Joe walked up the porch steps to tell Troy that Jake was waiting for him. It was the first time I'd seen Sheila's husband, but I knew it was him immediately since he was an enlarged duplicate of his son, Manuel.

Sheila put away the last of the dinner dishes and was ready to go home by the time Joe found Manuel. The three of them waved good-bye to me and made their way toward their quaint little cottage.

Later that night—

It was after eleven when Troy tapped on my bedroom door. I jumped up and, not wanting to appear too anxious, composed myself before answering.

"You ready?" He was bright and cheerful and seemed to be excited about being with me. Although a chill filled the air, a warm mantle of contentment shrouded me as we set out for our walk in the moonlight. A blanket thrown over his shoulder, we walked hand-in-hand down the lane leading to the creek.

Troy laughed. "This reminds me of how we used to sneak around because your parents wouldn't allow you to see me."

I grinned, remembering the fun times we'd been through together. The threat of getting caught had made it all the more romantic.

"Your parents sure didn't care for me much."

"Not until you had that little talk with Daddy." I recalled how Troy had walked three miles to my house to talk to Daddy. He was tired of sneaking around and was determined to set things straight with my parents once and for all. His rusty, beat-up old Mustang had died, but his strong determination had gotten him there by foot. I'd been sent from the room while they'd talked and to this day didn't know what had been said during that chat. Neither of them would tell me, but whatever it was had worked. When I'd reentered the room, Daddy and Troy had been shaking hands and joking around like old pals. "What did you two talk about, anyway?"

"Not much. He needed to know that I cared about you and would never do anything to hurt you. Once I'd convinced him of that, he was fine."

"Too bad you didn't mean it. Why did you go to all that trouble to get my daddy's permission to date me and then turn around and ditch me for my best friend? All that convincing went right down the tubes when Daddy saw how you hurt me. He hated you more after that than he ever did before."

Troy stopped walking and stared at me in disbelief. "I didn't ditch you." He looked angry as he defended himself. "Chloe wrote to me and told me that you were interested in another guy but didn't know how to break off with me. I simply gave you an easy way out by staying away and not contacting you."

I went pale, realizing that Chloe had double-crossed me. I stared at the ground in disbelief. Chloe was the only person I'd confided in about my feelings for Troy. Only Chloe had known how much I'd loved him.

My blood boiled. "I'll kill her. If I ever see her again, so help me I'll wring her scrawny neck!"

"What on earth is wrong?" Troy was stunned by my sudden outburst.

I turned on him. "What's wrong? That dear best friend of mine betrayed me, ruining my teenage years, and you ask what's wrong?"

"Hey, calm down. How did she ruin your life?"

"Don't you understand?" I was amazed at how thick-headed he seemed right now. "She lied! She knew how much I needed you, yet she told you I wanted to end our relationship. She also told me that you'd been trying to see her behind my back all along, and that you wanted to break up with me but were afraid of hurting me."

His expression showed that he finally grasped the whole picture, but instead of angry, he looked bewildered. "Why would she do such a thing? She was your closest friend. Did she hate me too, like your parents?"

My anger subsided as I chuckled at his stupidity. "You are so dense. She didn't hate you. She wanted you for herself, silly."

He almost choked on the thought of him with Chloe. "That's got to be the most ridiculous thing I've ever heard. I could barely tolerate being around her, much less want to date her. No man in his right mind could get serious with her. She was loony. She made a joke of everything, even the most serious subjects. How could you possibly believe such a thing?"

"Believe me, I fell for it all. She was very convincing."

He reached out and pulled me to him, hugging me close to his warm, hard chest. "I'd say we have quite a few years to catch up on, wouldn't you?"

We reached the creek, and Troy spread the blanket out over the sandy embankment. We sat and stared into the water, and I began to reminisce again. "Do you remember the last time we sat on a blanket beside a stream?"

"Yes, it was our very last date before I left for training." The affectionate tone in his voice caused me to glance up at him. The look in his eyes was so tender; I yearned for his touch.

"You know I was willing to make love that night."

"I know."

That night, so long ago, we had almost made love.

It was a cool evening in May. Troy drove us to a secluded spot by the side of a lake, armed with a couple of blankets. After spreading one of the blankets, he sat down and reached his hand out to me.

I thought I knew what he was expecting, and although

scared, I wanted to make him happy. I sat next to him and he wrapped the other blanket around us.

I waited.

He held me next to him. "I'm leaving in the morning."

"I know. I don't want you to go."

"I'll write, and I'll come back whenever I'm allowed to leave the base."

"I'm going to miss you." I was sixteen, but suddenly felt ten. I wondered when he would make his move. I'd already decided I loved him enough to give myself to him.

He said, "I need to know something."

"What?"

"Are you a virgin?"

I swallowed and looked at him. There was no need to answer. My frightened eyes told him.

He jumped up. "Get up and let's get out of here."

I stood and looked around to see if there was a policeman coming, but there was no one.

He snatched up the blankets and threw them into the back of the car.

Confused, I asked, "What did I do wrong?" but he wouldn't talk.

By the time we reached my home, I was crying, and he stopped the car on the side of the street to comfort me. He placed his arm tenderly around my shoulders and pulled me close. "Come on, stop crying."

"But I don't understand. What did I do?"

"You didn't do anything wrong. In fact, you're perfect, but I'm leaving tomorrow for training. I wouldn't feel right making love to you and then leaving. It's best if we wait."

Since that night, I'd felt a greater respect for him and my love had grown deeper because of it. I'd been haunted by that night and unable to get him out of my mind long enough to get involved with any other man. Now, here I was reliving it, but hopefully with a different ending.

My mind snapped back to the present as Troy's fingers stroked my skin, tenderly wandering over my flesh, sending a current through my entire being. He cupped my head in his hand and teased my lips with sweet light kisses, gently leaning me back onto the blanket.

A voice deep within me whispered, *You're a fool; don't give in*, but the throbbing of my pulse blocked out my instincts to stop him as his mouth caressed my lips, my face, my neck, and slowly made its way toward my breasts. I drowned in his warmth and wanted to release all the desires I'd held inside for so long, to feel the intense heights my entire being craved. I heard myself whispering, "I love you,"and I heard his rapid breathing. I realized if I didn't stop now, there would be no stopping him, no turning back. My instincts told me to pull away and run, but my entire being cried out to be consumed by him, to become one with his body. I was vaguely aware that my clothes had been peeled away, but I no longer cared. Eyes closed, I allowed myself to ride this wave of ecstasy, climbing higher and higher until we were both completely spent. I heard him groan. Then he rolled over onto his back pulling me on top of him. He smiled up at me. "Now *that* was worth waiting for." I laughed and rolled back to the ground, feeling more fulfilled than I'd ever believed possible. Without another word, Troy pulled me next to him, and we entwined ourselves together in a soft embrace. I closed my eyes, enjoying the tranquility that was ours alone, until Troy sat up and handed me my clothes.

I dressed, then sat next to him.

Troy was quiet. I studied his face. There was no smile, no frown, no expression. He sat with his arms wrapped around his knees staring into the stream.

"What's on your mind?"

Breaking from his trance, he shook his head. "Nothing. It's late, and we should be getting on back. I've got a lot to do tomorrow."

Saturday, June 5—

The sun shone brightly through the sheer, floral drapes. I sprang from the covers and opened the window to take in a large breath of fresh air. The sky was a brilliant blue with a wisp of soft, white clouds floating past. I felt weightless and could envision myself rising to drift among them. I rushed to shower and dress, then bobbed through the hall toward the study, yearning to see Troy again, to hold him as I had the night before.

Hesitating at the closed door of the study, pondering whether to knock first or walk in unannounced, I heard Troy's voice. My heart beat faster knowing he was only a few steps away. Placing my hand on the knob, I stopped when his voice amplified in anger. "That's your problem. You brought her here, now you take care of getting rid of her!"

I stood frozen, holding the knob, letting his sharp words soak in, trying to understand their meaning. I listened closely, trying to determine who he was speaking to.

"No, I never told you, or anyone else, to drop her off here at the ranch." There was a brief pause. "But the point is that she's here, and I need someone to get her off my hands." After another brief pause, he said, "Good, I'll expect you to come get her by tomorrow evening." I heard him hang up the phone.

I eased my hand from the doorknob and tiptoed back up the stairs to my room. I sat on the bed, trying to make sense of his words. Was he talking to Mitchell about me? I shook my head, not wanting to believe such a thing. *No, he loves me—doesn't he?* He was incredibly gentle and caring only a few hours earlier.

An unexpected realization stabbed through me. Troy never told me he loved me last night! I'd said I loved him several times, but he hadn't repeated those words. I remembered all the times in the past when I'd been so sure he loved me, only to have my heart crushed by him later. My eyes watered as I accepted the possibility that he was probably talking to Mitchell about getting rid of me.

I sat trying to reason things out. *Okay, let's be logical. What other explanation is there? Hadn't Mitchell surprised both me and Troy by dumping me off here at the ranch? Who else had been dropped off that he could want to be rid of?* The truth was, there was no one else. There was no other explanation.

I rolled over and began sobbing into the coverlet. *How many times am I going to make a fool of myself over him? I never learn. Now that he's gotten what he wanted, I'm of no more use to him. Well, Momma and Daddy, I guess you were right all along.*

Like a young child with a booboo, there was the sudden urge to turn to my parents for comfort. I dragged myself up and packed my suitcase, laying my airline ticket aside.

I sat on the edge of the bed trying to decide what to do next. *I can't call Mitchell. It's his fault I'm in this mess. How could he set me up like this? He knows Troy better than anyone. He should have known I'd only get hurt again.*

If I call Gina, she might tell Mitchell, then Mitchell would call Troy. No, I've got to do this on my own.

I hid the bags under the bed, rinsed my face with cold water, grabbed the airline ticket, and crept through the quiet house. There was no one around.

I slipped down the stairs, checked once more to be sure I was alone, then scurried to the telephone and retrieved the directory kept on the table next to the phone. I riffled through the yellow pages until I found the cab companies. *When should I have them pick me up, and where? I don't want anyone seeing me leave, so I'd better leave tonight after dark, after everyone has gone to bed. I don't want the headlights waking anyone, so I'll have to meet the cab at the gate at the end of the driveway.*

I called three cab companies before one of them agreed to my terms. The first wouldn't travel so far from the city limits. The second didn't have a car available for midnight. The third agreed to meet me at the gate at midnight to take me to the airport.

Placing the receiver back onto the cradle of the old-fashioned phone, I heard Sheila and Manuel enter through the back door. I slithered back to my bedroom.

Minutes later, Sheila knocked on my door. "Brianna? Are you okay?"

My mind raced to think of an explanation. "I'm not feeling well this morning. I think I need a little rest, so I thought I'd stay in bed for a while." This excuse gave me a chance to be alone so I wouldn't have to pretend to be in a good mood all day. Also, I wouldn't have to face Troy.

"Is it okay if I come in?"

I scrambled into the bed and threw the covers over myself. "Sure, come on in."

Sheila crossed the room and felt my forehead. "No fever. Do you feel like eating?"

"I'll be okay. I'm just tired after staying up so late last night."

Sheila gave me an understanding nod and left the room, returning a few minutes later with toast and juice on a tray. "You must have nourishment." She smiled, placed the tray beside me on the bed, and left to complete her chores.

Finally alone, I wanted to cry, but there were no more tears. I was totally numb. I tried to go to sleep but couldn't stop feeling sorry for myself.

"No!" My fist pummeled the pillow. "I refuse to be his victim again!" I shoved the self-pity aside and replaced it with determination. He'd made a fool of me again, but he wasn't going to have the satisfaction of seeing me hurt over him. Neither would he have the chance to jilt me this time, because I would dump him first.

Tears began trickling down my cheeks as I recalled how he'd become quiet after our lovemaking. He was probably trying to figure out how to get rid of me even then.

I remained under the covers, listening to the sounds of people walking through the house, dishes clinking in the kitchen, the grandfather clock striking every half hour until there was a rap on my door. I looked at the clock. Lunchtime. "Come in, Sheila."

The door opened, and when I saw Troy, my anger escalated. Suppressing it, I tried to appear poised.

"Hey, sleepyhead, what's wrong? It's a beautiful day."

"I feel like being lazy today. I haven't been sleeping much since I've been here."

"Okay. I need to go into town anyway. I'd almost forgotten that today is Manuel's birthday. I ordered his present a couple of months ago, and I have to go pick it up. Time slipped up on me with all the excitement you've caused by your arrival here, and then your accident." He hadn't made the remark with any malice, but I thought deep down he must have felt it.

I was glad I was going to be there for Manuel's birthday and became excited about it, putting aside my own heartache.

"What did you order for him?"

Troy's eyes flickered with the thrill of having something really special for Manuel. "His very own custom-made leather saddle. I hope he likes it. After I ordered it, he showed me a pair of boots he had his heart set on. I hope he won't be disappointed about not getting them."

"What are his parents giving him?"

A devilish grin crossed his face. "That's going to be a huge surprise. I'm not even going to tell you what it is. You'll see soon enough."

"And Uncle Jake?"

"He gave me money to buy something when I go into town, but it's not enough for those boots."

I had some of the money left that I'd allowed myself to spend on this trip, and since the trip was soon to end, I hopped from the bed and took out my purse. Making sure I withheld enough to get me home, I plunged the money into his hand, "Here, use this and add it to your uncle's money. Will that be enough?"

"Yeah," he said slowly, looking at my clothing. "What are you doing dressed and lying in bed. I didn't think you'd been out of that bed all day."

"Oh, I got up and dressed this morning, but felt so drained, I crawled back into the bed." I shrugged.

That seemed to satisfy his curiosity. He turned his attention back to the boots. "Bree, are you sure you want to spend so much on Manuel? You only met him this week."

"I know, but he's so adorable. Please buy him the boots. They can be from Uncle Jake and me."

He kissed my forehead and started out the door. "Are you sure you won't come with me?"

"I'm sure." The entire time he'd been in the room, I'd watched for any hint of pretense or deception, but he was slick. I was incredulous as he left the room. What an actor!

I tried to sing myself into a partying mood so I could greet Manuel with a smiling face. An air of pretense accompanied me as I walked down the hall, adding enough bounce to my step to appear happy. I found everyone gathered outside under a tree and they all turned to me with cheerful faces.

"Well, hello there," Uncle Jake was the first to speak. "Feeling better, I see."

"Yes, much better. I guess I'm not used to staying up so late."

Manuel was sitting on the ground, playing with his puppy.

"Happy Birthday, Manuel," I called to him.

He jumped up and ran to me. "How did you know it was my birthday?"

I looked down at him with a playful grin. "Because you no longer look like a four-year-old. Today you look big enough to be five." I reached down and mussed his hair, and he beamed proudly at the thought of looking older.

He turned to his mother. "When is it time for my party?"

"As soon as Troy gets back, we'll have some cake, okay?"

"Okay!" He tried to play, but every few minutes he glanced down the drive to see if Troy's jeep could be seen. It seemed an eternity before Troy finally returned. Meanwhile, Joe disappeared. "Now, where's Papa?" Manuel was frustrated that he couldn't get everyone together for his party.

"Here he comes." Troy pointed across the field. Joe was leading a pony across the pasture toward them. Manuel scampered to meet them, jumping and clapping as he ran.

"Fireball!" He stroked the pony's side. "I'm glad you brought Fireball to my party, Papa. Can I ride him?"

Sheila joined them, and Joe put his arm around her waist. "You can ride him all you want. He's all yours, son. Happy Birthday."

The dazed look on Manuel's face made my eyes water. I could tell this was a dream come true for him. Uncle Jake took hold of my arm and led me toward the pony while explaining, "Manuel went with us to look over some horses at another ranch a couple of days ago. He fell in love with this pony and was disappointed when we wouldn't buy it. Since Joe and Sheila had already planned to get him a horse of his own for his birthday, we arranged to have it delivered here early this morning."

Manuel stood by listening to the explanation and decided to add his own comments. "I sure do love this horse. I named him Fireball when I saw him because he was like Brianna."

Troy burst out laughing. "Fireball Chavis. That's a new one, but it does fit. Tell me, Manuel, how is Fireball like Brianna?"

"Because he's the same color as her hair. When the sun shines on him, he's the same color of fire; just like when the sun shines on Brianna's hair, it looks like a ball of fire."

Troy slipped away from the gathering and headed back to the jeep. He returned carrying a small saddle and horse blanket.

"Happy Birthday, buddy. Here's your very own saddle for Fireball." He showed everyone the saddle and then helped Manuel put it onto the pony. Manuel climbed up and rode around in a circle. Troy led them over to his jeep and everyone else meandered behind them. He took two wrapped packages from the front seat and held them up. "These are from Uncle Jake and Bree."

Manuel was overwhelmed at receiving so many big presents. He climbed down from Fireball and handed me the reins. "Hold him for me."

Instead, Joe took hold of the bridle and led the pony to the stables for Pete to check the shoes and give him some water.

Troy stood back to watch Manuel open the presents. "By the way, buddy, Mitch wanted to be here, but he had some very important business to take care of. He said he'd come see you tomorrow."

I looked at Troy. So Mitch was coming to the ranch tomorrow, not only to bring Manuel his present, but to collect me. Won't you all be surprised when I'm already gone!

Manuel ripped into the first present. "My boots!" He kicked off his shoes and put on the boots, then grabbed the other package and tore into it. It was a cowboy hat to match the boots. He'd been so involved with his packages, he hadn't noticed Joe leading Fireball away. He turned to me accusingly, "Where's Fireball? Did you let him run away?"

Sheila put her arms around him and told him where the pony was. "Why don't we let him have time to get used to his new home while we go eat some cake?"

He hesitated, then kicked at a rock on the ground and reluctantly agreed. He yawned as they all walked to the house. It had been a thrilling, but exhausting, afternoon.

I stood staring through the bedroom window into the blackness of the night. Everything was quiet except for the howling wind. Uncle Jake went to bed early, and Troy had tried hard to convince me to stay up with him, but I'd pretended to be exhausted and gone to my room. I'd been able to avoid him all day, and there was no way I wanted to be near him tonight. I sat quietly waiting and listening.

I heard Troy go to his room.

The hours ticked away; the clock struck nine, ten, eleven; finally, it was eleven thirty. I hadn't heard anyone stirring since Troy had entered his bedroom. Feeling it was safe, I checked to be sure I had all of my things, made sure I'd cleaned the room properly, and placed the simple note I'd written on the bedside table. Taking a deep breath, I gathered my bags and crept down the stairs and out of the front door. The howling wind helped disguise any noises I made.

I hurried down the drive toward the gate, fighting the wind, which whipped around me, making it difficult to carry the bulky baggage. My hair blew across my face and in an attempt to brush it aside, I dropped a piece of luggage. In my efforts to retrieve it, I dropped another bag. I finally surrendered them all to the ground and started over again, collecting them in my arms one at a time as tears dripped from my eyes. I neared the end of the drive, and a fine, misty rain began to fall. I was glad to see the cab waiting as promised.

The driver helped toss my suitcases into the trunk, and I climbed into the back seat for the long ride to the airport. Much to my chagrin, the driver loved to talk. He rattled on about the recent UFO sightings. "Since I drive a lot at night, I keep hoping I'll see one, but so far, I haven't. Have you ever seen one?" Not waiting for an answer, he continued. "I've talked to a few people that say they have, but you never know who to believe…" His voice droned on, and I wondered if he ever took a breath. During his monologue, he mentioned there were no flights going out of the airport during the night, and I would have to wait for morning before I could leave, so why would I want to go to the airport? "Never mind. That's none of my business. Did you hear about that pilot that saw a UFO? I saw him on the news, and he…" I was never so relieved to arrive at an almost deserted airport and escape his prattle.

Five hours later, I was boarding the plane that would get me back home after a six-hour flight. Exhausted, but unable to sleep, I looked through the airplane window, watching for UFOs.

Sunday, June 6–*New Mexico—*

Troy was anxious to make the most of the last few days of Brianna's vacation, hoping to somehow change her mind about going home and talk her into staying indefinitely. Mitch had been right all along. She was definitely the only woman for him, and he was determined never to let her down again. He dressed and trotted down the hallway to her room and knocked on the door. When there was no answer, he called out to her. Still no answer. He opened the door and found the room empty and the bed made. *Maybe she's already gone down to breakfast.* He jogged down the stairs and into the kitchen where Sheila was placing breakfast on the table.

"Good morning, Sheila. Have you seen Bree this morning? I wanted to see if she would go to church with me."

"No. I doubt if she is out of bed so early."

"Yes, she is. I went by her room and her bed is made. Maybe she went for a morning walk. I certainly hope she wouldn't attempt another horseback ride alone."

Uncle Jake, Joe, and Manuel walked in from their morning rounds and confirmed that none of them had seen her. Troy frowned. He couldn't imagine that she would take off on Misty again by herself, but the fear he'd felt the last time was still fresh in his memory.

"I'll eat later." He raced out to the stables only to find Misty casually grazing in the pasture. Pete was busy mucking out the stalls. "Pete, have you seen Bree?"

"No, sure haven't." A man of few words, he continued shoveling.

"Maybe she went for a walk." Troy surveyed the hillside, then started down the trail toward the creek. He searched the property until he found himself on top of the hill where they'd had their picnic. He stood looking over the ranch, hoping to catch a glimpse of her, but to no avail. *Maybe I missed her.* He started back to the house feeling sure he would find her waiting for him.

When he walked into the house, Sheila was descending the stairs. "She's gone! Her clothes and everything are gone."

Bewildered, Troy's mind raced to figure out a plausible explanation. *No, that can't be. How could she leave? She had no car.* He ran up the steps, taking two at a time, and burst into her room. He searched until he was satisfied that Sheila was right. *But how? And why?* He sat on the bed noticing the note on the bedside table. Picking it up, he read, *Thank you all for your hospitality. I must return home. Take care, Brianna.*

The phone rang, but Troy barely heard it as he struggled to make sense of Brianna's unexplained departure.

Sheila yelled up the stairs for him. "Troy, it's Mitchell."

Troy bounded back down the stairs and grabbed the phone. *Maybe Mitchell knows something.* "Mitch, where is she?"

"Who?"

"Bree. Didn't you come get her?"

"No. I don't know what you're talking about."

"She's gone. She left a note saying she had to go home. Why wouldn't she tell me she was leaving?"

"Did you two have a fight?"

Troy's voice was shrill. "No! We were doing great, or so I thought."

"I haven't heard from her. Let me give you her phone numbers, and I'll try to call her too. She couldn't be home yet, but maybe she'll answer her cell phone."

The rest of Troy's day was spent brooding. Several times he tried calling Brianna's cell phone and apartment, but there was no answer. He left several voicemails asking her to call him.

Manuel was also confused and hurt by her disappearance, and Troy attempted to make him feel better by making excuses for her. Finally, he took Manuel into town to get their minds off the situation. They went to a movie and stopped for a burger at a fast-food restaurant. The diversion helped Manuel, but it did nothing for Troy's state of mind.

Arriving back at the ranch, he ran to his room and searched through a box of keepsakes. He found his old address/telephone book and flipped through the pages until he found Brianna's old phone number, a number he had called so many times years ago when she'd lived at home with her parents. He raced back down the stairs and dialed, only to find the number now belonged to someone else. He called the operator and was told that Mr. and Mrs. Collin Chavis had an unlisted number. Another call to her apartment resulted with still no answer.

While he anxiously tried to get answers concerning Brianna, Uncle Jake was forced to take on all the duties of the ranch on his own. Joe bolted into the house hollering for help. Troy tore through the house and out the door to find Uncle Jake lying on the ground. He'd tried to make it back inside for help but had collapsed. His faithful dog, Rufus, whimpered and licked his face. Uncle Jake was unconscious, and there wasn't a pulse. Troy tried CPR, but it was too late.

Chapter 10

Eastridge—

The taxi pulled away from the curb, leaving my bags and me on the sidewalk in front of my apartment. I fumbled through my purse for my keys and opened the door. This no longer seemed like home. My shattered heart was still in New Mexico.

Feeling alone and empty, I placed my luggage in the foyer and knelt to pick up the mail from the floor. *One of these days I'm going to get a box to hang under the mail slot to catch the mail.* Among the numerous pieces of junk mail, there was a bank statement reminding me of my lack of funds, and two late notices. The one from the electric company informed me that the current would be turned off if the bill was not paid by April 30. I flipped the wall switch. Nothing happened; no lights. *How could this happen? I paid the bills before I left.*

Confused, hungry, jobless, alone, penniless, and overcome with helplessness, I took a deep breath. *Things are bound to look brighter after a nap.* I stretched out on the sofa, allowing myself to escape from reality as I succumbed to utter exhaustion and jet lag.

The shrill ring of the telephone jolted me from the land of dreams. I scrambled to the kitchen and grabbed the receiver, intent on stopping the infuriating noise.

"Hello?"

"Bree, you're home!"

"Hi, Momma. Yeah, I got in a while ago, but was so tired I fell asleep before I could call you."

"We weren't expecting you home until Tuesday, but Stacy called and said she saw a taxi in front of your apartment, and she thought you might be home. How was the trip?" Stacy was a friend of the family and one of my neighbors.

"Terrific!" I lied. I resolved never to tell my parents about seeing Troy again. No one needed to know what a fool I'd been. "I loved New Mexico. The weather was great, and the people were really friendly."

"Good, I'm glad you enjoyed it. I have to admit I'm glad you're home. When can you come over? We have a little surprise for you." Although she was upbeat about the surprise, there was a hint of sadness in Momma's voice.

Maybe she's tired. "What is it?" My curiosity grew.

"You'll see. I can still throw another steak on the grill if you want to come over for supper."

"I'm starved! I'll be right over."

Deciding to unpack later, I grabbed a clean pair of jeans and a shirt from the closet, placed them on the bed, and went to take a quick shower to revive my fatigued body. Cruel reality slapped me coldly in the face as I stepped into the freezing spray. "Okay, stupid, no electricity means no hot water." I grabbed a towel, deciding to shower later at my parents' house.

Sliding into the stale-smelling, pale blue interior of my Mustang, I noticed several envelopes on the passenger's seat; payments for the electric bill, the rent, and the auto insurance. *Great! I was in such a hurry to catch my flight, I forgot to put these in the mail.*

I drove along the familiar road through the small city of Eastridge—home. A comforting warmth enveloped me. I passed by all the places I'd known since a small child. There was Sharpe Styles, previously Lucille's Hair Salon, which had been owned by my grandfather's late wife and was my mother's first place of employment. When Lucille died, Beth Sharpe had taken over the business. Next I passed by the pizza shop, the police station, and the Italian Bistro. On the next street over, I could see Chavis Construction Company, which was next to the steel mill, both of which were owned by my Grandpa Raymond. Daddy had worked at the construction company for as long as I could remember and would inherit the company eventually.

As I entered the town square, there it was; the brand new, ultra-modern complex of Milliken & Chavis. In smaller letters were the words "Home of Milliken Fashions and Brittain Designs." Not much else had changed in Eastridge over the years, but this was a major triumph for my mother. Soon after becoming a partner in the business, they had designed and built this fabulous new building, changing the entire landscape of the town.

I drove through the residential part of the city, with beautiful trees lining the street and charming picturesque homes on either side. Turning into the circular drive, the stark-white Chavis mansion with its round columns welcomed me. A small, white car was parked where my brother Jesse's blue sports coupe usually sat. At eighteen, Jesse was living in a quarters over the garage. He'd helped on the construction sites since he was big enough to lift a brick.

I entered the house and yelled, "Hello?" Receiving no answer, I continued past the staircase and into the kitchen and heard voices in the backyard. The delicious aroma from the grill welcomed me as I crossed the yard. The picnic table, yard swing, and several chairs were arranged in a group near the brick barbecue grill. About a hundred feet away, down a gentle slope, was the in-ground swimming pool, gazebo, and pool house.

Momma was placing a tray of vegetables on the table and Daddy was grilling the steaks. Jesse was stretched out in a hammock doing absolutely nothing to help, as usual.

Trying desperately to hide my anguish from the emotional whirlwind I'd been through during the past two weeks, I faked a smile. "Jesse, I didn't see your car in the drive. I didn't think you were here." I thumped him on the head with my finger.

"My car is in the shop. I blew the engine at the drag strip yesterday."

"I thought a great mechanic like you could fix that without putting it in the shop."

"I thought I could too, but when I tried, I think I did more damage than good. Besides, it needed some body work too."

Assuming the little white car was a rental he was using until he got his car back, I went to give Momma and Daddy a quick "hello" hug. "Momma, what's the big surprise you were telling me about?"

Momma glanced toward the house. "Here comes the

surprise now." A door slammed, and I turned to see who was coming. Loaded down with steak sauce, salt, pepper, onions, paper plates, cups, and plastic-ware was my cousin, Lucy.

I ran to greet her and helped carry things to the table. "I walked through the house and didn't see you. Where were you?"

"Took a little break to answer nature's call." The two of us had been like sisters when we were kids, even though it had been a long-distance relationship. Lucy grew up in Austria where her parents, my Uncle Justin and Aunt Trisha, owned a small ski resort. Although that sounds impressive, it was a constant struggle for them to keep the resort out of the red.

Lucy could always make people laugh. I couldn't recall hearing her complain about anything, her happy disposition on display at all times. Even when her husband was killed, Lucy didn't let anyone see her cry. She'd married Brad at the delicate age of nineteen and was pregnant a year later. Before the baby was born, Brad was killed in an automobile accident. Lucy went into seclusion until the funeral. During the funeral, she was stoic, holding her head high and never breaking down in front of everyone. Since then, she'd been so busy working and supporting her daughter, Andrea, there'd been no time for visits to Eastridge. I had only received short, lighthearted letters with pictures of Andrea.

During the meal, I observed Lucy's short, wavy, blond hair, which surrounded her innocent-looking face. She had a fair complexion with freckles sprinkled across her cheeks and nose. Her laughing sea-green eyes caught my gaze.

"You look as if you can't believe your eyes." She giggled.

"I was actually thinking how terrific you look. I am a little surprised at your sudden appearance after not seeing you for several years."

"I thought it was about time everyone meet Andrea. I'll wake her up from her nap in a little while so she can eat."

"How old is she now, three or four?"

"She had her fourth birthday last month."

"So how long are you staying?"

"I'm here to stay. I arrived the day after you left for New Mexico and have been sleeping in your old room while looking for a job and an apartment. I finally found a job as a helper at a nursery school. It doesn't pay much, but I come out ahead since Andrea can stay there with me, and I won't have to pay for a sitter."

"What made you decide to move here?"

"If I stay in Austria, I'll never get away from that family business. I'm sick and tired of helping run the resort. I want to do something else. I'm not sure what yet, but I needed to get away and find out what else is out in the world. Besides, since Brad died, I've been at loose ends. I need a change. So here I am."

"How did the apartment hunting go?"

"Not good. There isn't much available in Eastridge. There's a young couple over on Maple Street willing to rent out a room of their home, but I need more space than that for Andrea. Besides, they didn't seem thrilled about having a child live there."

"Maybe we can find something together. It looks as if I might be homeless soon too." My lease was up in a month and the landlord was raising the rent to more than I thought the small one-bedroom apartment was worth.

Daddy looked at me. "So what's wrong with your apartment?"

"Daddy, I can't afford it anymore since they raised the rent, especially since I lost my job at the bank. I'm sure any job I find isn't going to start me at my old salary."

Momma's eyes twinkled the way they always did when she had one of her bright ideas. "I don't know why I didn't think of this before. Collin, how about Aunt Marty's place?"

I felt a ray of hope. "You mean the old millhouse?"

"Sure! It's sitting there empty. Aunt Marty didn't want to sell it because she's still hanging on to the idea of going home one day, but we all know that's not going to happen. She's in her late eighties now and too old to live alone. Taking care of her husband during his illness took its toll on her. Now that he's gone, she needs someone to take care of her. I'm sure she would agree to having you live there in her absence."

"So where is she today?" I looked toward the house.

"She went with your grandpa to a church social. They attend a lot of the senior functions together. It's good for both of them."

We heard the screen door slam and turned to see Andrea wandering across the yard. She hid behind Lucy, who helped her onto the bench. "Did you have a good nap, honey?"

The child's short red curls bounced around her head as she nodded. Hiding behind her mother, she peeked at me. She had Lucy's green eyes, fair skin, and freckles. I tried talking to her, but she backed away, tugging at Lucy's shirt.

After allowing the child to whisper in her ear, Lucy smiled and placed her napkin on the table. "Excuse us. We need to take a potty break."

Momma watched them enter the house, then explained, "Andrea is very withdrawn. She's been here for almost two weeks and still hasn't accepted any of us. She only speaks when she absolutely has to and hardly ever leaves Lucy's side. I guess the move must have been a traumatic experience for her. She's so little and probably doesn't understand the big change."

Momma stood up, hesitating as she clung to the table for support. "I'm feeling a bit tired. Bree and Jesse, could you help your daddy clean up here while I go lie down for a while?"

"Sure, Momma." I watched her slow and unsteady gait toward the house. "Daddy, is Momma okay?" I couldn't recall a time when my mother had not been strong and confident.

He watched his wife enter the house. "She hasn't been sleeping very well lately. She'll be okay after she gets some rest." His voice was laced with worry.

The following few days were busy ones as I attempted to pick up the pieces and put my life back in order. There had been several calls from Mitchell and Troy on my cell phone, but I refused to answer them. If they left any voice messages, I didn't listen to them. There was no need to torture myself. I was determined to get on with my life. I would miss Mitchell, but since he was such good friends with Troy, I was better off staying away from him too.

Feeling guilty about Mitchell paying for my airfare and my leaving without a word, I sat down to write him a letter. I didn't mention the real reason I'd left, but blamed my coming home on needing to find a job so I could pay my bills. I apologized for not saying goodbye to him and Gina and promised to pay him back for the plane tickets as soon as I had steady employment again. I mailed the letter, easing my guilty conscience.

I busied myself with packing and moving from my apartment back into my childhood bedroom at my parents' home, with high hopes that I wouldn't have to live there too long. Lucy had been staying in my room since she'd arrived, so now we were roommates. This would be an excellent test to see if we could get along well enough to live together.

Friday, June 11—

After four days of searching the paper and the Internet and pounding the pavement, I still had no job, no money. My finances looking more and more bleak, I was forced to cancel service on my cell phone.

Aunt Marty was being stubborn about the millhouse, still insisting she could manage living alone. "I might be old, but not so old that I can't do things for myself."

I sat back and watched while Momma tried to reason with her. "Aunt Marty, we love having you here with us. Why would you want to be alone? Besides, you can't possibly take care of that place by yourself."

"What I can't do, I can hire done. When I came here

to stay with you, it was to be a temporary arrangement, and that's the way I still want it."

Grandpa Raymond spoke up. "Marty, you can whine all you want, but you are not going back to living by yourself. If you can't be happy living here, then we will simply have to make arrangements for you to go into a home."

Aunt Marty wobbled around to face him with fire in her still-clear eyes. "Raymond Chavis, don't you dare threaten me like that! Before I let you do that to me, I'll have you committed. You're not that far behind me, you know, and I have a lot more influence around town than you do." The argument continued, the matter left unresolved.

Trying to remain optimistic, I headed downtown to continue my job pursuit. I could have settled for working as a sales clerk, but I was still hoping to find the perfect job.

Applying for several receptionist, filing clerk, typist, and other office positions, I received the same two responses over and over: "You are overqualified," or, "We'll let you know."

Market Street bustled with activity. I glanced at my watch—eleven-thirty. Futility set in. The blare of a horn intruded on my thoughts and, without breaking my stride, I looked back over my shoulder to see who was honking and collided into someone exiting a building.

"Oh, I'm so sorry. I wasn't..." I looked up and recognized my victim as the doctor I'd met on the plane. I reached back in my mind, trying to remember his name. Paul...

He grinned. "Well, hello again, Miss Chavis."

I smiled and extended my hand, remembering his last name. "What are you doing in Eastridge, Dr. Kellerman?"

"I liked your idea of me setting up a practice here in Eastridge, so I called Doc Wilson. It turns out that he's been wanting to retire for a while, but didn't want to leave his patients without medical care, so he agreed to let me take over his practice."

"Is it a done deal?"

"We finalized everything a few minutes ago, and now I'm going to celebrate by having lunch. Are you on your lunch break?"

"A permanent one it seems. I'm beating the pavement trying to latch onto a job."

"Are you hungry?"

"Sort of, but…"

"Then let's go." Seeing a break in traffic, he grabbed my arm and hurried me across the street. "I saw a little Italian restaurant earlier today that looked inviting. It's only about a block away."

Once we were safely onto the sidewalk, he slowed his pace and continued the conversation. "So you're job hunting. What kind of work do you do?"

"Nearly anything," I said with displeasure.

He glanced at me, one eyebrow raised and a sly grin touching the corners of his lips. "Oh, yeah?" His eyes fell briefly over my entire body leaving me blushing at his insinuation.

"I meant that I have done all kinds of office work. Secretarial, reception, bookkeeping, filing, veterinary assistant, and just about anything to do with a computer, including tearing them down and fixing them. Somehow, none of my jobs have been very satisfying. I wish I had gone further in college."

We entered the restaurant, were seated in a corner booth, and studied the menus in silence. The moment the waitress took our order and walked away, Paul wasted no time resuming the discussion. "I have the building for my clinic, which I'm going to renovate and put in more modern equipment. I've already got patients since Dr. Wilson is giving me all of his files, but I don't have any help. Doc Wilson's nurse, who is his wife, is also retiring. I'll need a receptionist to handle appointments, a bookkeeper for the billing, a file clerk for the patient's records, and someone who's really good on a computer. I don't seem to have any need for a veterinary assistant since I don't plan to treat animals, so I guess you're overqualified."

"If I hear that expression once more, I think I might scream."

He laughed. "I knew you must have heard that line a few times. It's the typical brush-off employers like to use."

"What baffles me is that I grew up in this town. Everyone knows me, or at least knows who I am, yet I can't get anyone to hire me."

"Why do you think that is?"

"The truth? Because they really do think I am overqualified. It's infuriating!"

Our salads arrived. After eating in silence for a few minutes, he spoke up again. "Seriously, I will need someone. Would you be interested?"

"Maybe. What could you pay?"

He smiled, swallowed, then commented, "You believe in getting right down to the important things, don't you? I won't know exactly how much I can pay until I get my books straight, but I assure you, I'll pay enough to live on."

"That sounds good enough. When do I start work?"

"How's Monday?"

"Perfect."

I burst into the house anxious to tell my news. Lucy met me, also delirious with excitement. "I got a job! I finally got a job! I start on Monday."

"And we have a place to live!" Lucy added her headline. "Aunt Marty said we can move in this weekend *if* we agree to let her move back in when she's ready."

"No problem! So what are we waiting for? Let's get packing."

Chapter 11

Sunday, June 20–New Mexico—

The funeral arrangements, taking care of Uncle Jake's outstanding business affairs, life insurance claims, and the execution of the will kept Troy busy for a couple of weeks. Brianna was constantly on his mind, but there was no time to do anything about it. There wasn't even time for him to grieve his uncle's death. Through it all, he also had to continue running the ranch. It wasn't a job that allowed you to take a day off. The animals had to be fed, exercised, and groomed, and maintenance of the grounds and equipment couldn't be ignored. Business transactions had to continue in order to pay the ranch hands and other necessary overhead.

Joe, Sheila, and Manuel were at church, and the ranch hands were busy with the chores of the day. Finally, alone in the quiet of the early morning, Troy sat at the kitchen table with his cup of coffee, sorting out any remaining details that needed handling.

He heard the front door open and someone walking through the house.

"Hello, anyone home?" came Mitchell's voice as he made his way toward the kitchen.

Troy smiled and arose from the table to greet him. "Hey there, buddy. It's good to see you. What are you doing way out here?"

"Thought I'd ride out to see how you're doing. I didn't get to talk to you much at the funeral."

"I know. Sorry about that. I've been having trouble coping with it all."

"I know. I'm going to miss him too."

Changing the subject, Troy had to ask the burning question, "Have you heard anything from Bree?"

"No. I've tried calling her, but she won't answer my calls. Now, her cell phone and the phone at her apartment have been disconnected. Troy, what on earth could have happened?"

"I can't figure it out. We were finally at the point that I thought we'd always be together. If I didn't believe that, I never would have..." Troy stopped himself. He was a little ashamed of himself and didn't want Mitchell to think he was bragging.

"Would have what?"

"Nothing."

"Don't say nothing. What did you do? Could it have anything to do with her leaving?"

Troy thought about it. *Would us making love be a reason for her to leave?* He couldn't see how, unless she was ashamed. "Maybe. I hadn't thought of that, but I guess it's possible."

"So what did you do?"

Troy sat down at the table, rubbing his forehead. "We made love the night before she left."

"So why would that make her leave?"

"I don't know. Maybe she was ashamed or something."

"Why would she be ashamed? Did she act any different afterward?"

"No. In fact, she seemed really happy."

"How did you act?"

Troy tried to remember. "I don't know. I guess I didn't act any different. I might have been a little quiet because I was worried."

"Worried about what?"

"We acted a little irresponsible, if you know what I mean."

"No protection." Mitchell understood.

"That's right." Troy stood and began pacing around the kitchen. "But even if she did get pregnant, I'd marry her. I'm not worried about that, but *she* might be."

"So what are you going to do now?"

"I've got to go find her. I've already hired someone to help Joe run the ranch, and now I'm ready to take a few days to go look for her."

"Good. I think that's a good idea. While you're gone, I'll keep an eye on things here."

"Thanks, Mitch. That would be a big help. How about a cup of coffee?"

"Sure."

Troy poured their coffee. "So, how are things at the base?"

"Not good. We've had some security leaks, so things are a little tense at work. That's why I had to bring Bree out here and drop her off. She was asking all kinds of questions, and with her curious nature, I knew she could cause trouble. Or even worse, get herself into trouble."

"So Sal wasn't arrested?"

Mitchell grinned. "No. Sal is clean. Sorry I had to lie to you. I've had to lie to Gina lately, too, and I don't like being in this situation. How did I get into this, Troy?"

Troy shrugged. "It's the government, but how does someone who is supposed to be an accountant get involved with government secrets?"

"That's what I want to know. I didn't seek this out. I got drafted into it by my superiors. I suppose they needed someone that wouldn't raise suspicion. Who better than a lowly accountant?"

"I guess. I wish you luck."

"Thanks. When are you leaving?"

"As soon as I can get packed."

A couple of hours later, Troy was cruising down the road in his jeep, headed out of New Mexico.

Monday, June 21–Eastridge—

Rachel forced herself to get dressed for work. It was tempting to stay home and enjoy the peace and quiet of the empty house. Her father and Aunt Marty were gone on a bus trip with the senior citizens group. Brianna, Lucy, and Andrea had moved into the millhouse. Rachel had been successful in hiding her symptoms from all of them, but it had been exhausting. Now she didn't have to worry about making excuses whenever she dropped something, or say she'd tripped when her leg gave out, causing her to fall into the wall.

It was difficult to keep the self-pity at bay and continue life as usual. Her right side didn't want to cooperate. Brushing her teeth or washing her hair was awkward without the complete use of her right arm. She'd never before realized how useless her left hand was and how much she depended on her right hand. *A simple thing like brushing your teeth shouldn't be so hard.*

Later that day…

Something was wrong with Momma. She was obviously distressed about something, and seemed to be tired all the time. I sat at the kitchen table sipping coffee with Daddy, trying to get answers from him.

When Momma arrived home from work, he shot her a concerned look of warning. "Here's your momma now. Maybe you should be asking her these questions."

Momma looked at me and placed her purse and keys on the kitchen counter. "What questions would that be?"

I stood and walked to the counter. "Before we get into that, would you like a cup of coffee?"

"No. I'd like to know what you were discussing."

"Momma, I'm worried about you. I've noticed you seem worried about something, and I've seen you drop things and look tired since I've been back from New Mexico. Are you alright?"

Momma took a deep breath and fixed herself a glass of water. "Okay, Bree. I guess I should have told you." She sat down. "While you were away, I went to the doctor. I'd been having problems with my right arm and went to have some tests." She hesitated and looked at Daddy.

"And? What did the doctor say was wrong?"

"He said he thinks it's MS. Multiple Sclerosis."

I didn't know how to react. I knew nothing about the disease. "What exactly is MS?"

"Well, the good news is that it's not a death sentence. MS is a chronic disease that affects the central nervous system."

"That doesn't sound like good news. It can be treated, right?"

Hope emanated from Momma's eyes when she smiled at Daddy and me. "Milly has found a doctor in Richmond that specializes in treating MS. She's going to call to get me an appointment."

Tuesday, June 22—

I arrived at the Medical Center building to find construction workers already busy with the remodeling. Men in hardhats carrying two by fours and sheets of plywood and drywall were everywhere. Paint cans and buckets of sheetrock mud littered the hallway. Carefully making my way around the scaffolding and ladders, I heard foul language coming from the next room. One of the workers near me shouted, "Hey, guys, a lady is present. Watch your mouths."

I found Paul talking with the electrician about what would be needed in each examination room. He was surprised to see me. "Hey, what brings you here this morning?"

"You don't waste any time, do you?"

"I got lucky. When I called Chavis Construction on

Friday, they said building has been slow and they could start right away. So here they are."

I eyed the electrician, who seemed annoyed at me for interrupting. "I'm sorry, I know you're busy, but I really need to talk to you about something."

He observed the worried look on my face. "You're not quitting on me already, are you?"

I gave him a half-hearted smile. "No, not yet anyway. I need some free medical advice first."

He turned back to the electrician. "Do you need anything else from me right now?"

"No, you go ahead. I think we're straight on what you need."

Guiding me through the maze of tools and materials, he joked, "Okay, madam, step into my office." He led me into a back room where there was a sheet of plywood laid across two sawhorses, along with a couple of metal folding chairs. A set of plans were spread out on the makeshift table. Offering me one of the chairs, he got to the point. "Okay, what kind of medical advice do you need?"

"I need to know whatever you know about MS."

He looked startled, but recovered quickly. "It just so happens that I know quite a bit about MS. What do you need to know about it?"

"Well, I already know that it affects the nervous system. How bad can it get, and are there treatments for it?"

"Multiple Sclerosis can be potentially incapacitating. It's an autoimmune disease, which means that the body's immune system attacks various parts of the body as it would attack a foreign substance."

"That sounds really serious."

"It can be. When I went to that conference in Phoenix, I learned that they've made a lot of advancements in the past few years in treating MS. Why all the questions?"

"My momma has been diagnosed with it. She's trying to get an appointment with a doctor in Richmond that specializes in treating it. The doctors here couldn't help her."

"See, I told you they needed another doctor in this town." His smile faded. "My mother has MS. That's what made me want to be a doctor, so I've sort of specialized in it myself. I'd like to see your mother." He indicated the incomplete surroundings and shrugged. "Obviously we're not ready to receive patients yet, but I could go to her home if she wants. Get her test results from her doctors so I can examine them."

I breathed a sigh of relief. "Thank you. I'll give her a call right now."

Unable to make herself go to work, Rachel wandered aimlessly from room to room, memories flooding her heart and mind. She studied the doorways to be sure a wheelchair could fit through the openings. She looked at the sweeping stairway and tried to picture a lift that could carry her to the second floor. A tune played in the distance and she remembered she'd left her cell phone in the kitchen. She ran to answer it. "This is Rachel."

"Momma, I've got good news."

"I could use some of that right about now."

Traveling over eighteen hundred miles, stopping only a few times along the way for gas, food, and sleep, forty-four hours after leaving the ranch, Troy made his way through the winding roads of the beautiful Appalachian mountains. It was a sunny morning, and the different shades of green and the splattered colors of flowers caught his eye, reminding him how much he'd missed this place he used to call home.

He'd prayed a lot during his long drive, but still felt his prayers weren't being heard. *Maybe my guilt is getting in the way of my personal relationship with God. I can't feel the Holy Spirit with me like I usually do.* He decided he should start by asking forgiveness. "Lord, please forgive me for my sins against you and against Brianna. I shouldn't have allowed my human wants and needs to overshadow what I knew was right. I should have waited until marriage. I know that. But I wanted her so much, I couldn't control myself. I'm sorry, Lord. Forgive me for my human frailties and help me find her so I can make things right again. In Jesus' precious name I pray, Amen." Troy took a deep breath and reminded himself that God always answers those who pray in faith. It was in God's hands now. *I know things will be alright. No matter what happens now, it will be God's will.*

He tried his cell phone, but was too far away from any towns with cell towers. It was useless in this remote part of the world. He stopped at a gas station, hoping to find a pay phone.

A scruffy old man sat in front of the station whittling.

When asked about a pay phone, he answered, "Nope, sorry. I got no phone here. There's another station about six miles fu'ther down the road and I believe they might have one."

Six miles later, a younger, but still unkempt attendant responded, "Sorry, the pay phone's not workin,' but you're welcome to use the phone inside thar."

"Thank you. I'll be glad to pay you for the call."

"Hep yoself."

Although Mitchell had told him Brianna's numbers were disconnected, he still had to try on the off chance that Mitchell could be mistaken. He called Brianna's apartment phone, but it was disconnected. Knowing it was futile, he tried her cell phone. Mitchell was right about that one too. It was no longer a working number. He purchased a soda and continued his drive to Eastridge, heading straight to the address Mitchell had given him for her apartment.

When no one answered his knock, he peered through the windows. There were no drapes, no furniture, nothing. The apartment was vacant. *Where could she have gone?* He sat on the steps trying to clear his head. He was tired and couldn't think straight.

After resting a few minutes, he realized she might have moved back in with her parents. He hopped into his jeep and drove toward the Chavis residence, stopping a block from the house. *Will her parents still hate me? Has she told them about seeing me again? What kind of reaction will I get when they open the door and find me standing on their porch?* None of that mattered. He had to find Brianna and find out why she'd left the way she had. Gathering his courage, he drove the last block and approached the house. He knocked. He knocked again. No answer.

Hopeless, frustrated, confused, and exhausted, he drove to a motel and checked in. Sitting in his room staring at the floor, the grief he'd been too busy to feel before now swept over him and swallowed him whole. The last few weeks had been difficult as he mulled over and over in his mind the last day he'd spent with Brianna, trying to come up with an explanation for her disappearance. He also relived finding his uncle sprawled out in the yard after his heart attack, and guilt consumed him. *If I hadn't made Uncle Jake do all the chores alone, he might not have had a heart attack. That's why he needed my help on the ranch in the first place. I really let him down.* Troy didn't feel he deserved his inheritance. *If Uncle Jake had known I was going to let him down like that, he never would have left me the ranch.* It was going to be hard to go back and face the pain.

Sleep had escaped him in the past weeks, and now his body collapsed from exhaustion. He began to tremble and sweat profusely. Crawling into bed, he fell into a fitful slumber. For days, too weak with fever to do anything else, he cried, slept, and wallowed in self-pity. His life felt void of anything that really mattered.

Wednesday evening, June 23—

Lucy and I finally had all of our boxes unpacked and our belongings put away. We were completely moved in at the old millhouse. Lucy sat cross-legged on the sofa after putting Andrea to bed. "This is a really cool place. I remember us coming here a couple of times when we were kids, but I'd forgotten how wonderful it was."

"I know. And the best part is it's already furnished! We don't have to worry about buying any furniture."

Lucy stared at the floor and then looked at me. Obviously something was on her mind.

"What?" I asked.

"Bree, I haven't seen you date anyone since I've been in Eastridge. What's the problem?"

"I've been a little busy, you know. Finding a job and moving twice, I haven't had time to think about a social life."

"No, it's more than that. I know you. There's something wrong, so what is it?"

It had been almost three weeks since I'd returned from New Mexico. I needed to talk to someone and face what had happened. Lucy was the only person I truly felt I could talk to about it. "When I went to New Mexico, something happened that made me not ever want to get involved again with anyone."

"Maybe it would help to talk about it."

Taking a deep breath, I began telling about the painful experience. "When I left here, I thought I was only going to visit Mitch."

"Your mom told me that he sent you an airline ticket to fly out there. So what happened?"

"What I didn't know was that Mitch was setting up a surprise reunion for me and Troy Garrison." I waited for Lucy's response.

"Troy Garrison! The same Troy Garrison you went with in high school?"

"The very same."

"But why would he do such a thing? How did he even know about Troy?"

"I met Mitch through Troy, remember? He was, and still is, a good friend of his."

"Then he must have known how Troy treated you before."

"Yes, but he thought he was doing us a big favor by getting us back together. He believes in destiny and thought he would help it along."

"How do you feel about destiny as far as Troy is concerned?"

"I believe people are destined to be born and to die. What happens in between is strictly up to us."

Lucy shrugged off any further philosophical discussion. She was anxious to know what had happened. "So what happened when you saw Troy?"

"I've never gotten over him, and when I saw him, I knew I still loved him as much as ever. He seemed to feel the same way. We had such a great time together while I was there." I became quiet as I fought back tears, but Lucy wasn't going to let me stop there.

"So what happened to destroy it?"

"He made love to me."

"Oh. Well, I wouldn't put up with that!" She was being sarcastic. "Come on, Bree, give me the bottom line. Was he that awful or what?" Lucy was tiring of having to pry the story from me, but she was trying to be patient and understanding.

"No, it was great, or at least I thought so at the time. Then the next morning, I overheard him talking to Mitch on the phone. He'd gotten what he wanted, so he was ready to get rid of me."

"What exactly did you hear him say?"

"He was talking about how he never asked Mitch to bring me to the ranch and how he wanted him to get rid of me." All the pain I'd been holding inside since that awful day now surfaced and tears began to flow.

Lucy put her arms around me, and her comforting embrace caused me to begin sobbing uncontrollably. I know she wanted to say something comforting, but there was nothing she could say. Nothing could erase the hurt I was feeling. "Did you talk to him about it?"

"No. I just left. I never gave him a chance to see me cry. I ran out on him before he could have the pleasure of dumping me again."

"But, Bree, is there any chance you could have misunderstood what he said to Mitch?"

"No, it was very clear. Mitch dropped me off at the ranch because his roommate was arrested for drugs, and he didn't want me getting involved in that mess. Troy was stuck with me. He had no choice." When she didn't say anything, I continued. "I guess I wasn't really surprised. I had a feeling he was going to hurt me again. He's always meant trouble for me. Why should a few years have changed that?"

"So now what? Are you going to pine over him for the rest of your life and never go out with anyone else?"

"No. I don't know. Why does life have to be so cruel?"

"Because that's how we learn."

I glared at Lucy as if she'd lost her mind. "What is that supposed to mean?"

Lucy jumped up. "I'll be right back." She disappeared down the hall and soon returned with a small pocket-sized Bible. She flipped through it until she found a small slip of paper stuck away in its pages. "Here it is. When Brad died, this helped me to understand why we go through so much pain. There's also a Bible verse that helped me that I've marked."

She opened the little Bible and began looking for the verse while I took the paper and read: *Happiness comes from sadness - For only through sadness-can we know what happiness is - We first must know it. - But never should we pursue happiness - For it will flee from us - But look to other things - And it will come and land on our shoulders.*

"Here's the verse I was looking for." She pointed out the verse as she held the little Bible for me to see.

I shoved the book away and went into the kitchen to grab a soda. "I don't want to be quoted Bible verses, okay? Troy is all into that crap too, but did it stop him from being a total jerk? No."

"You can't blame God for Troy being a jerk."

"Maybe not, but after hearing him talk about his holier-than-thou beliefs and then having him treat me the way he did doesn't give me that warm and fuzzy feeling for religion."

"I suppose I can understand why you feel that way. All I know is that I wouldn't have made it through Brad's death and the funeral if I hadn't been able to lean on Jesus through it all." Lucy stared at the floor, obviously remembering the pain. It had been four years, but the pain could still be seen in her eyes.

Feeling guilty about being so insensitive, I sat back on the sofa and sighed. "Okay, let's hear the verse."

Lucy hesitated, then opened the little Bible again to look for the verse. "Let's see. It was in Romans, chapter 5, verse 3. Here it is. 'We also rejoice in our sufferings, because we know that suffering produces perseverance; perseverance, character; and character, hope. And hope does not disappoint us, because God has poured out his love into our hearts by the Holy Spirit, whom He has given us.' So see? By suffering we learn to persevere, which builds character and gives us hope for our future." Lucy continued to try to make me see her logic. "Even though it seems awful now, something good will come of all this pain. We have to trust that God will teach us something from it."

"Yeah, He's taught me something alright. Not to get mixed up with the opposite sex."

"Oh, come on, Bree. Not all men are bad. You've got to get past the hurt and try again."

I smirked. "No thanks. I'll pass."

Thursday, June 24—

I waited in the kitchen for Paul to finish examining Momma. I'd spent the past two days procuring the MRI reports, X-rays, and lumbar puncture report from the doctor who had diagnosed her with MS. All morning, Paul had studied the films and reports, but refused to discuss his findings until after he'd given her a thorough examination.

I paced the floor, looking through the window and then into the refrigerator, with no idea what I hoped to find. I wasn't hungry, merely anxious. Paul and Momma had been in the other room for almost two hours. What could be taking so long?

Momma had asked me not to say anything to Daddy about this appointment with Paul. She didn't want to raise his hopes, only to be let down if there was nothing that could be done.

The door opened and Momma emerged, tears streaming from her sparkling eyes, and a huge smile across her face. "Bree, Paul says he's pretty sure I don't have MS! My problems are coming from a deteriorating vertebrae in my neck."

Paul walked into the kitchen behind her. "It's difficult to see on the films, but I believe there is a deteriorated disk that is putting pressure on the nerves. I'd like for you to have another MRI so we can be sure. If I'm right, I will refer you to a neurosurgeon who can perform the surgery to correct the problem."

I've never seen my mother so happy. This glimmer of hope had given her a new lease on life. Momma's smile stretched all the way into her glistening eyes as she said, "God truly does work in mysterious ways."

I didn't see the connection. "Why do you say that?"

"Do you think it was a coincidence that Paul moved here, of all places, and that he happens to be so knowledgeable about MS? No, Bree, I believe him coming here was an answer to my prayers. It had to have been."

I turned to Paul. "So, Paul, is Momma right? Did God send you to our little town?"

Paul shrugged. "All I know is I was looking for a small town to start a practice, and I met you on the plane. That's when I did a little research on Eastridge and learned that the local doctor was retiring. Maybe it *was* a part of some greater plan. Who knows?"

Chapter 12

Friday, June 25—Eastridge—

Troy stared into the mirror at his image, not recognizing himself. He hadn't shaved or combed his hair in almost a week. He looked worse than death, his hunger the only thing forcing him from his seclusion. He cleaned himself up and pulled himself together. Life had to go on. He wasn't giving up yet. He would find Brianna, but first, he had to find food.

Walking along the sidewalks of town, he not only looked for a place to eat, but kept his eyes peeled for a glimpse of Brianna. He came to a small bistro. *This is new. It wasn't here last time I was in town.* He reached for the doorknob, glancing across the street. His heart skipped a beat. Her back was turned, but that long reddish-brown hair had to be hers. He released the knob and ran across the road, almost being struck by a delivery truck. The woman turned at the sound of the horn and tires squealing. His heart sank. It wasn't her.

He gorged himself with enough food for three people, returned to the motel for his jeep and drove back to the Chavis home. No cars were in the driveway and all was quiet. He knocked and listened. He knocked again. Nothing. He jumped back into his jeep and drove back toward the motel. Passing by the Milliken & Chavis building, he considered stopping to find her mother's office. *Mrs. Chavis has never liked me much. I'll probably never be able to get in to see her.* He took a deep breath and turned into the parking lot. *She can hate me if she wants to, but I've got to find Bree.*

He marched into the building and searched the names listed on the wall with office numbers. Beside "Rachel Brittain Chavis" was "Top Floor." *Makes sense since it's her building.*

Entering the elevator, he punched the button for the top floor and was impressed with the quick, but smooth, ride. The elevator doors opened and straight ahead was a huge mahogany reception desk. A pleasant young lady greeted him. "May I help you?"

"I'd like to see Mrs. Chavis, please."

"Do you have an appointment?"

"No. It concerns her daughter."

"Your name?"

He hesitated. He could lie and that might get him further than telling the truth. *No, that's only asking for more trouble when she finds out it's me.* "Troy Garrison."

"Okay, Mr. Garrison. Please have a seat and I'll see if she's in."

He listened as she placed the call. "Mr. Troy Garrison is here to see Mrs. Chavis. He said it concerns her daughter." There was a short pause. "Okay." She hung up the phone. "Mr. Garrison. Mrs. Chavis's assistant will be out momentarily."

Milly debated if she should disturb Rachel or not. She knew Troy Garrison was not one of Rachel's favorite people, but if it concerned Brianna, it might be important. *Probably not. I'd better find out more before disturbing her with this.* She walked into the reception area. "Mr. Garrison?"

Troy stood and walked toward her. "Yes."

"Ms. Chavis is busy in a conference at the moment. May I take a message for her?"

"I'm looking for her daughter, Brianna. Do you know where I can find her?"

"I'm sorry, Mr. Garrison. I can't give out that kind of information unless you tell me what it is you want with Miss Chavis."

"I understand. Sorry to bother you." He turned to leave, then stopped and turned back to Milly. "But if you would please ask Mrs. Chavis to call me when she gets out of her conference, I would appreciate it. Here's my number." He jotted down his cell phone number and handed it to her. "Thank you."

Milly went back to her desk, looked at the phone number, then threw it in the wastebasket.

Recalling friends Brianna had known in high school, Troy made a list of names. He searched the phonebook to find their numbers. What he couldn't find there, he tried to get from information, but it had been a long time since high school. He could only come up with a few numbers. Most of them were probably married, changing their names, or had moved away. He tried the ones he'd found, and finally got one of them to answer.

"Tiffany?"

"Yes, this is Tiffany."

"This is Troy Garrison. I don't know if you remember me, but..."

"Sure, I remember you. You dated Brianna Chavis back in high school, didn't you?"

"That's me. As a matter of fact, Bree is the reason I'm calling."

"Did you two ever get married?"

"No, but I am trying to find her. I guess you haven't heard from her lately." The answer was already obvious since Tiffany didn't know they hadn't married.

"Gosh, no. I haven't heard anything from her in ages."

"Can you think of anyone that might have?"

"No, I'm sorry, Troy. I don't keep in touch with anyone since my accident. I sit here in this house and watch a lot of TV. I get on the computer and go into chat rooms to pretend I'm someone else with a real life." There was a sad, broken giggle in her voice.

Troy had forgotten about the accident. *How could I have been so stupid?* The poor girl had been with friends, drinking and driving after the high school prom. She'd been left a quadriplegic after the crash. "I'm sorry, Tiff. I guess you think I'm an insensitive jerk."

"No, not at all! It's actually really great to hear from someone. Everyone else has forgotten I exist. Have you tried calling Brianna's parents?"

"Yeah, I haven't been able to reach anyone there." After more apologies, he ended the call and tried the other numbers, but could get no humans to answer. He didn't want to leave messages. How could he explain the situation on a voice message? He glanced at his watch, 3:45 on

Friday afternoon. *Most people would be at work at this hour. I'll try again later.*

He remembered the apartment rental office. *Maybe they have a forwarding address.* But that was another dead end.

Still weak and tired, he flopped back on the unmade bed, realizing Brianna may not even be in Eastridge anymore. *She could be anywhere!*

Although he had faith that Joe and Sheila could handle the ranch for a while without him, he felt obligated to go back soon. He hadn't contacted them since he'd left. He could run away for only so long. *Tomorrow is Saturday. I'll try again then, and if I can't find out anything, I'll have to get back to the ranch.*

Rachel emerged from the steaming shower and reached for her towel. Her right arm tingled, then felt as if an electric shock ran through it. It fell limp at her side and she couldn't move it at all. She began crying, panicking, and calling for Collin.

Collin ran into the bathroom. "What's wrong?"

"My arm. I can't move it!"

"Does it hurt?"

"I don't know. I mean it feels strange, uncomfortable, but it's not really pain. I can't describe it." She tried to move her fingers, but the limb was completely dead. She'd lost complete use of it. The surgery was scheduled for next Friday, one week. "Collin, I don't know if I can stand this for a whole week."

He helped her into her nightgown. Within fifteen

minutes, her arm began to tingle again and the same strange electrical shock ran through it. She wiggled her fingers, then lifted her arm. After several minutes, the tingling stopped, leaving only numbness. She continued to prepare for bed, reaching for her toothbrush. She placed the toothpaste on the brush, but when she tried to put the brush to her mouth, her arm went in the opposite direction and she dropped the brush. She could move her arm, but she couldn't control what it did. It was as if it had a mind of its own.

She crawled into bed and waited for Collin. An hour went by before he finally came back into the bedroom. "Where have you been?"

"I was on the Internet. I learned that the hot shower is probably what caused your arm to go haywire. People with nerve damage can be much more sensitive to heat, and it can cause a number of symptoms to occur, including what happened to you earlier."

"So no more hot baths or showers for me?"

"No, at least not until after your surgery. You might also want to stay in the air conditioning during the heat of the day."

Saturday, June 26—

Fire alarm! No, alarm clock. Troy drifted back into consciousness and realized the piercing noise was his cell phone. He glanced at the clock—8:02 a.m. "Hello?" His voice was still scratchy.

"Troy?"

"Yeah, Joe. What's up?"

"I'm sorry, Troy, but we really need you to take care of some things here. That guy you hired to run things hasn't been back here since Monday, and the ranch hands are upset because they didn't get paid yesterday. Also, some guys have been coming by to purchase horses. Then yesterday this banker came by and said they are going to auction the ranch since Jake is gone. I told them you were taking over, but they need to hear it from you. They said they need you to sign some papers."

Troy took a slow, deep breath, disappointed that he would have to give up his search for Brianna. "Okay, Joe. I'll head back home today. I should be there late tomorrow if I drive straight through."

"Good. Thanks, Troy. We'll see you tomorrow."

He sat on the edge of the bed, slumped over, rubbing his head. *I knew I'd forgotten something. I never sent the papers to the bank to let them know I'd inherited Uncle Jake's ranch.* He dialed Mitchell's number.

"Hello," Mitch sounded hurried.

"Hey, bud."

"Troy, where are you?"

"Still in Eastridge."

"Did you find her?"

"No, but I know I could if I had one more day to look. In a town the size of Eastridge, there can't be many places to hide."

"Exactly. You've been there a week and haven't found her yet?"

"I actually didn't get here until Tuesday, then I got sick and was in the bed for three days, so I haven't been searching but two days."

"Are you okay now?"

"Sure, I guess it was a virus. Or maybe my body couldn't take anymore and needed the rest, but I'm better now."

"Did you go talk to Mr. and Mrs. Chavis?"

"I tried, but no one was home. So I went to Mrs. Chavis's office, but couldn't get past her assistant. I left my number for her to call me, but she hasn't yet."

"Did Joe call you?"

"Yes, so now I need to stop looking and get back to the ranch. I can't believe I forgot to file those papers at the bank. They're signed and sitting on the desk."

"Okay, I can take care of that. I'll go to the ranch and pick them up, then take them to the bank on Monday."

"No, I've still got to come back anyway. You can't take care of the payroll. I didn't make any arrangements for that because I thought I'd be back in time to do it myself. I never dreamed it would be so difficult to find Bree or that I would be sick in the bed for three days."

"So you're heading back?"

"Yeah, I should get there by tomorrow night. Are you doing okay? You sounded upset or rushed when you answered the phone."

"I'm fine. Gina's getting ready to leave on vacation with her parents for two weeks. We were packing her things into the car when you called."

"What about the restaurant?"

"Her cook, Luigi, knows plenty about restaurant management, so she's leaving him in charge."

"Are you okay with her going?"

"Of course. She could use some R&R. If anyone deserves to get away and enjoy themselves, it's her."

"Tell her I said to have a good time. I'll see you soon."

"Okay. I'm sorry you have to come back without finding Bree."

"Me, too, but it can't be helped. I can't let Uncle Jake down again by losing the ranch."

"You never let him down, Troy. Don't even think that."

"You go give Gina a proper good-bye. I'll see you in a couple of days."

Troy gathered his things, threw them into the jeep, paid his bill, and drove out of town, searching the streets and sidewalks as he went. Upon reaching the interstate, he shifted gears, his focus changing from Brianna to the problems at the ranch.

Several miles of monotonous highway later, he saw a flash of light. Hovering in front of him was a metallic oval with glowing orbs, emitting a peaceful aura. Transfixed, he stared into the light while the jeep swerved off the road and headed toward a ravine. There were sounds of crunching metal and breaking glass, then total quiet. Troy reached up to feel his aching head. Woozy, but trying to focus, he glanced around, seeing nothing except trees and dirt. He pulled at the door handle and pushed against the door, but the door wouldn't open. Unbuckling the seatbelt, he cranked the window down, then climbed through it. *Thank God I don't have electric windows.*

He surveyed the damage; flat tire, broken headlights and windshield, and busted radiator. He reached into his pocket for his cell phone, but it wasn't there. *I must have left it on the passenger seat.* Pain seared through his entire body as he edged his way around to the passenger door, yanked it open, and searched for the phone. *It's not here. Where could it be?* After looking everywhere in and around the jeep, he gave up and started making his way up the hill to the road.

Monday, June 28–New Mexico—

Mitch hurried through the ranch gates in answer to a phone call from Joe informing him that Troy had not shown up as promised. Joe stood on the front porch with several ranch hands around him, their arms flailing like a flock of geese about to take off. When he stepped from the car, he could hear them yelling obscenities and threatening to quit.

He rushed to Joe's rescue. "Calm down, men. You know Joe can't do anything about this, so get off his back. I'm sure Troy will be here soon. He probably stopped to get some needed rest. He's been ill while away and was probably unable to drive straight through. Please, go back to work and be patient."

"What if he doesn't show up? Then what? We got families to feed," yelled out one of the men.

"I know. If he doesn't show up, we'll figure out a way for you to get paid. I promise." Mitch gave them a reassuring smile and nod, then went into the house, motioning for Joe to follow him.

After closing the door, Joe gave Mitch a puzzled look. "You have a plan, right?"

"No, Joe, no plan. Just faith that Troy will be here. In the meantime, let's get those papers to the bank."

Joe shook his head. "I hope you're right and he gets here soon."

Two days later, it was obvious that Troy wasn't going to show up. When Mitch left the base on Wednesday, he drove straight to the ranch and found Joe handing out paychecks. He stood back and watched in amazement, then followed Joe into the house.

"How did you get the money to pay them?"

"I mortgaged my home. When Mr. Garrison gave me that house and the property, he gave it to me free of liens. I called the bank and asked them if there was any way I could use it to get money to pay the men. They didn't care what I did with the money. They gave me plenty to last for a while, at least until I can sell some horses and get this ranch back to making money."

"So you're going to take over running the ranch?"

"Somebody's got to. Mr. Garrison had faith in me and was really good to me and my family. I have to do this for him."

"I know you loved Uncle Jake. He would be very proud of you." Mitch frowned and sat down at the kitchen table. "Have you tried to call Troy?"

"Of course, several times. I get his voice message, but he doesn't return my calls."

"Yeah, me too. I wonder what's going on? I'm really worried. He would have called if he wasn't coming home. Something is very wrong."

Friday, July 2—hospital in Roanoke—

"Rachel. Rachel, you can wake up now." The distant voice was persistent. "Come on, wake up. It's all over. Rachel? Come on, honey, wake up now."

Rachel opened her eyes and tried to focus. The nurse was standing over her, patting her hand. "There you are. Your surgery is over."

"Already?" Her voice was scratchy and her throat sore.

"Yes, already. You're in the recovery room. The doctor will be in to talk to you once you're fully awake."

Rachel lifted her right arm and wiggled her fingers. It felt normal. She smiled up at the nurse. "My arm feels normal again. It must have worked." She reached up and felt the hard collar around her neck. Prior to the surgery, the doctor had explained how he would be entering from the front of her throat to get to the vertebrae. Although it sounded frightening, he assured her that he'd had great success with the procedure.

The curtain parted. Collin and Brianna appeared by her side, smiling.

Collin took her hand. "Hey, there. The doc said everything went as planned. How do you feel?"

"Wonderful," she croaked. "I can move my arm and hand again, and it's not numb at all. The surgery worked."

I spent the next eight weeks tending to Momma through her recuperation and working at the clinic setting up files, organizing the accounting system, and remodeling the old building into a doctor's office. The clinic took a lot of long, hard hours to get established, but every now and then, I allowed myself to daydream about Troy coming back into my life, begging my forgiveness, and how I'd cut him down to size.

Chapter 13

Friday, August 13*—Alamogordo, New Mexico—*

Mitch sat in the conference room watching the men from D.C. arguing with the upper brass of the Air Force. Tempers were flying over the breach in security.

The agent from DIA *(Defense Intelligence Agency)* pounded his fist on the table. "We've had complete success keeping things under wraps for a half a century, but someone on this base has jeopardized all of that. And now our EMP *(electromagnetic pulse)* program is also at risk." He aimed his comments at the major.

Major Bradford didn't flinch, but held his ground, staring him down. "I have complete confidence in the men on this base, Sir. I do not believe the leak originated here."

"In order to prove that, the Secretary of Defense has ordered that you will provide to the DNI *(Director of National Intelligence)* and the FCI *(Foreign Counterintelligence Investigations)* a list of any and all personnel that had access to the information, from generals to janitors."

"Of course. That will be done right away."

"Also, the NSA *(National Security Agency)* will be sending agents here to investigate and they are to be given access to all buildings and personnel. No one outside of this room is to know that they will also be using Echelon to monitor any and all communications from this base. Is that completely understood?"

"Yes, Sir." Everyone answered in unison.

The meeting over, Mitch sat at his desk. He reached into the drawer and pulled out the envelope he'd received earlier in the week. It contained a check and a simple, impersonal note that read, "Sorry I had to leave the way I did. Enclosed is a check to reimburse you for the airline ticket. Love, Bree." *I'll be glad when they lighten up on the security around here so I can take a few days' leave to go find her. Maybe she'll know what happened to Troy. If she'd only answer my calls!* Frustrated, he placed the check back into his desk drawer with no plans to cash it.

Early September–Eastridge—

Now, with autumn approaching, the medical practice was in full operation. Paul was treating Doc Wilson's regular patients, and more were coming in every day with colds, flu, and viruses.

One of our favorite and most colorful patients was Mrs. Perkinson, a lovable lady of eighty. She came in the first day the clinic opened to the public. Before Paul examined her, she took me aside and whispered, "He isn't one of them fresh doctors, is he? I get tired of going to doctors that get fresh with the ladies, always pretending they can't find your heartbeat and pushing your blouse open and putting that cold stethoscope farther and farther down. I really don't think all of it is medically necessary. I'm not a dummy; I know what they're up to."

I contained my hysteria until Paul had escorted his patient safely into the examination room. There was nothing wrong with the woman except a severe case of loneliness. Since that day, she'd become a regular visitor, always complaining about headaches, sore knees, backaches, and anything else she happened to read or hear about. She had a definite case of chronic hypochondria, and Paul prescribed "ascorbic acid pills," commonly known as Vitamin C, for her condition. She was satisfied that the medication was curing her symptoms.

My days were hectic, keeping the patients' charts in order and the billing adjusted properly while attempting to be friendly and helpful in greeting the patients. My mornings began at the office at eight o'clock, organizing the day's appointments and records. At nine, we started with the first patient, and from then until lunch it was a steady stream of sick people. During lunch, I usually called to remind people of their appointments for the next day, and it started all over again; pulling files, taking temperatures, comforting children, and settling billings; over and over until four thirty, at which time we would lock the door and work on the filing, bookkeeping, and other paper work. Finally, I would reach home around six-thirty, where Lucy normally had dinner waiting for me. Although tempted to collapse onto the sofa and fall asleep, I dragged myself to night classes to learn more about the world of medicine.

Friday, September 24—

Blinded by the brilliant sun, I stepped into the building to begin another full day. My eyes adjusting to the artificial light of the room, I stood admiring my handiwork.

Shiny mobiles hung from the ceiling of the waiting area to brighten the atmosphere. In the corner was a child's table and chairs with coloring books and crayons, stuffed animals, storybooks, and puzzles so the little ones could entertain themselves while waiting for their parents to be treated.

Entering my office, I found a cup of coffee and the newspaper waiting on my desk as usual. Paul was pouring his own cup and turned to welcome me as he did every morning. "Well, good morning, Sunshine."

Sunshine! The nickname reminded me of Uncle Jake at the ranch, which reminded me of Troy, which caused my blood to boil. "Don't call me 'Sunshine,' and the only thing good about this morning is that it's Friday."

"My, my, you're grumpy today," he remarked as he left the room.

I knew my outburst was uncalled for, and I owed him an apology. After all, he had no way of knowing about the nickname. "Paul," I called to him and followed him into his handsome office with its leather furniture and impressive plaques and certificates lining the walls. A deer head was mounted on one wall; an eight-pointer he'd killed during hunting season a year ago. "I'm sorry, I didn't mean to be so rude. I didn't sleep well last night. Andrea cried most of the night. I guess she's gotten a virus or something. Lucy might bring her in for a check-up today."

"Do we have a place on the appointment schedule for her?"

"I'll fit her in. The child is sick and that's what we're here for. Sickness doesn't wait for appointments, you know."

"Yes, but other people are sick too. We can't have preferred customers."

He was apparently striking back at me.

"Paul, I said I was sorry about snapping at you. What's your problem?"

He slammed a book down on the desk. "It has nothing to do with this morning. You've been driving me to a point of frustration for the past few weeks. I've practically begged you to go out with me and so far you've allowed yourself to have lunch with me twice. I'd like to know why?"

"Maybe because I was hungry."

He sighed. "I'm trying to be serious here. Why do you keep turning me down? I'm not accustomed to being turned down by women so consistently. Most women happen to believe I'm fairly good-looking."

What an ego! I reminded myself that he was my employer, not just another playboy. I'd managed to keep our relationship cool, but friendly, and I didn't want to jeopardize the friendship now. I loved my job. It was fulfilling to be able to help people, and it kept me busy enough so I didn't have to worry about my inactive social life. "Well, you're not too hard to look at, but by the time I finish up here and go to school at night, when I do have free time, I want to relax. Maybe after things slow down we can go out sometime."

He rolled his eyes and shook his head, seeing right through my tactful brush-off. Before anything else could be said, I retreated back to my own office.

The morning schedule was booked, but the late afternoon was free. During a light lunch, I called Lucy and told her to bring Andrea in at 4:00, then settled down to the computer to work on the accounting.

It was a quiet afternoon until Mrs. Perkinson waddled in looking weary.

"Hello, Mrs. Perkinson. Did you have an appointment?"

"No, but do you think the doctor could see me anyway?"

"What's the problem?" I always tried to take the woman seriously because the day might come when she would have a legitimate complaint.

"I've got a rash breaking out, and I was afraid it might be cancer."

I smiled. "No, I doubt if it's cancer, but I will have Dr. Kellerman look at it for you." I left to find Paul in his office.

"Paul, your girlfriend is waiting to see you," I teased. "She says she has a rash and is afraid of cancer."

He nodded. "Send her back to room number two." He was curt, obviously still upset with me and in no mood for joking around.

"Yes, sir," I muttered, heading back toward the waiting area.

Twenty minutes later, Paul entered my office. "Please refill this prescription of ascorbic acid for Mrs. Perkinson."

"Did you find her problem?"

"I believe it's only a skin irritation, maybe from the soap or talcum powder she's using, but I'm going to take a blood sample anyway." He took a few things from the cabinet and started back toward the door. He glanced back at me and I gave him a sly grin and whispered, "Now don't you get naughty in that secluded little room."

He attempted to keep a straight face, but the corners of his lips twitched.

Paul tried all afternoon to talk me into having dinner with him and going dancing afterward. I'd turned him down and was attempting to come up with a believable excuse when Lucy popped into my office. "Anybody home?"

"Sure. Where's Andrea?"

"She spotted a stuffed animal in the waiting room and is sitting in the floor playing with it. She's feeling so much better, it almost seems silly to bring her in, but she hasn't had a check-up in a while, so I'd like to have the doc look at her since we're here."

Paul appeared in the doorway and I noticed Lucy's startled expression, her gaze traveling over Paul's physique.

"Lucy, this is Dr. Paul Kellerman. Paul, meet Lucy Anderson, my cousin."

"So my new patient is in the waiting room, huh? Well, I guess I'll go take a look at her." But he didn't move.

An awkward silence permeated the room until I spoke up. "Lucy said Andrea seems to be feeling better, but she would still like for you to give her a check up if you don't mind, right, Lucy?"

Lucy was mute, nodding her head.

Shaking himself from his trance, Paul agreed, "Of course I don't mind. I'll go get her."

He left Lucy staring after him. She whirled around to face me. "Why didn't you tell me your boss was so gorgeous? You've been working for him for how long, and you haven't hooked him yet? What is wrong with you?" I smiled. Maybe now I wouldn't have to think of an excuse not to go tonight. Instead, I would offer to babysit Andrea.

"Is he married or something?" Lucy was still trying to figure out my problem.

"No, he isn't married. He's not my type, that's all."

"Good, because he is definitely my type. Do you have a mirror around here? I didn't expect to meet the man of my dreams at a doctor's office. What do I look like?"

"You look great. Besides, the first impression has already been made. If I know Paul, you passed inspection."

The sound of a giggling child came from the hallway. Lucy looked amazed. "Is that Andrea?"

"I've never heard her laugh like that. She sounds so happy."

Paul came around the corner riding Andrea on his shoulders.

"Look, Mommy. I'm riding the horsy," she giggled.

Paul reached up and hoisted her down, "Okay. The horsy is played out," he looked at Lucy, "but little Andrea here is the picture of health. She probably had a little virus or something, but she's fine now."

Lucy's astonishment was reflected in her voice, "She sure is. I've never seen her so full of life. What did you do?"

Kneeling on the child's level, he grinned. "Oh, Andrea is my favorite little patient. We're buddies, right Andrea?"

Her red curls bobbed as she nodded her little head. "That's right." She gave him a tight hug around the neck.

"Now, why don't you run along and find that stuffed doggie you liked," he suggested.

"Okay," and off she ran.

"Lucy, would you consider going out with me tonight?"

Lucy looked stunned and I knew her first concern would be Andrea. "Go ahead, Lucy. I'll keep Andrea for you if you want—"

Paul interrupted, "No. We can go out to eat and take Andrea to see that children's matinee all the kids have been talking about. If we leave now, we can make it an early evening so Andrea could get to bed at a reasonable hour. How about it?"

"Sounds terrific! I know Andrea will love it."

"Okay, let's go." He strutted down the hall, calling over his shoulder, "Brianna, can you lock up?"

"Sure," I yelled back. "No problem. Have a good time." I wondered if he was trying to make me jealous and laughed at the thought. Rather than jealous, I was relieved. At least now I wouldn't need to make excuses for not going out with him. However, I couldn't help worrying about Lucy. I didn't want to see her get hurt by anyone, much less an arrogant peacock like Paul.

Four hours later, Paul carried Andrea into the house and helped get her into her pajamas and into her bed. She'd fallen asleep on the way home, exhausted by her exciting evening. Lucy told me how much Andrea had loved the play, and from the twinkle in Lucy's eyes and the glow on her face, it was apparent that she had enjoyed the night even more.

Paul didn't tarry long, but before saying goodnight to Lucy, he made plans to spend the next day with her.

Too keyed up to sleep, Lucy spent most of the night talking about Paul.

Chapter 14

Saturday, September 25—

Saturday was a long and lonely day for me. Paul, Lucy, and Andrea were hiking at Snowshoe Mountain for the day, and I was left with a lot of time to think. Although thoughts of Troy were never far from my mind, tonight they were more persistent, reminiscent of the time when we intuitively knew when the other was hurting or in trouble. Could he be in trouble? Is that why I'm feeling this way again?

Attempting to shove Troy from my mind, I wondered about everyone else at the ranch, especially Manuel. I'd never said good-bye to any of them and wondered what they must think of me for disappearing like that. After a long debate with myself, I decided to call Manuel. Desperately hoping Troy wouldn't answer, I dialed the phone before I had a chance to talk myself out of it.

"Hello," came Sheila's voice over the line.

"Sheila, this is Brianna Chavis. I was calling to see how Manuel is doing."

"Hello, Brianna. Manuel is not doing very well. He's very upset about everything that has happened." Sheila's tone was stiff.

"What do you mean? What has happened?"

"Not long after you left, Jake had a heart attack. Troy

blamed himself for his death because he had let him do the evening chores alone that night just before the attack."

My face felt flushed and my heart was heavy. "Uncle Jake is dead?" My eyes burned and tears began to well up in them.

"Yes. Then soon after the funeral, Troy disappeared. Manuel feels that everyone is deserting him. First you, then Jake, and now Troy. Naturally, he is very depressed."

"What do you mean, 'Troy disappeared'?" Now my heart was pounding. Maybe he was in trouble and that's why he's been on my mind.

"He left and never came back. It has been many months since we heard anything from him. We have tried calling his cell phone, but he does not answer or return our calls. We have been very worried but did not know what to do."

"When did you last hear from him?"

"We called him the end of June to tell him there were problems here at the ranch that needed his attention. He said he would return immediately, but he never did. We have not heard from him since that phone call."

"Have you reported him missing?"

"Yes, Joe called the sheriff. He said he would see what he could do to find him."

"Where was he when you talked to him last?"

"It was on his cell phone, so he could have been anywhere. We do not know where."

"Yes, but the sheriff should be able to get that information from the cell phone company. They might even be able to track his cell to see where it is now."

"They can do that?"

"Yes. Did the sheriff get his cell information from you?"

"Only his phone number. Is that all he will need?"

"I think so. Let me know if you hear anything." After giving Sheila my number, I hung up and sat motionless for several minutes in a state of shock and remorse. It was hard to accept that Uncle Jake was dead. My heart ached with sorrow for Manuel, knowing the hurt he must feel. I'd been so selfish, thinking only of protecting my own pride. It had never occurred to me that my leaving could contribute to Manuel's unhappiness. I was angry with myself for being so inconsiderate. Where did Troy go? Everything happened soon after I left the ranch, which was over three months ago. *Where is he?*

I sat on the sofa, darkness filling the room. The door blew open and laughter gushed in as Lucy flipped the light switch so Paul and Andrea could see to enter. The laughter stopped when they noticed me.

I tried to shake my mood. "Hey, you guys sound like you had a good time."

Lucy nodded slowly, peering at me. "Yes, we did, but why are you sitting here alone in the dark?"

I wanted to talk to Lucy about Troy's disappearance, but not in front of Paul and Andrea. It could wait until later. "Oh, I dozed off and only woke up when you came in. No biggy."

"You won't believe what we saw!" All three of them gathered around me and exclaimed in unison. "We saw a UFO!"

"You what? Where?"

Andrea's eyes were wide and her voice shrill with excitement. "Up on top of the mount'n! It was willy sumfin'!"

I smiled at the limited vocabulary of a four-year-old, but I had to hear the details from an adult. I switched my focus to Lucy and Paul. "Tell me what happened!"

They began to talk at the same time, but Paul yielded to Lucy. "We were hiking along the top of one of the peaks and heard a strange high-pitched sound. It wasn't loud but noticeable because it was so quiet up there. We saw the sun reflect off something in the sky, like bouncing off a mirror. At first we thought it was an airplane, but it came closer and we could see that it was flat and oblong and almost white like a cloud. Even though it was closer, it didn't get any louder. Then in a flash, it went straight up and was gone out of sight."

"Were you frightened?"

"No. It wasn't threatening at all. In fact, it was calming somehow. I can't really explain it, can you, Paul?"

"The only way I know to explain it is that I felt like I was looking at an angel or something. I felt at peace."

Andrea jumped into Paul's lap. "I liked it. Can we go see it again?"

Lucy looked at Paul and shrugged. "Well, I don't know, honey. It might not be there next time we go."

"Why?"

"Because we don't even know what it was. We've never seen one before."

"It liked us, so it'll come back," Andrea assured them.

Paul stood, picking her up. "Maybe so, Peanut, but right now I think it's probably past your bedtime."

With Andrea tucked into bed, I retired to my bedroom so Lucy and Paul could have their privacy. I unsuccessfully attempted to read, paced for a while, and tried desperately to make sense out of Troy's disappearance. A couple of hours later, I heard the front door open and close. Now I could talk to Lucy.

I walked down the short hallway only to find Lucy gone. Sneaking a peek through the window, I saw her standing by Paul's car kissing him good-bye, so I walked across the cobblestone floor to the kitchen to prepare coffee and wait.

I had the cups out and was pouring the aromatic brew when Lucy returned.

"Would you like some coffee?"

"I thought you'd gone to bed. What are you doing up so late?"

"I need to talk to you. I called the ranch and got some disturbing news."

"About Troy?"

I nodded. "And his Uncle."

"Oh? Okay, pour me a cup." She flopped down in a chair at the wood plank table.

"Uncle Jake died right after I left the ranch."

"Died? What happened?"

"He had a heart attack."

"Is Troy taking it hard?"

"I guess so. He's disappeared."

"What do you mean 'disappeared'?"

"Sheila said he left the ranch and never returned. They called him on his cell back in June and he said he was going to be returning immediately, something about some ranch business that needed to be handled, but he never showed up. They haven't heard from him and have no idea where he is."

"That is strange. Maybe he simply decided he didn't want to run the ranch anymore. With his Uncle Jake gone, he could have lost interest."

"Yeah, but he wouldn't leave Joe and Sheila holding the bag like that. And he loves Manuel. I can't believe he would desert him. If he didn't want to run the ranch, he would have sold it or something, not up and leave, right?"

"Hey, this is a guy who acted like he cared about you but was trying to get rid of you at the same time. Who knows what's really going on with a person like that?"

"True, but it doesn't fit. Something has got to be wrong."

"I'm sorry, Brce. I know that Troy's disappearing is upsetting you, but I can't wrap my mind around anything else right now other than that UFO. It was amazing! I honestly never believed in them, but there was no mistaking what we saw. Do you think we should tell anyone? I mean, won't people think we're crazy or making it up to get in the news?"

"Probably. That's what we've always thought of other people who have claimed to see them. I'd be careful about who you tell."

"I guess. How do you keep something like this to yourself? I wish I'd had a camera. Well, actually we did have a camera, but we were so stunned and mesmerized, we didn't think to take pictures of it."

"That's too bad. Troy told me he's seen one, but he acted like it was no big deal."

"Troy saw a UFO?"

"That's what he told me, but he didn't elaborate."

"I wonder where they're coming from, or if there were people or beings of some kind aboard."

We pondered the thought for a while before Lucy continued. "You know, the Bible says Christ will return on a cloud. Did you ever think that the 'cloud' could be a UFO? Back when the Bible was written, they wouldn't have had any words for such a vision. I guess they could have described it as a 'cloud.' Just like the 'giant fire-breathing locusts' could be what we know as helicopters."

I cut my eyes at her. "Now I know you're tired. It's late, so we better go to bed and save the speculation for when we're thinking more clearly."

I stood on top of a dune in White Sands. A bright light streaked across the sky and disappeared behind a far-off mound. This time, I was determined to see what it was and walked through the sand over dune after dune, each time hoping this would be the one where I'd find it, but there would be nothing, so I continued to climb the next hill.

I never found the shiny object, but I came to a cantina. I walked inside and there was Troy singing "Electric Breeze." I was so excited about finding Troy, I forgot about the glowing object in the dunes. I listened as he finished the song, then walked up to him with open arms to give him a hug. He smiled, put down his guitar, and placed his arms around me. My head pressed against his chest, my eyes closed. I was at peace.

I opened my eyes to see sunlight filtering through my bedroom window. It was only a dream, but it was so real. It was an hour later before the peculiar feeling of being in another world finally faded away.

Lucy and Paul's sighting and my dream sparked my curiosity about UFOs again. The following Saturday afternoon, I drove to Snowshoe Mountain and trekked along the trails, hoping to see a flying saucer. I sat at a lookout point and watched an eagle circle above. I dug into my knapsack for my peanut butter sandwich, banana, and bottle of water. Watching the eagle renewed a peace within me that I'd been missing. Life was so hectic, I'd forgotten how to enjoy the little things. I took a deep breath, realizing I needed to get back into practicing yoga.

The sun was beginning to sink low in the sky. Suddenly, something glistened to my left. I eagerly watched. It came closer and was becoming larger, until I could see its silver wings. Only an airplane.

I sat there until dusk, then started my hike back to my car. I should have known I wouldn't see a UFO, but it was a wonderful day nonetheless.

My curiosity with unidentified flying objects didn't go away. I continued surfing the Internet and researching the subject. I learned there were a large number of mountain people, some near where I live, who have claimed seeing them. I also found a UFO Center website and information about an organization called MUFON (Mutual UFO Network), set up for the scientific study of UFOs.

Chapter 15

Saturday, October 9—

I sat at the kitchen table drinking my morning coffee, staring at the pumpkin Lucy planned to carve for Andrea. The last two weeks had been difficult. I wasn't concentrating at work and had made several errors on patients' files. Luckily, none were critical mistakes, but enough to show me, and everyone around me, that I was not my usual efficient self.

Where on earth could Troy be? I needed to talk to Mitchell but was embarrassed to call him after all this time. My mind suddenly recalled the conversation I'd had with Troy about Mitchell's beliefs and Troy's religious transformation. Would prayer help me? Probably not. It had been years since I'd tried to pray. God probably wouldn't recognize my voice anymore.

Swallowing my pride, I reached for the phone and dialed Mitchell's number.

"Hello," came his sleepy voice.

"Mitch?"

"Bree?" His voice was now wide-awake and strong.

"How've you been?" I wasn't sure what to say now that I had him on the phone.

"How've I been? I've been going crazy, that's how. Why wouldn't you return my calls all these months?"

"I'm sorry. I guess I didn't want to have to explain

myself. Truthfully, I still don't, but I do need to talk to my best friend."

"Okay, I won't ask for any explanations. I just thank God you finally called. I've missed you."

"I've missed you too." There was a comfortable pause. "Have you heard anything from Troy?"

"No. We still don't have any idea what happened to him. He simply disappeared off the face of the earth. I can't imagine where he must be. It's been months now."

Now I was really worried. I'd hoped that Troy had taken a trip to escape the pain of Uncle Jake's death, but he would never have stayed away this long. He certainly wouldn't have deserted Manuel and the ranch like that, would he? I shrugged. Maybe he would. I obviously hadn't known him at all. "I've been getting the feeling that he needs me. You know, like I used to years ago. It's like I know he's in trouble, but I don't know how to find him. What can we do, Mitch?"

"I wish I knew. The police are supposed to be searching for him, but I don't know how much even they can do."

"Have you been to the ranch?"

"Not lately. I probably should visit to check on them, but Joe seems to have everything under control."

"What about Manuel? Is he okay?"

"It's been hard on him, but he's in school now, so that helps take his mind off things."

Feeling better and reconnected, I was glad I'd called. "How's Gina?"

"She's fine."

"Tell her I said hi. Mitch, keep in touch, and let me know if you hear anything about Troy."

"Okay. Thanks for calling."

After hanging up, I felt better than I'd felt in months. At least I had my best friend back. I smiled at the thought that Mitch had been so easy to talk to and so willing to accept me back with no questions asked. He was truly a rare breed. How many people would be that understanding and accepting?

Other than a few decorations at the clinic and noticing Andrea's fairy princess costume, Halloween came and went without receiving much attention from me. I didn't even bother attending the annual Chavis costume ball.

Thursday, November 4—

Several weeks had passed since Lucy and Paul began dating, and they'd been together almost every night and every weekend. I returned from work expecting Lucy to be anticipating another evening out, but instead found her in her robe and curlers.

"Aren't you seeing Paul tonight?"

"No. We've been on the go every night, so I decided to take a night off."

"You're not getting tired of him, are you?" I would understand if she were. Paul's ego was pretty hard to take after a while.

"No, of course not."

"Well, I would get sick of his conceited attitude if I were dating him. How can you stand it?"

"Haven't you ever heard that when you love someone, you love him as he is?"

"Love? Are you telling me that you've fallen in love with him?"

"Dearheart, I fell in love with him when I first laid eyes on him."

"Has he given you any idea of how he feels?"

"I'm not sure. I think he loves me. He has spent a lot of time with me, and he hasn't been seeing anyone else. I think that's a good sign, don't you?"

"Don't ask me. I'm the one that got dumped on by another smooth talker, remember? But Paul does seem to care about you and Andrea."

"He's terrific with her, isn't he? She's much happier and better adjusted than she's ever been in her life."

"I sure hope things work out for you, Lucy. Not only would a heartbreak hurt you now, but it would devastate Andrea."

Lucy waved me away. "You're such a pessimist. Life is a gamble. We all take chances. Either we win or we lose, there are no guarantees. So enjoy what you've got while you've got it and stop worrying about what tomorrow will bring. As for Andrea, she'll be okay. She has to grow up in this world, and it won't hurt her to learn to take the hard knocks at a young age. I've always heard that the very young are resilient and can adjust to difficult situations much easier than we adults."

"Maybe you're right. I can't get over the three of you. What a trio! You're carefree and crazy, Paul is serious and stuck on himself, and little Andrea is so quiet and innocent."

"We're like a knife, fork, and spoon. All different, but when you put them all together, you get a great combination." She flopped down on the sofa and hugged a pillow, her laughing eyes sparkling so that I could almost swear I saw stars in them.

"The great philosopher strikes again," I quipped.

Lucy giggled and threw the pillow at me. It felt good to see Lucy back to her old self. It had been a long time since I'd seen the happy, carefree girl I used to know.

"Hey," I changed the subject. "Do you realize it's November already? Christmas is only a few weeks away. Why don't we go shopping tomorrow night?"

"How about making it Saturday? Tomorrow is Friday, and Paul and I are going out to celebrate."

"Celebrate what? There's a Friday in every week."

"Yes, but this Friday we will have known each other exactly six weeks. He's planned a special night." Her hand flew to her mouth as she remembered something. "I almost forgot. I'm supposed to get a sitter for Andrea. Could you babysit?"

"Sure, why not? I've got nothing else planned."

"I didn't think you would. When are you going to start living again?"

"Hey, no lectures, please. I promise you that I'll make that my New Year's resolution, okay?"

"Okay, but I'm going to hold you to it. By the way, have you heard anything about Troy and where he disappeared to?"

"No, I want to call but don't know if I should."

"Of course you should. Showing concern is never wrong. If you don't call, it looks as if you don't care."

"That's my point. I don't want Troy to think I care. It

would only make his head swell to think I would be worried about him."

"Then don't ask about him. Call to see if Manuel is better."

"Good idea! I would like to know how he's doing." I ran to get the phone number and dialed.

"Hello?" It was Sheila's sweet voice.

"Sheila, this is Brianna."

"Brianna! Have you heard from Troy?" she asked anxiously.

"No, I was calling to see if you had."

"Oh," her disappointment was obvious. "No, we haven't heard a thing from him. We're very worried."

"How's Manuel?"

"Still not good. He's not adjusting in school very well because of his depression."

"I wish there was something I could do."

"I don't think anything will help except for Troy to come home. If you hear from him, please let us know, and tell him how much he is needed here."

"I doubt if I'll be hearing from him. If I do, I'll be sure to tell him, and I'll call you right away."

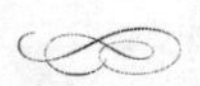

Friday, November 5—

It was a cold and rainy night. I answered the knock on the door. "Come on in, Paul. Lucy will be ready in a minute."

Andrea ran through the room and landed in mid-air into Paul's arms. She clearly loved him, and I wanted more than anything for things to work out for the three of them, but I didn't trust Paul's intentions. For that matter, I didn't trust any man.

Lucy made a grand entrance in one of Milliken's designs. It was a lovely, emerald green evening gown with a plunging neckline. It hugged her petite body down to the waist and then fell into a soft, flowing skirt to the floor. It was accented by long, tight lace sleeves and a dark velvet sash, drizzled with rhinestones, at the waist. She'd added a gold necklace and earrings, and the effect was breathtaking. Her eyes appeared greener than ever before.

Andrea was as overcome with admiration as Paul and I. "Mama, you're pretty," she said in her tiny, awestricken voice.

"Gorgeous!" Paul agreed and helped her with her coat. He hesitated, "I hate to cover up such beauty. What you need is a mink to wear tonight."

Lucy laughed, "Even if I owned a mink, I wouldn't wear it in this weather."

Andrea cried when they left without her but soon fell asleep in my arms. Looking at the sweet face of the child made me believe in angels. Angels, God, Jesus. What do I believe? Troy certainly seemed convinced, but how could someone be a Christian and deceive another person the way he had deceived me? And Mitchell, his beliefs are different, but who's to say he's wrong? Momma and Daddy had always gone to church, but they never talked much about what they believed. And then there was Lucy, whose faith had sustained her through so much, but is it only a crutch? I tried to say a prayer but felt the empty words falling into the barren air around me.

I went to bed soon after tucking Andrea in but awoke

with a start when my bedside lamp clicked on. Lucy was standing over me full of excitement. "I'm sorry, but I had to wake you. Look!"

My eyes adjusting to the faint light of the small lamp, I saw an elegant diamond cluster staring at me from Lucy's left hand. I sprang up and flicked on a brighter light so I could inspect it more thoroughly. There was a half-carat diamond in the center with six tiny diamonds surrounding it, set in a silver inlay with a gold band.

"Oh, Lucy, it's beautiful! I need to ask Paul for a raise. If he can afford something like that, we must be doing better than I thought."

"I'm so happy. Andrea was delighted when she learned that she will finally have a daddy."

"Andrea? You've already told her?"

"Of course. Paul wouldn't even put the ring on my finger until he okayed it with her. He wanted to see if she would accept him as her father before he could finalize the engagement, so we woke her when we got home and told her."

"What did she say?"

"She was too sleepy to say much, but when we told her good-night, she called him 'Daddy.'"

"I'm so happy for you. When is the wedding?"

"We haven't decided for sure yet, but we talked about the first of January. You will be my maid of honor, won't you?"

"Are you crazy? Of course I will! But that doesn't give us much time to plan a wedding."

Saturday, November 6—

The department stores were crammed with shoppers. While Lucy looked over the dolls and dollhouses, I browsed through the rest of the toys, inspecting all the new electronic gadgets. Then I caught sight of a beautiful model of a horse exactly like Manuel's Fireball. I glanced around and saw Lucy was already at the checkout counter loaded down with gifts for Paul and Andrea. Snatching the horse from the shelf, I hurried to join her.

Packages loaded into the car, we started home. "How are we going to sneak this stuff past Paul and Andrea?" Lucy mulled over her problem as she drove. Paul was at the mill-house watching a football game and babysitting Andrea.

"Why don't we go by Momma's and wrap everything before we go home," I proposed.

"Great idea!" She made a quick U-turn and headed back up the street.

The house was dark and the doors were locked. I rang the doorbell. Several minutes passed before Aunt Marty opened the door. "Bree, why didn't you use your key?"

"I don't like to use it if someone is home. It doesn't feel right to walk in unannounced."

"Nonsense. You're family." The old woman's mind was still sharp even though her body was weak and wobbly. "So what brings you girls here?"

"We were Christmas shopping and wanted to wrap the gifts before we go home so Paul and Andrea won't see what we got them." We hauled the packages into the dining room and stacked them on the table. "Where are Momma and Daddy?"

"Your mother had a banquet for work and Collin accompanied her. They are presenting Rachel with some type of award, I think."

Lucy looked impressed. "Wow, that's great!"

I smiled. It had been a common occurrence during my life for my mother to be winning awards. "Momma's always winning some kind of award. I mean, it's great that she's so good at her job, but how many awards can one person get anyway?"

Aunt Marty was looking at Lucy's finger. "Is that an engagement ring, dear?"

Lucy beamed. "It sure is!" She held it up for her to get a better look. "By the way, Aunt Marty, I've always wondered why it took you so long to get married. Until you met Mr. Jamison, you stayed single. Why is that?" Aunt Marty had been in her sixties when she'd met her husband.

"Well, because I don't believe two people should try to force themselves to stay in a relationship just because they get married."

"What do you mean?"

"See, when two people get together, it's usually because they have somethin' in common—a physical attraction or a mutual interest in a hobby or job. Eventually that mutual interest is gonna change, and when it does, they'll start to drift apart. Now unless they continue to find mutual interests to keep that bond between 'em, they'll grow in separate directions and become like strangers living under the same roof. That's why there are so many divorces. I've studied people all my life and have only seen a few couples who were truly meant to be together. Like Rachel and Collin. They are soul mates. I never met my soul mate, not until I met Jamie." There was a pregnant pause as she thought about her deceased husband. "So, Lucy, is this fella your soul mate, ya think?"

Lucy didn't seem shaken in the least by the older woman's depressing commentary on relationships. Her love for her fiancé was spelled out clearly in her smiling face. "Yes, Aunt Marty, he is definitely my soul mate. I loved Brad, but my feelings for Paul are different, deeper somehow. It's like we know what each other is going to say before we say it. Sometimes it feels as if we could communicate telepathically."

And I'd thought Troy and I were the only ones that experienced that feeling. *So much for soul mates*. Obviously, that didn't protect one from having her heart broken. These thoughts went through my mind as I listened to Lucy and Aunt Marty.

"Good for you, sweetie. I wish you both well. I'd like to meet this young man of yours."

"Oh, you will. If you don't meet him before then, you'll meet him on Thanksgiving. He'll be coming with me for Thanksgiving dinner."

Lucy and Aunt Marty continued talking as I finished wrapping Manuel's package and wondered when I should send it. Although I normally didn't like to give gifts too far ahead of Christmas, with Troy gone maybe it would help lift Manuel's spirits if I went ahead and sent it. I looked up to ask the other two women for their opinion but thought better of interrupting them and made the decision to mail the package in a couple of weeks. Besides, I didn't want to explain who Manuel was to Aunt Marty.

We arrived back at the millhouse with wrapped packages in tow. Paul met us at the door. "Andrea is asleep. Let's put her packages in my car, and I'll keep them at my place until Christmas."

"Perfect. I was worried about where we would keep them. There isn't much storage space in this place; nowhere to hide stuff."

Gathering the packages in his arms, Paul said, "By the way, Bree, someone named Gina called and wants you to call her as soon as possible. It sounded pretty urgent. Her number is by the phone." He and Lucy hauled the packages to his car while I went to call Gina.

"Hello." I recognized Gina's southern drawl immediately.

"Gina, this is Brianna. Has there been news about Troy?"

"Not exactly. The state police called Joe and said they found the jeep. It was abandoned in a ravine by I-81 near Roanoke, Virginia. There was no sign of Troy though. But, Bree, I actually called about Mitch." She sounded worried.

"What about him?"

"Have you heard from him?"

"No. Why?"

"He's gone. I haven't seen or heard from him in a week. He seems to have disappeared too."

"Gina, what's going on? First Troy, and now Mitch? Do you have any idea what could be happening?"

"No. I wish I did. None of this makes any sense to

me. Mitch wouldn't up and leave without saying anything. And his car is here. I even tried to get in touch with his roommate, Sal, but he's gone too. If you hear anything at all from Mitch, please call me."

"Of course. Keep me in the loop too. I really wish I knew what's going on."

I had another restless night. I desperately tried to think of a reasonable explanation for Troy, Mitch, and Sal to have disappeared. My mind kept going back to the UFO sightings. I shook off the idea that they had been snatched by beings from outer space. *I've seen too many sci-fi movies.*

Sunday, November 7—

As the sun peeked over the horizon, I dragged myself into the kitchen to perk the coffee and wait for a reasonable hour to call the ranch. Maybe Joe and Sheila knew more about Troy by now. I busied myself with making a big Sunday breakfast for Lucy and Andrea, hoping it would help time pass more quickly. Now breakfast was ready, but the other two sleepyheads were still in bed, so I wrapped the food and placed everything into the warm oven and glanced at the clock. 7:20—close enough! I grabbed the phone and dialed. There was no answer. Of course not, it was too early for anyone to be at the main house. I wished I had Joe and Sheila's phone number. I waited for the voice message to finish its spiel and left a message for them to call me.

Lucy and Andrea were finishing their breakfast when the phone rang. I grabbed it on the first ring. "Hello."

"Brianna?"

"Hi, Sheila. Thanks for calling me back. I wondered if you've heard anything at all from Troy."

"No, but the police did find the jeep he was driving."

"That's what Gina told me. They found it near Roanoke?"

"Yes, in Virginia. The state police found it down in a deep ditch behind some trees, so they don't know how long it was there."

"What do they think happened to Troy?"

"They don't know. They didn't know anything about Troy. They said the jeep was registered to Mr. Jacob Garrison, so they called here to let us know they had found it. We told them that Mr. Jake was deceased and that Troy was the driver, and they should be looking for him. We have not heard anything more."

"Did you know that Mitch has disappeared too?"

"Yes, Gina called here looking for him. This is so strange. We don't know what is happening."

"Let me know if you hear anything."

"I will."

"Sheila, before you go, how's Manuel?"

"He's doing better in school, but he's still not himself. He's very lonely without Troy. If it wasn't for Shadow, I don't know what he would do."

The next day, I dropped Manuel's package by the post office. I wished I knew if my little gift would make him happier.

Chapter 16

Thursday, November 18—

Troy crossed the Arkansas/Oklahoma border, trying desperately to keep his speed within the limits of the law. The rental car was a lot smoother ride than Uncle Jake's old jeep. *Four-and-a-half months.* He had been cut off from everyone, unable to let anyone know where he was. *What must everyone think? I wonder if Bree has tried to contact me. And the ranch. I hope the bank hasn't foreclosed.* Eagerness to get back and make things right again compelled him to skip meals and continue driving for hours without resting.

His heart pounded when he finally saw the gates of the ranch. It was the dinner hour and he hoped to find Sheila in the kitchen, but the house was locked and empty. He ran to the stables and was relieved to find old reliable Pete sitting by the barn door working on a broken bit.

"Pete, where is everyone?"

Pete, intent on his chore, was startled by Troy's voice. He looked up and beamed at the sight of the returning vagabond. "Well, well. You finally decided to come home?"

"I'm sorry for the disappearing act, Pete. I'll explain later, but tell me how everything's going here?"

"Oh, we just been going about our usual chores. There's been a few problems, but Joe can catch you up later. I'm sure glad you're back. We was plum worried sick about you. I hope you're staying put for a while." He looked up at Troy with a question in his eyes.

"I hope so too, Pete. Where are Joe and Sheila?"

"Oh, they're down at their place. They don't bother coming up here unless Sheila is gonna clean or somethin.'"

Troy grabbed his saddle and saddled one of the horses. He wasted no time getting to the little cottage.

"Hey! Anybody home?" He jumped from the horse and tied the reins to a hitching post beside the picket fence.

Manuel bolted from the house, followed by Sheila and Joe. Jumping into Troy's arms and squeezing him until he choked, Manuel's eyes danced with excitement.

After the initial greetings were over, Troy looked at Joe. "Tell me about how things stand here at the ranch. What happened with the bank?"

Joe looked at him, his face stern. "You have some nerve! Disappearing like that, then showing up here asking questions like you actually care."

"I do care, Joe. I didn't disappear because I wanted to. I was on my way back here after you called, I swear I was."

"So what happened?" Joe was still miffed.

Troy was tired and hungry. "I'll fill you in later. I'm exhausted, and it's a long story. Can we go inside and get something to drink? I'm really thirsty."

Walking into the house, Troy turned to Sheila. "Have you heard from Brianna?"

"Yes, she's called a few of times."

Tears came to Troy's eyes as the desperation he'd felt for so many months gave way to reassurance. "What did she say? Where is she? Why did she leave?" His questions spilled out.

Sheila smiled sadly and shook her head. "Slow down, Troy. First, we have a lot of questions for you to answer." She knew her husband's questions would not wait for idle talk about Brianna. It would only serve to make him more angry.

Sheila sat another place at the dinner table while Troy played with Manuel and tried desperately to explain why he'd left the way he had. "I left to go find Brianna, but I never found her. The rest of the story is long and complicated, so I'll have to tell you about it later. I'm sure glad to be home." Manuel looked confused, but his joy at having his Uncle Troy back overpowered any other feelings and soon everything was forgotten.

They ate in silence. Joe was obviously still waiting for an explanation. "Joe, if I could have, I would have been home months ago. I was unavoidably detained. I don't want to say any more than that right now." He glanced at Manuel.

Sheila understood that he didn't want to discuss it in front of her son. She tried to change the subject. "I just remembered, a pretty package came for Manuel. I thought it was from you, maybe?" She looked at Troy inquiringly.

"No. What was in it?"

"I don't know. It was wrapped in Christmas paper, so we put it in the closet to go under the Christmas tree thinking it was from you."

Manuel slipped away from the table and ran to get the package. When he returned, he handed it to Troy. "Can I open it now?"

Troy looked at the return address. There was no name, but there was a return address, 812 Market St. in Eastridge. Troy looked at Manuel and grinned from ear to ear.

"No, don't open it yet. We'll put it under the tree and open it together Christmas. Okay?"

"Then it is from you?" Manuel's bright eyes were filled with love and expectations.

"No. I believe it's from Brianna."

Manuel looked down and bit down on his bottom lip.

Troy picked him up and sat him on his knee. "Come on, little buddy. What's with the pouty lip?"

Manuel just shrugged and continued to stare at the floor.

"Manuel, I don't know why she left, but now I know where she is, and I will find out what's going on with her. When I do, I'll bet she'll want to see you. She wouldn't have sent you a gift if she didn't care about you, you know?"

Again, Manuel shrugged. "I guess."

Sheila began clearing the table. "I promised Brianna I would call her if I heard from you. Do you want me to call her, or do you want to do it?"

"You mean you have her phone number?"

"Oh, yes, did I forget to mention that?" she teased.

"I'll be making that call, thank you very much."

"I left the number up at the main house by the phone."

Troy was anxious to go back to Eastridge and find Brianna, but he'd been away from the ranch far too long already. Things here needed his attention. The ranch had meant everything to Uncle Jake, and it was important to Troy that he make sure it continued to prosper. That was the only way he could make up for what he'd done. Besides, Manuel would never forgive him if he left again this soon. He walked out onto the porch and looked up at the early evening stars. *I have to concentrate on getting things back on an even keel here before I take off again. But, Bree, I will get there soon, whether you like it or not.*

Joe joined him on the porch, along with Manuel.

"Joe, do you want to tell me what's been going on here?"

"I handled everything with the bank. I found the papers on the desk in the den that were supposed to go to the bank, so I delivered them. Then they said they would need the payments for two months that had been missed. I didn't have the money, so I mortgaged my home to pay the payments."

Troy sighed. "I'm sorry, Joe. I'll pay off that mortgage for you."

"Most of our ranch hands were threatening to quit, so I had to use more of the mortgage money to keep them paid too."

"What happened to that guy that I hired to manage things?"

"He quit after the first week. Just walked away and didn't come back."

"Joe, I don't know how to thank you for all you've done. I'll make it up to you somehow."

"I did it for Jake."

"I know you did."

By the time Troy and Joe finished catching up on everything that had happened in the past few months, it was too late to call Brianna. The next morning, he met Joe bright and early to ride around the ranch to see what needed to be done now that he was back.

He hurried into the back door, glanced at the clock—9:45, and headed for the phone in the hallway. He found Brianna's phone number beside the phone as Sheila had promised. Heart racing, he dialed the number. It rang, and rang, and rang. "You have reached the home of Bree and Lucy. You know the drill."

He hung up when he heard the beep. *I can't leave her a message. What would I say? "Hi, Bree. Sorry I haven't called, but I've been locked away for over four months?" I'm sure she'd love that.*

There was so much to do in order to whip the ranch back into shape, there didn't seem to be enough hours in the day. Between the banks, the disgruntled hired hands, the property maintenance, the horses that were about to foal, the injured horses, and the sales that needed to happen in order to bring in the funds to keep the ranch running, Troy's schedule didn't allow much time for brooding over Brianna. He attempted to reach her several times but could never catch her at home.

He tried again on Thanksgiving Day, but when he heard the voicemail message again, he realized she was probably at her parents' home for their big Thanksgiving feast.

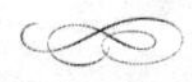

November 25–Thanksgiving in Eastridge—

The house was alive with music and laughter. The holidays were always festive around the Chavis household. Anyone and everyone who had nowhere else to celebrate Thanksgiving was invited. The entire Chavis family was there, but so were several other people who were strangers to me. Extension leaves had been added to the dining room table to accommodate the crowd of guests. Food streamed from the kitchen to keep up with the demand of the ravenous throng. In spite of the lavish home setting, there were no formalities, just good home cooking and revelry. I smiled at the warm scene surrounding me. *This is what Thanksgiving is all about; family and loved ones sharing in their joy for all the blessings God has given them.* Daddy said a quick prayer before we began eating to remind us of why we were gathered. My parents were kind and generous, and although there were a few in town who were jealous of all they had accomplished, they were beloved by those who took the time to get to know them. I was proud of both of my parents and wondered if they knew that.

Hours later, the party dwindled until no one remained except the immediate family sitting around the den watching the flames of the crackling fire in the fireplace and enjoying the wonderful feeling of fulfillment. Not only were our bellies full, but our hearts glowed with the contentment of being with loved ones.

Daddy broke the silence. "Bree, I've been meaning to tell you about a visit I had from Sheriff Rudy a few weeks ago concerning Troy Garrison."

I tried to hide my emotions, but my heart pounded with expectation as adrenalin coursed through my veins. I still hadn't told my parents about seeing Troy during my trip to New Mexico. Knowing they wouldn't approve, I didn't want to discuss it with them. "What did the sheriff have to say?"

"He said the state police found a jeep by the Interstate near Roanoke that was registered to a Mr. Jacob Garrison in Lincoln, New Mexico. They learned that he was deceased, and when they called his home, they were told that Troy Garrison, his nephew, had been driving the vehicle and no one had heard from him for a couple of months. They came by the house to see if we'd heard anything from him."

Momma chimed in. "Why would they think we'd heard from him?"

"They knew he'd been in Eastridge because he was registered at the hotel. They were checking with everyone in town, not just us. Of course, I told him we hadn't heard from him in years." Daddy was watching me closely for any trace of reaction.

I exchanged a glance with Lucy. "So did the sheriff know anything else?"

Daddy noticed my guarded demeanor, but Andrea began patting him on the leg to get his attention, causing him to lose his train of thought. "About what?"

"Like what might have happened to him?"

"No. They didn't have a clue. It's no telling with that boy." Daddy abandoned the entire conversation and turned to Andrea. "Come here, Pumpkin."

I glanced around the room. Aunt Marty appeared deep in thought. "Aunt Marty, are you okay?"

Shaking her head and waving me away, she tried to dismiss whatever was on her mind. "It's nothing. I'm fine."

Momma had also noticed. "Aunt Marty, you seem bothered about something. What is it?"

With a deep sigh, she relented. "I'm wondering if I should go see the sheriff and tell him about that young man coming by the house a while back."

She now had everyone's attention. In unison, we said, "When?"

"Oh, it was a few months ago. The azalea blooms were long gone and the daisies were starting to bloom, so it must have been toward the end of June."

Momma coaxed, "What did Troy say when he came by?"

"I didn't answer the door. I was the only one home, and I certainly had no dealings with him."

"Are you sure it was Troy?" I was frustrated, anxious, and angry. Why would he come here? What could he want? And where did he go?

"Oh, sure, it was him. I'd recognize that troublesome boy anywhere—"

Daddy's voice of logic interrupted. "I think you should go to the sheriff and let him know about this. I don't know if he's learned anything since I talked to him or not. That was several weeks ago. But if this boy is still missing, it might help them to know you saw him. It would help them out a lot more if you knew exactly when it was."

Aunt Marty looked miffed. "Young man, I know that! Do you think I learned nothing when I was mayor? Don't treat me like an old fool." She hobbled out of the den and down the hallway to her room.

I was anxious to get home so I could call to find out if anyone had heard from Troy or Mitchell. I'd called a couple of times in the past few weeks, but there'd been no news. Now I felt a renewed urgency to know what was going on. "Momma and Daddy, this was wonderful, but I'm getting tired, so I think I'm going to head home." After the usual remarks such as, "Don't rush off," and,

"How about another dessert before you go?" they finally surrendered and said their good-byes.

Back at the millhouse, I looked up Gina's number and dialed.

"Hello?"

"Gina?"

"Hi, Bree. Have you heard from Mitch?"

"No, I was hoping you had."

"No, not yet, but Troy is home."

"He is?"

"Yeah, he showed up last week, but he has no idea about where Mitch has gone."

"Where has he been?"

"I don't know. I haven't talked to him except to see if he's heard from Mitch. I'm glad he's home, but I don't care about anything except where Mitch is. We were getting along great, so I know he wouldn't leave like this of his own free will. Something is wrong, yet no one seems to want to help. The police have been no help at all. They keep saying it's a military matter."

"I'm sorry, Gina. I wish there was something I could do. What about his superiors at the Air Force Base? Can't they help? Is he considered AWOL or what?"

"They won't talk to me. They won't tell me anything."

"That's fishy. If he was AWOL, they would definitely want to talk to you, wouldn't they?"

"I don't know. They treat me like I'm a nutcase or something."

"Have the police tried to trace his cell phone?"

"It's here. He didn't take it with him. He never went

anywhere without that phone. Nothing is right about any of this."

"Please let me know if you hear anything. No one called to let me know Troy was home and I've been worried sick. Please be sure to call me if you hear anything about Mitch, okay?"

"Okay. Thanks for calling."

New Mexico—

The phone rang as Sheila was cleaning up the dinner dishes. Troy answered, "Hello."

"Troy, it's Gina. Have you heard anything from Mitch yet?"

"No, I can't imagine where he could be. Do you think his unit was called out and he went AWOL to avoid going?"

"No. I checked on that. They are acting very strange at the base though. I think they know something. Maybe it has something to do with the top secret stuff he's been involved with in D.C."

"Maybe. If that's the case, there's probably not much we can do."

"I'm so glad you're home. Where were you anyway?"

"That's a long story for another time."

"I talked to Bree tonight."

He perked up. "You did? What did she say?"

"She called to see if I'd heard from Mitch. I told her you were home, so don't be surprised if she calls the ranch."

"I hope she does! I've been trying to call her for a week and can't catch her at home."

Well, Bree, I guess if you want to talk to me, you'll call. I'll wait to see if you do.

Friday, December 3—Eastridge—

After a long, hard day at the clinic, I reclined on the sofa and watched Andrea play with her doll. "Andrea, are you excited about seeing Santa tonight?"

"I guess, but he scares me a little."

"Oh, you don't need to be afraid of Santa. He loves little children and all he wants to do is make you happy. He would never do anything to hurt you."

"I know, but he's scary looking and sounds scary too."

I laughed. "Yes, I guess he is a little loud with his 'Ho ho ho,' isn't he? But remember that he's really a very nice old man."

"Will he bring me presents if I don't talk to him?"

"Sure he will. You don't have to talk to him if you don't want to."

"Good. But I might anyway."

After Lucy, Andrea, and Paul left, I changed into my flannel PJs and curled up on the sofa and surfed through the TV channels. Bored with finding nothing worth watching, I stopped on a news channel. I was about to turn it off when a picture of Mitchell in his Air Force uniform popped on the screen. I turned up the volume. "The FBI rolls up Air Force spy. Details when we return." Then a commercial. And another. And another.

I let out a guttural groan. "Come on, stop with the commercials and get to the news!"

The picture of Mitchell was back on the screen. "America is sold out by one of its own." The word "Espionage" appeared, splattered across Mitchell's picture.

I couldn't believe my eyes and ears as the anchor gave his report. "Staff Sergeant Mitchell Sibley of the U.S. Air Force has been accused of selling government secrets. The FCI has been investigating a leak from the Holloman Air Force Base for the past year. They are not releasing any details regarding the nature of the information sold at this time. Sergeant Sibley faces charges of treason and espionage. Article 3 of the Constitution states the penalty for treason is a minimum of five years imprisonment and a maximum penalty of death, a minimum fine of ten thousand dollars, and the convicted party shall lose all rights to ever hold office in the United States. To date, no one has been convicted of treason in this country, thus the espionage charge, which is more likely to get a conviction. Now for the local news…"

I sat staring at the screen in shock. This was crazy! Mitch would never do something like that. There's got to be some mistake! The telephone rang. Still dazed, I reached to answer it. "Hello."

"Bree, this is Gina."

"Gina, I'm so glad you called. Have you seen the news?"

"No, not yet. I was hoping to tell you before you saw it."

"They're accusing Mitch of espionage!"

"I know. I can't believe this nightmare. Mitch couldn't have done this, I know he couldn't. They finally allowed him to call me today before the news broke. He told me he was innocent and not to worry."

"Of course he's innocent! We know that, but how is he going to convince the FBI or the FCI? What is the FCI anyway?"

"The FCI is a branch of the FBI. It stands for Foreign Counterintelligence Investigations. He's been working with the higher ups at the Defense Intelligence Agency and he thinks they'll help him prove his innocence, but I'm afraid they may be the ones that pointed the finger at him to begin with. Who else would have?"

"Do you know what evidence they have against him?"

"I don't know much. He wasn't allowed to talk very long when he called. I hope they'll let him call again soon."

"Is that where he's been all this time?"

"I guess. I was so shocked by the accusations that I didn't even ask him about that. After we hung up, I thought of a million questions I should have asked."

"Hopefully, you'll get the chance soon. Do you know where he is?"

"Somewhere near D.C. That's all I know."

The trip to visit Santa had worn Andrea out, and they returned home early. Paul told them goodnight and left. I waited for Lucy to tell Andrea her bedtime story and return downstairs. "Lucy, you're not going to believe what was on the news tonight."

"What?"

"It's Mitch. He's been arrested for espionage."

"What is espionage? I've heard the word and I know it's a serious crime, but what is it exactly?"

"They said he sold top secret information to other countries, making him a traitor to this country."

"What kind of top secret information?"

"They didn't say, but they said he could get a minimum of five years in prison, or as much as the death penalty if found guilty of treason. I can't believe this is happening to Mitch. He's the last person anyone would ever suspect of something like this. I, for one, do not believe he's guilty of anything."

Lucy became quiet.

"Are you okay?"

"Sure, I'm fine. I was going to talk to you about something, but you've got enough on your mind."

"That's okay. What is it?"

"I was thinking about a conversation I had with Paul tonight. He was upset because a good friend of his from back in Chicago just died from AIDS."

"That's awful!"

"It is, but it also made me think about a conversation you and I had some time ago."

"What conversation? I don't recall us ever discussing AIDS."

"Back when we first moved in together, you told me about you and Troy making love."

"Yeah, so?"

"Under the circumstances you described, I was wondering if either of you thought about protection? I mean, you know what a playboy he's always been."

The thought had crossed my mind a few times. "I know. I was relieved when I wasn't pregnant, yet I know there are other things I should be concerned about. I thought about getting tested, but I didn't want to talk to Paul about it. I didn't feel right going somewhere else when I work in a doctor's office."

"You should get tested, either at your office or at the hospital. Please do it."

"You're right. I will."

The following week, I went to the hospital and was tested for AIDS and for STDs. During the days that followed, waiting for the results consumed my thoughts. When I was finally told all the tests were negative, I swore I would never have sex again without protection. The worry and stress and risks were not worth it.

Chapter 17

Monday, December 20—

My Christmas shopping complete, wrapped presents waited under the tree for the days to pass. At the clinic, I added a few decorations to the tiny tree in the waiting room. Mitch was once again on my mind, as he had been for the past couple of weeks. I wished there were something I could do to help him. Poor Gina. She must be going out of her mind with worry.

Paul burst through the door, singing "Jingle Bells." He stopped singing when he saw me. "Bree, I want to see you in my office right away." He didn't sound angry. In fact, he was acting rather jolly.

Curiosity drove me to drop what I was doing and go straight to his office. "Okay, I'm here."

"Efficient as always. I think you've earned a vacation. You've slaved in this office for six straight months without a break and have done a fantastic job. Now you deserve a rest. I want you to take off from this Wednesday through the third of January. Besides, you'll need the time to help Lucy with the last-minute details of our wedding. I want her to have the most perfect wedding ever."

"So much for a rest! Planning a wedding isn't exactly relaxing, but it *is* a task I'll enjoy. I could definitely use a break from this office. Those end-of-the-year reports are going to need an alert mind when I get back."

"Let's worry about that after I get back from my honeymoon. Your only concerns are celebrating the holidays and helping with the wedding right now, nothing else."

Thoughts of the holidays were depressing. Except for the traditional large dinner with my family, I had no plans and felt the loneliness of the season bearing down on me.

Tuesday, December 21—

The day was hectic; getting paperwork caught up, patients flocking in to see the doctor before the clinic closed, and Mrs. Perkinson showing up as I was about to lock up for our holiday break.

"How are you today, Mrs. Perkinson?"

"I'm fine."

I was shocked. I couldn't imagine her coming in with no complaints.

"I dropped by to give you one of my homemade fruitcakes. You can share it with Dr. Kellerman if you will. I didn't think either of you would need a whole one, so you can split it."

"That's very sweet. Thank you so much." I walked her to the door and gave her a hug. "Have a Merry Christmas."

"You too, dear," and she was gone.

I went back to my office to finish my filing. Paul sat at my desk making notations on patients' files. The door slammed in the outer room, and I realized I'd forgotten to lock the door when Mrs. Perkinson left.

"I'll be with you in a minute," I shouted, placing the last file into the cabinet. I started toward the reception area and caught a glimpse of the new arrival through a mirror. Troy? I froze, did an about-face, and ran back into my office. Holding onto the file cabinet to steady myself, my mind raced. I'd never expected to see Troy again, and now, with no warning, he'd returned to complicate my life. Why?

"What's wrong?" Paul jumped up to help me to my chair. "You look as if you've seen a ghost. What happened?"

"Troy," I whispered.

"What?"

"Troy," I repeated, pointing toward the waiting room. I knew Lucy had told Paul all about me and Troy.

Paul strode from my office and into the front room. The men's muffled voices drifted through the building.

"I'm Dr. Paul Kellerman. How can I help you?"

"I'm looking for Brianna Chavis. I understand she works here."

"She does, but I suggest you leave her alone."

"I'm not leaving until I see her."

"She doesn't want to see you, so I think you'd better leave. Now."

"Please, I just want to talk to her."

"Do you understand English? I said she doesn't want to see you. I'm going to say this one more time. Get out." Paul's voice grew loud and angry. I dashed through the hall to stop the quarrelling before it escalated.

"Okay," I said as I entered the room. "You wanted to see me? Here I am. Now what do you want?"

Paul stormed, "Look, buddy, this is my clinic and I'm telling you to leave!"

Troy looked at me to see my reaction to Paul's edict.

When I didn't say anything, he nodded his head, turned, and left.

My need for answers overrode my fear of facing the source of so much of my grief. I rushed out into the brisk air after him. "Troy, wait!"

He stopped, turned, and waited for me to catch up. There was an awkward silence as we stood face to face.

I finally spoke. "I heard about Uncle Jake. I'm sorry."

He stared at the ground with sorrowful eyes but remained silent.

"So why did you want to see me?" I asked.

"We need to talk." Puffs of white vapor rose from each breath.

"Okay. Let me go back to my office to get my coat and I'll be right back."

"Your boyfriend might object."

"He's only trying to protect me, but he's not…" I turned and rushed back into the building without finishing the sentence. So what if he thinks he's my boyfriend. What does it matter anyway?

He escorted me to his rented car and drove to a little eatery we'd frequented years ago. We sat in the small café pretending to concentrate on the menu, neither knowing how to begin a normal conversation.

Once the waiter had taken our order, I broke the silence. "Have you heard anything about Mitch? It's been a couple of weeks since I last talked to Gina."

"I haven't heard anything more than what was on the news. Even the news media can't dig up anything about it."

"I know. I noticed they haven't reported any new information. I was expecting to hear all kinds of garbage out of the press about Mitch's background, but they haven't said much."

"I'm sure they tried to dig up some dirt, but there's nothing to dig up. Mitch is about as straight an arrow as they come. You and I both know he didn't do this."

"You're right, but there's not much we can do. How can we convince the government that they're wrong?"

Troy looked determined. "I don't know, but I do know Mitch is being framed and there's got to be some way to prove it."

The food was served and the conversation lulled while we concentrated on our meal.

I tried to figure out why I was there with him. Why did I run after him? He said we needed to talk, but what is there to say? Obviously, there was nothing left to talk about, or we wouldn't be behaving like a couple of strangers silently devouring our dinner.

His gaze penetrated my thoughts, causing me to glance up into his sad eyes.

He sipped his iced tea, then broke the silence. "You looked deep in thought just then. Can you tell me what's on your mind?"

"Nothing special."

"I'll bet. You were thinking about your doctor friend, weren't you?" Venom dripped from his words. "He's not your type, you know. He's going to drop you so fast that your head will spin when he's through squeezing all he can out of you."

Heat rushed through my veins, my heart pounding. I

sprang from my chair, throwing my napkin onto the table. Fire leaping from my glaring eyes, I hissed, "What right have you to tell me what's right for me after everything you've done?" I glanced around the restaurant, planning to make my departure as unnoticeable as possible, but the adrenalin coursing through me made me lose focus. In my escape, I clumsily knocked over an empty chair, then bumped into another occupied one, causing the gentleman to spill his coffee. Angry, and embarrassed by my awkward departure, I fled out to the sidewalk.

The cold air smacked me back to my senses, and the adrenalin turned to tears. Then came the realization that I'd ridden with Troy to the restaurant and now had no way home. Delving through my purse, I grabbed my cell phone and called Lucy. I leaned against the building to wait, feeling desperately alone.

The restaurant door swung open, and I was again face to face with Troy. I walked away to avoid him, but he followed.

"Hey, I'm sorry. I had no right to say anything about your boyfriend."

"He's not my boyfriend, as if it were any business of yours."

"So why are you so angry? At least tell me what I've done to upset you."

I continued to walk determinedly away from him, not bothering to answer his question.

He grabbed my arm and whirled me around to face him. "Look, you were the one who deserted me. I should be the one who's upset. At least tell me why you took off without even saying good-bye."

I sneered at him, ready for battle. "You can't stand it, can you? I beat you to the draw. For once in our lives, I finally got to lay the final blow."

"Is that all you wanted? To get back at me for the past? Is that all the time at the ranch meant to you? What about the night before you left, the night beside the creek. Was that your way of making the last blow that much harder?" His neck muscles tightened as his jaws clenched in anger, his face scarlet.

I knew he was trying to make me feel guilty, but there was no way I would let him succeed. Hands on hips, I stood my ground. "Listen, don't you try to lay any of this on me. You got what you wanted and then you were ready to toss me aside."

Lucy's little white car pulled up at the corner and I rushed toward it, adding over my shoulder, "And don't try to deny it either. I heard you talking to Mitch the next morning, telling him to get rid of me, so I saved both of you the trouble."

I scrambled into the car and slammed the door, leaving a bewildered Troy staring after the car.

Wednesday, December 22—3:00 *AM*—

Ripped from a deep sleep by loud banging noises, I bailed out of bed and shuffled through the dark house into the living room, groping for the light switch. I found the switch and was panic-stricken when another hand fell over mine. I heard Lucy shriek and the glow of the light revealed both of our terrified faces.

"What the devil is going on?" Lucy inquired, short of breath.

"I don't know. It's three o'clock in the morning. What idiot would be banging on our door at this time of night?"

The banging continued, and Lucy went to stand near the door. Her hand on the knob to be sure it was locked tight, she called out, "Who's there?"

"I want to see Bree."

Recognizing Troy's voice, I sank down into the armchair. "Go away, Troy! I don't want to see you. Get out of my life!"

"I'm not leaving until I talk to you. I'll stand out here and yell all night if I have to."

"Okay. Make your noise. I'll call the police."

"Bree, please," he pleaded.

Concerned about Andrea, Lucy was disgusted with the entire situation. She spoke quietly, "Why don't you talk to him and get rid of him. What can it hurt? At least then we can get a little sleep." When I didn't answer, she jerked the door open. "Okay, get your big mouth in here and quiet down. Say what you have to say, and then get lost."

"Lucy!" I was shocked that Lucy had opened the door without my approval.

"Goodnight," Lucy excused herself and yawned lazily as she trudged off to her bedroom.

"Okay, Troy. Talk." I gripped the arms of the chair with determination.

"I want to know what you meant by that remark about hearing me talking to Mitch? I don't even remember talking to him. What is it that you think you heard?"

"Don't play dumb with me. I know what I heard. I heard you telling him about how he'd brought me there, and how you wanted him to get rid of me."

He looked dumbfounded, trying to recall that morning over six months ago. Then, looking as if he'd been slapped, he closed his eyes and buried his head in the palm of his hands. "Oh no. I don't believe I've been going through hell all this time because of that." Suddenly, he burst out laughing at the situation. Failing to see the humor, I felt humiliated by his outburst. I held my temper at a slow simmer, waiting for him to stop laughing.

He shook his head and gained control of his hysteria. "Did you ever think that maybe you misunderstood that telephone conversation? That just maybe I wasn't even talking about you?"

"Oh come on, Troy. Who else could you have been talking about. Who else got 'dropped off' at your place that you could want to get rid of. I was the only one there besides family and ranch hands."

"A horse."

"What do you mean?"

"I was talking about a horse."

"What lies are you trying to concoct now?"

"Really! The day those ranch hands from Jessup's ranch dropped off Manuel's pony, they also dumped an old nag into our pasture. I phoned them that morning to get them to come back to pick it up. That's what you heard when you eavesdropped."

The realization that he could be telling the truth made me feel more foolish than I'd ever felt before in my life.

For six long months I'd suffered because of my own stupidity and insecurity. I attempted to regain my dignity. "Why did it take you six months to tell me? If you really cared, you could have at least called me."

"I had no idea why you left. I tried to phone you at your apartment, but you weren't there. When I tried again a few days later, your phone was disconnected. After my uncle's funeral, I came looking for you. I tried your old apartment, but you'd moved out. Then I tried your parents' house, but no one was ever home. I tried the phone company, but neither your number nor your parents' number were listed. I even called Tiffany because she was the only one who answered her phone. Believe me, I tried everyone I could think of. But then Joe called and said they needed me to get back to the ranch. On the way back, I ran off the road and...well, that's another long story. My point is that I really did try to find you."

"If you couldn't find me then, how did you find me now?" I wanted to catch him in a fib so I wouldn't feel so dumb, but so far everything he'd said made sense.

"When you sent Manuel that gift, it had your office address for the return address. Then when you caught your ride after running away from me at the restaurant, I followed you home so I would know where you live."

"Why did you wait until three o'clock in the morning to show up?"

"I was confused. I couldn't figure out what you were talking about. I couldn't sleep because it was driving me nuts trying to figure it out. I had to find out what you were so angry about, and I didn't want to wait until daylight."

"Troy, I feel like a real dope. I was so afraid that you were going to hurt me again that I jumped to conclusions. In all fairness, you have to admit that what I overheard sounded like it had to be about me. I believe anyone would have thought the same thing I did."

"Next time, come and talk to me. Don't you realize that all of the pain you've been through, that you've blamed on me, was caused by misunderstandings? I never did anything to hurt you. First, it was lies that Chloe told you that caused us to spend years apart. Then you overhear a piece of a conversation and jump to a wrong conclusion. You really need to start trusting me, you know?" He reached out and took my hands gently. "I love you, Bree, and I always have. I promise that I will never hurt you."

Those three lovely words echoed in my head. I'd waited nine years to hear him say he loved me and I couldn't believe he'd finally said it. "You love me?"

"Of course! Do you think I've searched for you for the past six months for nothing?"

"But you never told me before."

"I know. I don't believe in throwing that word around. I wanted to be positive before I ever said it to anyone, but now I have no doubts. I do love you, and I don't ever want to lose you."

His tear-filled eyes glistened as he pulled me to my feet and held me close. My ear pressed against his chest, listening to his heart pounding rapidly beneath his sweater. Déjà vu? The dream. Afraid I might be dreaming again, my eyes flew open and I looked up at him. His lips claimed mine as he reclaimed my heart. This time I knew

I would never have to fight my feelings for him again. At that suspended moment in time, I relinquished my entire heart to him, and with it, my trust. My fears were washed away by those magic words, and as I remembered them, I whispered, "I love you."

He clung to me, his body trembling, and for the first time I could feel that he needed me and that I could trust him.

Chapter 18

I awoke when the sunlight splashed across my face and opened my eyes to see the most beautiful sunrise. Troy still slept, his head resting on the back of the sofa, one arm draped over my shoulder. I'd had lots of questions for him, but we were both so exhausted, we'd fallen asleep before I could get the answers.

I inched my way from beneath his arm, trying not to waken him. He groaned, rolled over, and curled up in a fetal position. I grabbed the afghan from the armchair and covered him, then retreated to the kitchen to start the coffee maker.

Showered, dressed, and ready to face the first day of my life as a confident and loved woman, I descended the stairs. Gone were all the insecurities that had haunted me most of my life. All of the doubts I'd had over the years about Troy had been caused by figments of my own imagination, instigated by lies, and misunderstandings. Never again. From now on I'll trust my heart. My heart never stopped loving him and aching for him. It was my head that had kept me doubting.

Troy stood and stretched. I stood behind him admiring his silhouette in the sunlight filtering through the window in front of him.

"Coffee is ready, if you want some."

"Smells great." He sauntered over to me and wrapped his arms around me in a warm bear hug. "This feels so perfect." We stood there, eyes closed, gently swaying, relishing the moment.

I broke away from the embrace and led him into the kitchen. Pouring the coffee and placing the cups on the table, I frowned. "You still have a lot of explaining to do."

"Oh, come on, Bree. I thought we got through all of that last night."

I gave him a reassuring smile and quick kiss before sitting at the table. "Yes, we're fine, but I still want to know where you were all those months you were missing in action."

"I told you, it's a long story."

"So? Have you got a bus to catch?"

He laughed. "Okay, but it sounds like a work of fiction. You'll never believe it. No one would. That's why I've avoided talking about it."

"I'm listening."

"I came here to Eastridge to try to find you but didn't have any luck. Then Joe called and said they were having problems at the ranch. I couldn't let my uncle down again by losing the ranch, so I started back. I was almost to Roanoke when I saw a UFO. It was right there in front of me, hovering. I couldn't take my eyes off it. The next thing I knew, I ran off the road and down into a ravine. The jeep was totaled."

"Then what? Don't tell me you were abducted by aliens."

"No, of course not, but not far from it."

6 *months earlier—Saturday, June* 26—

Troy left his wrecked jeep and began hitchhiking. An eighteen-wheeler finally stopped. "Hey, buddy, need a lift?"

"Thanks!" Troy ran around to the passenger side and hoisted himself up into the lofty cab.

"Where you headed?" The hairy trucker's massive body was covered in tattoos, and Troy had the impression he was more suited to a Harley than an eighteen-wheeler.

"You can drop me at the next bus station or car-rental office. I need to get to New Mexico."

"Hey, I'm headed to Albuquerque and don't mind the company. My name's George."

"I'm Troy, and if you get me to Albuquerque, I can get the rest of the way home with no problem."

Two hours passed and the scenery became more boring with each mile as they made their way deep into Kentucky.

The driver, who had been quiet for several miles, now spoke up. "Gonna have to stop for gas soon."

Troy noticed a small sign indicating there was a gas station at the next exit and pointed it out. Easing the big rig over to the right lane and downshifting, they were soon off the interstate and headed down a deserted, narrow two-lane back road. About to give up on finding a gas station, they passed a small green sign that read "Banyon Forge."

Blue lights began flashing in the side mirror and George looked disgusted. "Great!" Rather than pull over, the burly driver revved the engine, shifted gears, and sped down the road through the small town of Banyon Forge.

Troy couldn't believe he was involved in a police chase. "What are you doing? Why didn't you simply pull over?"

"Can't do that." George's black hair shook wildly back and forth as he concentrated on driving the rig as fast as possible.

Troy was at the mercy of this maniac and his lethal vehicle. He stared ahead, begging, "Please, man, stop this thing. Before you know it, you're gonna have an army after you. You're going to get us both killed." Troy imagined this man must be a wanted criminal.

"Oh geez, why did I have to pick up a sissy. Okay, I'll stop, but you back up whatever I tell this guy."

"Sure, whatever you say."

The deputy approached and ordered the driver to climb down from the cab, not noticing Troy. Troy listened to the conversation.

"Hey there, Officer. I apologize for not stopping back there. I was on the telephone with my woman and she was giving me a bunch of lip, ya know. I didn't even notice you back there until my buddy here told me you was there. Had the radio blastin' and the wife nagging."

The mention of his "buddy" now had the officer looking to see who else was inside the cab. He ordered Troy to exit the driver's side so he could keep an eye on both men. A second police car arrived and the other officer made George open the rear doors of the trailer so he could see what was inside. Moments later, Troy and George were being cuffed and escorted to the police car as they were read their rights.

Troy protested. "What's the charge? What's going on?"

The two officers looked at each other and shook their heads. "As if you didn't know."

"I don't. I just met this guy. I was hitchhiking and he gave me a lift."

"Sure. Tell it to the judge."

It turned out that there was a stash of drugs inside the trailer that George was hauling across country. He was on his way to pick up an additional shipment in Albuquerque.

Wednesday, December 22–Eastridge—

Troy looked at me, bringing himself back into the present, obviously not wanting to relive anymore of the harrowing experience. "So I was cooling my heels in a little cell in downtown Banyon Forge for four and a half months, trying to prove I was not involved with the drugs."

"For four and a half months? Didn't they allow you a phone call?"

"Technically, yes. I used my one phone call to call Mitch, but he didn't answer and his voicemail never picked up. When I explained that to the sheriff, he said that was my tough luck. I'd had my chance and I wasn't getting another one. He said, 'You're in Banyon Forge now, son. We don't put up with no druggies here. We're gonna lock you up and throw away the key.'"

"Didn't they let you get an attorney?"

"They assigned me a court attorney, which was a joke."

"How did you finally get out?"

"I'd been telling them about how I wrecked the jeep. Obviously, I didn't mention the UFO. That would have thoroughly convinced them I was using drugs. I asked them over and over again to check with the Virginia State Police about locating my jeep, which would prove I was telling the truth. They refused. When I finally got to court in November, the judge insisted they make the phone call. When they did, they learned that the jeep had been found right where I said it would be. So, after over four months in a cell, I was finally found not guilty and released. By the end of September, I was ready to give up. I became so depressed and thought I was never going to get out of that place."

I remembered feeling he was in trouble. Wishing I'd been able to help, I reached up and placed my hand on his cheek, wanting to comfort him. "Why didn't you, or someone, call and let me know you were home? I had to learn it from Gina a week after you got there."

"I did call. I didn't want to leave a message, and I couldn't catch you at home. I tried several times, then decided to come find you instead. I didn't know why you'd left, or how you were going to react towards me."

"You've been home for over a month." I wanted to understand. *No more misunderstandings or wrong conclusions*, I reminded myself. *I've got to trust what he tells me.*

"I've been trying to straighten out things at the ranch. There were a lot of problems that needed to be dealt with there. I'd been gone for over four months, and poor Joe had done the best he could but there were some things he couldn't handle."

"I know you had a lot to handle, but someone should have called me."

"I know, but then Gina told me she talked to you, so I knew you already knew I was home. I figured you would call me if you wanted to talk to me."

Lucy, in her pink fluffy slippers and blue chenille housecoat, shuffled into the kitchen and looked at Troy, her sleepy eyes still half closed. "You still here?" She poured herself a cup of coffee.

"No, I left. You're only dreaming because you want me to be here."

"Funny. Bree, what's he still doing here?"

"He explained everything, Lucy. Remember the phone call I overheard that was supposedly to Mitchell?"

"Yeah."

"It wasn't to Mitchell, and it wasn't about me."

After listening to the explanation of the misunderstanding, Lucy excused herself. "I need to go get ready for work. Troy, try to behave yourself."

"I'll try, but I can't promise anything." Left alone, Troy turned to me. "So where do we go from here?"

"Where do you want to go from here?"

"I'd really like for you to go back to the ranch with me."

"I'd like that, but I'm in the middle of helping Lucy with her wedding. She's getting married in only ten days. I can't possibly leave now."

"Only a couple of days? Spend Christmas with me at the ranch, then you can come back here and help with the wedding. You can't do much on Christmas day anyway, right?"

"That's true," I said slowly, thinking through my

options. I would have to miss my family's Christmas gathering. My parents! I groaned. "Troy, how am I going to explain this to Momma and Daddy? They have no idea I've seen you. I never told them you were in New Mexico."

"You've got a lot of 'splainin' to do, as Manuel would say."

I smiled at the thought of Manuel. I would love to see him again, and it would be a special treat to spend Christmas with him. "Okay. We'll have to visit Momma and Daddy tonight when they get home from work and try to explain it to them."

"We?"

"Yes, you're going with me. Maybe if they see how much you've changed, it will make it easier for them to accept."

Standing on the porch of my parents' home, I held tight to Troy's hand and took a deep breath before ringing the doorbell.

Daddy opened the door, looking from me to Troy, and back to me.

"Daddy, you remember Troy, don't you?"

"Of course. So you're still alive, I see."

Troy held out his hand. "Yes, sir. It's good to see you again, Mr. Chavis."

Shaking his hand, Daddy looked stern. "I wish I could say the same."

"Daddy! Don't be rude. We would like to talk to you and Momma about something."

"Alright. Come on in. Your mother is in the den."

Momma turned off the television as we entered the room. "Hello Bree, Troy." She nodded her greeting.

Daddy sat in his recliner. Troy and I sat on the sofa facing him and Momma, whose matching chair sat next to Daddy's.

"Momma, Daddy, there's something I didn't tell you about my trip to New Mexico." I hesitated, glancing at Troy for courage. "Mitchell's entire reason for inviting me there was to get Troy and me back together."

Daddy stared at me. "So you were going to see Troy, not Mitchell?"

"No, I had no idea Troy was down there. I went to visit Mitch. I was there for several days before I even knew Troy was living there."

Daddy turned his attention to Troy. "How about you, young man? Were you in on the scheme?"

"No, sir. I had no idea either. Mitch surprised both of us."

Momma, who had been sitting back taking it all in, finally spoke up, "So why are you telling us this now?"

I took a deep breath, looking from Troy to Daddy, and then Momma. "Because I want to go back to New Mexico to spend Christmas with him."

It was Momma's turn to take a deep breath. "I see. So, Troy. Last I heard, you'd disappeared, abandoning a jeep in a ditch along the highway. What was that all about?"

Daddy stood up and began pacing. "Who cares about all that? He's obviously not missing, and he's here wanting to take our daughter back to New Mexico!"

Momma used her soft voice, the voice of reason. "Collin, our daughter is a grown woman. She will make her own choices. All we can do is try to help her make the right ones, and getting angry won't help."

"Then you talk some sense into her." Daddy strutted from the room and we heard the back door slam.

Momma remained composed. "He'll be okay. Troy, you convinced him years ago you wouldn't hurt his little girl. Then we had to watch her suffer when you did just that."

"I know, Mrs. Chavis, but if I'd known back then what I know now, none of that would have happened. It was all a huge misunderstanding."

"That's between you and Bree. Bree, is there anything I can say to change your mind about going to New Mexico during Christmas?"

"I don't think so." I smiled at my mother. "This is something I have to do."

Momma knew me well and could see the love between the two of us. "What about Lucy's wedding?"

"We're not leaving until Friday, and I won't be gone but a few days. Almost everything is already done, and nothing is going to get done during Christmas anyway. Lucy and I are going to go over everything between now and Friday. Don't worry, it's all under control."

I spent the next day going over the details of the wedding with Lucy and doing last-minute Christmas shopping. Now that I'd be at the ranch for Christmas, I needed to buy gifts for Troy, Gina, Sheila, and Joe.

Chapter 19

Friday, December 24–New Mexico—

Only a few days ago I'd been depressed because my holiday plans had looked so bleak, and now Troy and I were on our way to spend Christmas at the ranch. It was hard for me to contain my excitement over seeing Manuel's sweet little face again, and I was anxious to try to make up for any pain I might have caused him.

Gina greeted us at the airport terminal gate. "Welcome back."

I could tell Gina was struggling to be upbeat, but it was obvious that worrying over Mitchell had taken its toll. She was thinner than before, and the gleam was missing from her eyes.

On our way to baggage claim, I thought about Gina's little car. "How are we going to get all of our luggage and the three of us into your little VW?"

Gina gave me a weak smile. "I already thought about that. I didn't bring the VW. I have Mitchell's car."

"How did you get his car? Have you seen him?"

"No. When he disappeared, he left behind his cell phone, his car, his keys, everything. He left with nothing but the clothes on his back. And I'm only assuming he had clothes on."

I missed Gina's joviality. Her weak attempt at a joke

only served to emphasize how difficult this was for her. She was almost lifeless, her spirit wrung from her body by sorrow and worry. "Gina, I wish we could do something to help."

Troy gathered the luggage from baggage claim. "We will do something, but first, let's get all of this to the car. What is all of this, anyway? I thought you were only staying a couple of days."

"It's Christmas. I had to bring gifts."

When we approached the car, I remembered the first time I'd seen that beat-up old station wagon. Tears filled my eyes as I thought of Mitchell and the mess he was in.

After loading the luggage, Troy handed the keys back to Gina. "You drive. Bree, you sit up front with her so you girls can talk. I'm going to sit in the back so I can take a nap." As we pulled from the parking lot, I heard him calling Sheila on his cell phone, letting her know we would be arriving at the ranch soon.

Feeling compelled to lighten the mood and keep Gina's mind off of Mitchell, I talked above the squeaks and rattles of the car. "How is Jacques doing? Is he going it alone as a solo act at the restaurant?"

"No, he left town and went back to France."

Surprised, my voice changed to a higher pitch. "When?"

"Back in October, right before Mitch disappeared."

A trace of suspicion entered my mind. "Oh, really." So much for casual conversation. All avenues led right back to Mitchell and his strange disappearance. I glanced into the back seat to see Troy's reaction to this bit of news, but his eyes were closed and he didn't appear to be listening.

"Didn't you mention to me on the phone that Sal was also gone?"

"That's right. He left around the same time Mitch did, but he was always taking off, so that didn't seem unusual. Then last week, they discovered his body. It washed ashore on the bank of the Rio Grande."

Even more suspect. "Do they know what killed him?"

"I haven't heard anymore about it. I suppose they're still investigating."

I attempted to wrap my mind around all the facts and piece them together. "Okay, explain to me again how Jacques and Mitch met."

"I had an ad in the newspaper for musicians to entertain at my restaurant. They both answered the ad."

"How did Mitch know Sal?"

"I don't know how they met. Mitch never said. He was living with Sal when I met him, but he'd only been living with him for a couple of weeks. In fact, he said it was Sal that showed him my ad in the paper."

Interesting. "Do you know if Jacques and Sal knew each other?"

"No. I believe they met later after Mitch and Jacques began performing together at the restaurant."

"Are you sure?"

"I guess. They certainly didn't act like they knew each other. In fact, I don't think they liked each other very much. They weren't friendly at all."

Again I turned to look at Troy. He was listening, and when our eyes met, I knew he was following my train of thought. He nodded slowly, his eyes boring into mine, and then looked at Gina and back to me, encouraging me to continue pursuing answers.

"You know, Sal, Mitch, and Jacques are so completely different. Didn't it ever strike you as odd that Mitch could be friends with someone like Sal and with someone like Jacques?"

"Of course not. You know Mitch. He's the type of guy who can be friends with anybody. He accepts people the way they are, no matter how strange or different they might be."

"That's true." I couldn't shake the idea that one of those two men was the key to Mitchell's arrest for espionage. I had no hard proof, but the fact that they both disappeared around the same time as Mitchell spoke volumes.

We dropped Gina off at the trailer park where she'd left her car and continued our journey in Mitchell's car with Troy now in the driver's seat. It was well after dark by the time the lights at the ranch came into view. My heart throbbed with anticipation as the car rattled and squeaked through the gates and down the drive to the main house. I felt I was coming home. As I reached over and took Troy's hand, he smiled and gave my hand a comforting squeeze.

Sheila, Joe, and Manuel were waiting in the yard.

"Your rooms are all ready for you, and your dinner will be on the table in about twenty minutes." Sheila headed toward the kitchen.

Joe helped with the baggage and Manuel tugged at me. "Come on. I want to show you something," he begged.

Troy took my bags. "You go ahead and see whatever it is he wants to show you. I'll take your things to your room for you."

The grandfather clock in the hallway struck nine o'clock as I followed Manuel through the kitchen, stopping a few minutes to chat with Sheila. "Isn't it a little late for you to be cooking dinner?"

"Yes, but when Troy called, we were getting ready to eat, so I kept it warm for you. I knew you would be hungry. I've heard that airplane food is not very good."

Manuel was pulling impatiently on my arm. "Come on!" I laughed and allowed him to lead me into the study.

He stood proudly pointing at the Christmas tree with its blinking lights and homemade ornaments. "I helped decorate it. Mama and me made those gingerbread men and Papa and me made those wooden decorations."

"They're beautiful. Did you help paint them too?"

"Uh huh, and I put the present you sent me right here in front."

Although delighted that Manuel had accepted me back as a friend, I still felt I owed him an apology. "Manuel," I knelt to his level and held his hands, "I'm very sorry I left the way I did without saying good-bye. I was upset about something and wasn't thinking clearly at the time. I hope you can forgive me."

He threw his arms around my neck and hugged me, using all the strength in his tiny body. "I'm glad you came back. I don't want you to go away like that again."

"Okay. If I have to leave again, I'll make sure I tell you good-bye, and I will always come back to see you. That's a promise." I poked him in the belly causing him to topple onto the floor giggling.

The house was quiet. Joe, Sheila, and Manuel had gone home to their cottage for the night, leaving Troy and me alone in the spacious, old home. I glanced around the den at the bookcases, then the green recliner. "It's strange here without Uncle Jake." Then I realized I hadn't seen Uncle Jake's old dog. "Where is Rufus?"

"He didn't last long after Uncle Jake died. He stayed beside that chair, grieving and refusing to eat until he pined away. We buried him next to Uncle Jake. It took some persuading to get permission to put him in the cemetery, but the church finally relented."

Troy grabbed a spiral notebook and a pen from the roll-top desk. "Come with me. We've got some things to figure out." He led me into the kitchen and sat at the table. "I've been thinking about your conversation with Gina on the way from the airport. Let's try to make a list of the information we have so we can make sense of it all."

Anxious to prove Mitchell innocent, I sat across from him. "First, we know Mitch is innocent."

"Yes, but to prove it, we've got to figure out who is guilty. Who had the opportunity to get information and use it to frame Mitch?"

I remembered going to Mitchell's office with him. "When I went to the base with Mitch, he had a briefcase. He left it open on his desk and really freaked out when he saw me standing beside it. He even accused me of snooping through it, saying there was top secret stuff in there, and that he had been careless leaving it out like that."

Troy picked up on my train of thought. "So anyone

with access to that briefcase might have been able to get the information. That makes things more difficult. I thought we would be looking at someone with access to the base, but it could be anyone who knew Mitch. I wonder if Gina has his briefcase. She said he left his keys and phone and everything else there." He jotted down a note to check with Gina.

Jacques and Sal were still on my mind. "I find it strange that Jacques left town right before everything hit the fan. And what happened to Sal? I know he was involved in drugs, but maybe he was involved in more than that."

"Oh, about that. Sal was never involved with drugs."

"But I thought they found drugs when they searched his car?"

"Mitch made all of that up to get you to stay here."

"You mean Mitch lied to us? He's the most honest person I've ever met. Why would he do something so out of character?"

"Because you were asking too many questions. He was worried you would get yourself into trouble if his superiors caught wind of your inquiries."

"Questions about what? I don't recall asking anything to do with his job other than the fact that he worked weird hours for an accountant. I thought it was strange, but I certainly was no threat to national security."

"I know that, and so did Mitch, but he said you were too smart and too curious. He couldn't take the chance that you would get involved."

"If Sal wasn't involved with drugs, why is he dead?"

"That's part of what we need to find out. Maybe he was involved in this somehow."

"Troy, we're talking about espionage here, not a simple theft. When I think of espionage, I think of James Bond-type people. People with connections, like politicians. How would Sal or Jacques fit into that category?"

"Bree, we don't know that much about Sal or Jacques. Where did they come from? Are they US citizens? And if not, how long have they been in this country? Why were they here? These are things we need to know before we can rule them out."

"We know that Jacques came from France. Isn't that one of the countries mentioned in the news reports that purchased the information?"

"Yeah, France and China. Coincidence?"

"Gina said Jacques went back to France. I often wondered why he was here to begin with? He always seemed out of place."

Troy wrote down Jacques's name with a big question mark. "We'll ask Gina how much she knows about him." Then he wrote down Sal's name with "murdered?" beside it.

I looked at Sal's name written on the paper. "Did you ever meet Sal?"

"I saw him a couple of times when I visited Mitch, but I didn't get to know him. He seemed to be kind of a loner, not too friendly."

"I saw him once at the restaurant. I thought it was strange because, according to Mitch, he was supposed to be in jail at the time. Sal. What kind of name is that?"

"I think it's short for Salvatore or something like that. He looked Italian maybe." Troy's mind was not on the conversation. He was trying to think of other clues to add to his list. "While you were here, did you see Mitch talking with anyone else? Anyone that we might add to this list?"

"Mitch talks to everybody. He's the friendliest person I know. At the restaurant, he seemed to know everyone there, and if he didn't know them, he would before he left that night."

"Yeah, but was there anyone suspicious, anyone that he seemed closer to than the others?"

"Only Gina."

"Should we add her to the list?" Troy held his pen, ready to write her name.

"Of course not! If she were involved, she wouldn't be so worried about him."

"You don't think that could be an act?"

"No way. She's too real. There's nothing fake about her," I said.

"I guess you're right. Let's think about how all these people met. Gina placed an ad in the paper for musicians. She had no way of knowing Mitch would answer her ad. Jacques answered the ad having no way of knowing Mitch would. Then Sal showed Mitch the ad and encouraged him to call about it." He threw his pen down on the table. "None of it adds up. It was all chance. We need to pin down someone who manipulated their way into Mitch's life. The only one I can connect that way is Sal."

"How did Sal and Mitch meet?"

"I'm trying to remember. I know Mitch was staying on the base when he first arrived here. Then he moved out here to the ranch with Uncle Jake. He loved living here. But then one day he said he'd met this guy, Sal, who had offered to let him live in his trailer. Since it was more convenient to the base, he decided to take him up on it. I don't think he ever said how he met this guy, but I do know he wasn't looking to move until Sal suggested it."

"Gina said she didn't know how they met either. That does seem odd that some stranger would show up out of nowhere and offer Mitch a place to live when he wasn't even thinking about moving. Write that down on your list."

Mitch circled Sal's name. "This is our number-one suspect. Let's start here."

"Great, but what do we do now?"

"Now we get some sleep so Santa won't catch us awake." He threw down the pen and stood, stretching. "This can wait until after Christmas. There's nothing we can do tomorrow anyway."

Saturday, December 25, Christmas morning at the ranch—

Troy ripped me from my slumber before dawn the next morning. "Come on, sleepyhead. We're going for a ride."

"So early?"

"Sure! The sunrise is the most beautiful part of the day. You wouldn't want to miss it so you can be lazy for a few more minutes, would you?" He started back out the door. "Meet me at the stables in ten minutes."

"Ten minutes? At least give me time to get dressed, will you?"

"Okay, fifteen, but no longer." He winked at me and strutted down the hall, whistling contentedly.

By the time I reached the stables, the horses were saddled and Troy was perched on Stormy's back, waiting.

"You're late. It's been sixteen minutes."

"I beg your forgiveness, master," I joked.

"Okay, I'll forgive you this time." He handed me Misty's reins and I stroked the horse's nose. Misty nudged me as if she remembered me.

We rode to the top of the hill where we stopped to watch the sunrise. Troy helped me dismount and stood holding me in his arms for a few minutes before twirling me around. Standing behind me, his arms still wrapped tightly around my waist, he pointed to the ranch house and the land surrounding it.

"Look down there." His voice was soft and gentle in my ear. "I brought you here to give you a bird's-eye view of your new home; that is, if you'll marry me."

I turned to look at him, surprise frozen on my face.

"Well, will you?"

"You don't waste any time, do you?"

"Actually, I've wasted several years. You know we're meant to be together, so what do you say?"

"Of course I'll marry you!" I flung myself unmercifully at him, smothering him in a bear hug. His strong arms encircled and squeezed me until I was gasping for air. After he'd relaxed his grip enough for me to turn around to look at the house nestled farther down the hill, the reality of what he'd meant by my "new home" struck me. "We're going to live here?"

"If you think you could be happy here."

I looked up at him, my eyes luminous. "I know I could."

"Uncle Jake left me the house and half of the land, and

the other half he left to Joe and Sheila. They were the only family he had for many years, and they were always very loyal to him and this ranch. Uncle Jake gave his entire life to this place, and I think I love it almost as much as he did. I want to keep the ranch going if at all possible."

"Then that's what we'll do."

The sun was a giant red ball peeping over the horizon, changing the sky into a pallet of purple and pink hues.

Troy cooked breakfast for the two of us. "Sheila will be here later to fix Christmas dinner, but she's taking time this morning to spend with Manuel so he can open all his Santa gifts."

I thought of my family and how they would be gathering to celebrate the holiday.

Troy noticed my sudden change of mood. "Missing your family?"

"Christmas has always been my favorite holiday. Momma's parties are so public the rest of the year, but Christmas Day is reserved for family only. This year, I'm right where I want to be; right here with you."

"Good. Then come with me." He took my hand and led me into the den. The tree was lit and Christmas carols were playing.

"When did you do all of this?"

"While you were freshening up after our ride."

"But you were cooking breakfast."

"Yes, but I slipped in here for a second to turn things on. I can multi-task, you know."

"Wow, a man who can do that is quite a catch. I'm such a lucky girl."

"Well, lucky lady, this is for you." He handed me a small wrapped package.

"When did you go shopping?"

"I didn't. This is something very special that I want you to have."

I tore the paper from the small box and opened it. There sat a vintage ring, gold filigree with an oval diamond nestled between two clusters, each with two smaller diamonds and a ruby. "Oh, Troy. It's gorgeous!"

"We might have to get it sized. It belonged to Uncle Jake's wife, Elissa. Since he said you reminded him of her, I thought it would be appropriate for you to have it as your engagement ring. Let's see if it fits." He took the ring from the box and tried it on my finger. It was a perfect fit. "See, it was meant to be."

Overwhelming emotion rendered me speechless. I threw my arms around him and gave him a warm, tender kiss.

We heard the back door open with a blast of noise, the pounding of running feet, and Manuel's little voice calling out to us, "Troy! Brianna! Where are you?"

"We're in the den, little guy," Troy yelled back.

The child appeared in the doorway, teeth shining and eyes bright with excitement, carrying a remote-control monster truck. "Look what Santa brought me! It'll climb over almost anything!" He handed the truck to Troy. Sheila and Joe stood in the doorway of the den smiling down at their beloved son.

Troy knelt down and examined the truck with Manuel.

"This is really cool. We need to go try this out in a little while."

"Now! Come on!" Manuel insisted.

"In a few minutes. Be patient. I have some news you might like to hear." Troy sat on the sofa, arms spread across the top edge of the backrest.

Manuel looked around at all the adults. "You're not going away again, are you?" He looked from me to Troy and back to me.

"Well, Bree might have to leave to go home for a few days, but she'll be back."

"Are you sure?"

"I'm very sure. You know how I know?"

"How?"

"Because she's going to be my wife. We're getting married." He watched Manuel, anticipating his joy.

Manuel's eyes looked huge in his little face as he looked up at me. "Really?"

I walked over and stood behind Troy, my hands on his shoulders. "That's right, and we're going to live right here."

"Wow! Cool! That's the best Christmas present ever!" Manuel ran around to the back of the sofa and hugged my legs.

Joe and Sheila congratulated us and retreated to the kitchen to begin preparing Christmas dinner.

Manuel looked at the tree and realized he still had one more present to open. "Brianna, can I open my present from you now?"

"Of course. I hope you like it." I watched him tear the paper and rip into the box. There sat the small replica of his pony.

"It's just like Fireball!" He threw the box down and picked up the monster truck. "Troy, can we go play with my truck now?"

Troy looked at me. "Sure, buddy, but first you should thank Bree for the nice gift."

Manuel ran over and grabbed me around my neck as I kneeled to his level. "Thank you. I'm glad you're gonna live here too. I love you." He turned to Troy. "Now can we go play?"

I smiled and nodded at Troy. "You go ahead. I'm going to help Sheila prepare dinner." I watched them scurry from the room. *I love you too, Manuel.*

The afternoon was spent preparing a Christmas feast that took several hours to make and twenty minutes to devour, but it was well worth the effort.

When the meal was over and everything cleaned up, Joe and Sheila gathered their coats to leave.

I held up my finger. "Don't go yet. Wait here for one minute." I ran into the den and grabbed two little gifts I'd brought from Eastridge for them. Returning to the kitchen, I handed them their presents. "It's not much, but I wanted to get you something."

Sheila opened her matching necklace and earrings, and Joe his pocketknife. The modest couple expressed their gratitude by hugging me, the joy in their faces filling me with delight. "I'm so glad you like them."

"The gifts are wonderful, but the true gift is that you thought of us. Thank you." Joe didn't express himself often, but when he did, it was from the heart.

Troy and I sat in the den staring at the Christmas tree. There was one little gift still under it. Troy cocked his head at the unfamiliar little present. "Where did that come from?"

"Now you didn't think I'd forget you, did you?" I went to retrieve the beautifully wrapped little box. "Merry Christmas." I handed it to him.

Inside the box was a gold bowling-ball miniature clock.

I grinned. "Reminiscent of our first date." When I'd purchased it, it seemed like a good idea. "It seems silly now."

"Not at all. I love it. It will serve to remind me how precious our time together is so I don't waste a second of it." He kissed me and went to place the little clock on the desk.

The sad truth entered my mind. "Speaking of our time together, I've got to go home tomorrow. First, there's Lucy's wedding, and then I'm going to have to take care of things at work. I can't leave Paul in the lurch right after his wedding. I'll have to stay long enough to hire and train someone to replace me."

"How long do you think that will take?"

"I don't know. Is there any way you could come up there for a little while?"

"Bree, you know I can't desert the ranch again right now. If we're planning to keep the ranch going, I've got to be here."

"I know, but what about New Year's?"

"I'll fly up for New Year's and stay a couple of days. Then I'll have to come back here. Not only for the ranch, but I've got to work on proving Mitch's innocence."

My mind switched gears as I remembered some

thoughts I'd had during the night. "About that, I was thinking about a couple of things last night."

"Like what?"

"I remembered a conversation I had with Jacques. I asked him what he did for a living. He was a little evasive, saying he worked for the government. When I asked what he did for the government, he said he was in acquisitions. Acquiring what? Information maybe?"

Troy went back to the desk and grabbed a pen and some paper, jotting down this new bit of information. "Did he say anything else?"

"No, but it was obvious he was skirting the subject of his employment. I didn't think much about it at the time, but it struck me last night how odd it was."

"You said there were a couple of things you remembered. What was the other?"

"On our way to the ranch the day Mitch brought me here, he stopped at a tavern to pick up a package for Sal. He said that Sal's uncle owned the tavern."

"What was the package?"

"I don't know, but it looked about the size of a brick and was wrapped in plain brown paper. What do you think that could be?"

"Well, we know Sal wasn't doing drugs, so it couldn't have been a stash. I'll go talk to the uncle and ask some questions." He wrote down more notes. "Where was the tavern?"

"About halfway between here and Mitch's trailer. It was a little log building nestled among the rock along the side of the road."

"I think I know the one you're talking about. I'll check it out."

Chapter 20

Sunday, December 26—

Troy's usually intense brown eyes peered up at me like a sad puppy. "I don't understand why you didn't give Gina the Christmas gift when she picked us up from the airport." Although his tone was calm and caring, there was a hint of frustration.

"Because I want to see her open it. What fun is it to give a special gift to someone and not have the pleasure of seeing them open it?"

"I don't want to miss church today, but there's no way we can leave church, go to Gina's, and still make your flight at 1:35."

I couldn't understand why Troy couldn't see the obvious solution. Keeping my voice quiet and steady, I explained as if speaking to a child. "Why don't you simply drop me off at Gina's and go to church, and then pick me up after church and take me to the airport?"

"But I wanted you to go to church with me," he whined.

"Yeah, but I really don't want to," I whined back.

Gina tore the wrapping from the shirt-sized box. I anticipated her inevitable surprise as she lifted the lid to reveal the genuine Brittain jeans, specially designed by Rachel

Brittain Chavis. "Oh, Bree, I can't believe it. How can I ever thank you?" She checked the size, which I knew was right because I'd watched her closely when we'd gone shopping for the cheaper knock-offs.

"No thanks necessary. I get things wholesale, you know." We laughed and she gave me a big hug. It felt good to see a smile back on her face, and I was glad I could do something to make that happen.

Gina frowned. "I'm so embarrassed. I don't have a gift for you. I haven't been much in the mood for Christmas this year and never went shopping. I'm sorry."

"Don't be. The smile on your face when you opened those jeans was the best Christmas present I could have received."

After seeing Brianna off on her flight home, Troy returned to Gina's. "I need to ask you a few questions. I'm determined to help Mitch prove his innocence."

"That's great! I'll do anything I can to help."

"Good. The first thing I need to know is whether he has an attorney."

"Yes, but I don't recall his name. Mitch said he'd be callin' me again soon, so when he does, I'll find out."

"Okay. Do you know anything about a package Mitch picked up from Sal's uncle's tavern?"

"No, I'm afraid I know nothin' about that."

Troy took a slow, deep breath, glancing at his list of questions. Gina wasn't much help so far. "What about Mitch's briefcase. You said he left his cell phone, his car keys, and everything else. Do you have his briefcase?"

"No. That was the one thing that was missing. He told me they confiscated it when they arrested him."

"When you spoke to Mitch, did he say anything about what happened to Sal?"

"He was upset about it, and I got the impression that he knew why he was killed, but we didn't talk about it. When he calls, do you want me to ask him about Sal?"

"Yes. Get all the information you can. How much do you know about Jacques?"

"He was a good musician. He was French. That's about it."

"He was from France, but was he a US citizen?"

"No. He wasn't."

Troy jotted down a few notes. "Back to the briefcase. Was Mitch careful with it? I mean, did he leave it laying around the trailer where Sal, or anyone else, could get into it?"

"No, he was very careful. He kept it locked and under his bed." She looked thoughtful, then said, "I don't know if this helps or not, but talking about Sal and Jacques reminded me. I heard my cook and Jacques talking in the kitchen one night, and it was apparent they'd known each other before working at the restaurant."

"What's this cook's name?"

"Luigi Benotti. He was actually the one who suggested I hire musicians to play in the restaurant. He came from Italy, just like Sal, and he wasn't a US citizen either. He'd only been in this country for a couple of months when I hired him."

"So can I find Luigi at the restaurant?"

"No, he went back to Italy about the same time Jacques returned to France."

Gina had given Troy a few things to look into. Over the next couple of days, Troy visited the base, where he was denied entry, made phone call inquiries to every official he could imagine, and tried to locate anyone who knew Sal, Luigi, and Jacques. Next, he stopped by the little tavern where Brianna had seen Mitch pick up the package for Sal.

It was dusk when he stepped into the dimly lit, beer-stenched bar. Barbaric-looking men glared at him as his boots hammered across the old wooden floor.

The man behind the bar used a dirty bar towel to wipe the inside of a mug. "Can I help you, mister?"

"I hope so. I'm trying to help out a friend of mine. Do you know Mitchell Sibley?"

The man grinned, suddenly a lot more friendly. "Sure I know Mitch. That's some mess he's gotten into, isn't it? I hope you can help him out. He's good people. He don't deserve what's happenin' to him."

"Are you Sal's uncle?"

"Sal? No, don't know no Sal."

"Mitch came by here and picked up a package, which he said he was picking up for Sal. What do you know about that?"

"Don't know nuthin.' The only thing he ever picked up from here was fruitcake. I make a mean fruitcake, and Mitch loves it. He might have picked one up for his friend."

Troy smiled. He knew Mitchell well enough to know the package had probably been a part of his stupid lie to Brianna about Sal's involvement in drugs. *Fruitcake. The size of a brick. Leave it to Mitch to authenticate his lie with a prop. He knew Bree, with her inquisitive mind, would later question if that package might contain drugs.*

Arriving back at the ranch, Troy phoned leasing agents until he located the person who'd rented the trailer to Sal. He learned Sal had signed the lease about the same time the cook had shown up in town. Both being Italian raised his suspicions, especially since Sal had suggested Mitch answer Gina's ad for a musician.

The ringing of the telephone broke his train of thought. "Hello."

"Hi," came Brianna's sleepy, sultry voice.

"Hi, beautiful." He glanced at the clock. "What are you doing up? Isn't it a little late there?"

"Yeah, but I couldn't sleep. What are you up to tonight?"

"Getting ready to turn in. It's been a busy day of investigating."

"Did you learn anything new?"

He explained about the fruitcake caper. After a good laugh, he continued to tell her about the rest of his day.

She tried to connect all the pieces. "Okay, so your theory is that this Luigi and Sal were working together to get Mitch to work at the restaurant, but what purpose did that serve?"

"I'm thinking maybe it would get Mitch away from the trailer at pre-determined times, so Sal could search his briefcase and belongings for information."

"So Jacques doesn't figure into it at all?"

"Actually, he might. It turns out that the cook also knew Jacques. Gina heard them talking in the kitchen and realized they'd known each other before working there."

"Is the cook still working for Gina?"

"No. He left and went back to Italy about the same time Jacques left to go back to France. I have some other things I'm going to check into tomorrow."

Friday, December 31*–Eastridge—*

I stared at the creek from my bedroom window of the millhouse. It was going to be a big weekend. Rehearsal dinner tonight, then the famous Chavis New Year's bash, and Lucy's wedding tomorrow. The past week had been filled with finalizing the details of the wedding and making sure nothing was forgotten.

I reached into the drawer of my bedside table and removed the ring box. Not wanting to overshadow Lucy's big event, I'd removed the ring and remained silent about my engagement when I'd arrived home from New Mexico. I knew my news might upset my parents, and I didn't want anything to spoil Paul and Lucy's day.

Uncle Justin and Aunt Tricia had flown in from Austria for their daughter's wedding and were staying with Momma and Daddy. It was wonderful seeing them again. I smiled as I remembered the ecstatic expression on Lucy's face when they'd arrived.

My cell phone rang, pulling me from my thoughts. "Hello."

"Bree, it's me." Troy's voice caused my heartbeat to quicken. "I'm at the airport in El Paso and should be arriving there around 4:30 this afternoon your time."

He sounded rushed, so I didn't waste time telling him

how much I missed him. "Okay, I'll meet you at the airport. Which flight?"

"East-Air Flight 689."

"I hope your flight's on time. The rehearsal starts at 6:30, and I have to be there."

"If the flight is late, I can rent a car at the airport. You go on to the rehearsal, and I'll catch up with you at your parents' after the rehearsal dinner."

"I'll be at the airport, but if your flight doesn't get in by 5:30, I'll have to leave."

"Okay. Gotta go. They're calling my flight now. I love you."

I snapped my phone shut and felt newly energized. Time to get busy.

Somewhere over Oklahoma—

Troy rubbed his hands over his face. It had been grueling getting checked in and boarded for the flight. New Year's Eve was not a choice travel date.

The lights in the plane flickered, then went out, leaving only the sunlight filtering through the windows. Troy looked around when he heard people rushing past him. A few men were making their way toward the cockpit. He watched them closely, vaguely aware there was a disturbance going on behind him. Panic set in when someone grabbed him from behind and placed a knife to his throat. He could feel the man's breath in his ear. "You think you're so smart, but you should have kept your nose out of things." It was a French accent. Troy closed his eyes. *Lord, I could sure use your help right now.*

A cell phone rang behind him and he heard another voice answer, speaking in French. Troy wished he'd taken French in school rather than Spanish. Although he didn't know French, he did recognize one word, *Jacques*.

Roanoke Regional Airport—

The flight was late. The flight monitor showed the flight as delayed but didn't have an arrival time posted. I waited until 5:35 but couldn't stay any longer. Lucy was depending on me, and it was a long drive back to Eastridge.

Although late for the rehearsal, I hadn't missed anything. Everyone stood around waiting to be told what to do without a clue about where to start, until Momma and Aunt Tricia arrived. Between their organizational skills and the minister's expertise, they were able to pull it together.

The catered dinner, held at Momma and Daddy's home, transitioned into the New Year's Eve celebration. Practically the entire population of Eastridge had been invited, and the house overflowed with guests. Chamber music filled the air from the corner of the spacious living room. Waiters worked the room with serving trays of food and drinks. It was a familiar occurrence for me, being the daughter of the town's most elite couple. The Chavis home was known for its lavish parties.

I paced the hallway, checking my cell phone for messages. Where was Troy? I tried his cell phone for the third time, but continued to reach his voice mail. "Troy, please call me. I'm getting worried."

Hours ticked by. The mantel clock struck 11:00. Still no Troy. I slipped into my mother's study to get away from the festivities. Grabbing a phonebook from the desk, I looked up the number for the airport. Wanting to save my cell battery, I used the desk phone.

"I need information concerning East-Air Flight 689. It was due in at 4:30 this afternoon. Has it arrived?"

"I'm sorry, that flight has been delayed." It was the voice of a well-trained operator.

"Delayed? It's almost seven hours late!"

"The pilot had to make an emergency landing. We expect the flight to resume within the hour." The voice was controlled and sugary sweet.

"What happened?"

"That information is not available." Now the woman sounded like a recording.

"Where did it land?"

"Hold please." I listened to bad music for several minutes before Jesse burst into the study.

"Here you are. Everyone's lookin' for you. Whatta you doin' hidin' out in here? There's a party going on, you know." His words were slurred and he stumbled across the room.

"I'll be there in a minute."

"No, not in a minute. Come on, who could you be talkin' to? Everyone's here."

"Not everyone. Now please go back to the party and I'll join you after this phone call."

"Nope. You're coming with me now." He placed his finger on the receiver button. "Oops, phone call over."

He grabbed my arm and pulled. I jerked away from him, causing him to topple over onto the desk.

"Jess, you'd better leave me alone and sober up. If Daddy sees you in this state, he's going to kick your butt." I helped him to the small sofa. "You stay here, and I'll go get some coffee." Before leaving the room, I turned to make sure he was staying on the sofa. He was passed out, not going anywhere for awhile. Shaking my head, I rejoined the party.

I mingled, making sure I spoke to all the guests, satisfying my family that I was in attendance and doing fine. It was now 11:45. Frantic, I grabbed my cell phone and walked onto the front porch, dialing Troy's number again. No answer. But wait! I thought I heard a phone ringing in the yard. Peering through the glare of the porch and yard lights, I saw movement.

"You didn't think I would miss our first New Year's Eve together, did you?"

"Troy!" I leapt from the porch and into his arms. "What happened?"

"It's been quite an adventure. I'll tell you all about it later, but right now it's almost midnight, and we have some celebrating to do." He led me into the house and found the caterers passing out champagne. Everyone gathered around the television watching the ball begin to drop in New York. Then the countdown began. 10–9–8–7–6–5–4–Troy didn't wait. He grabbed me and kissed me with more passion than I'd ever experienced. The celebrating went on but faded into obscurity as I closed my eyes and dissolved into Troy's arms.

Saturday, January 1, 1:30 *a.m.*—

I arrived at the millhouse and headed for the kitchen to brew coffee. Troy was following close behind in his rental car. With all the revelry at the party, there'd been no opportunity to discuss Troy's delayed flight, and my curiosity wasn't going to let me rest. No matter how long the day had been, or how long the day ahead would be, we needed to talk.

Lucy had been the first to leave the party and was already in bed in an attempt to get plenty of rest before her wedding. Andrea was spending the night with her Grammy and Gramps at her Auntie Rachel and Uncle Collin's house. Grammy, Gramps, Auntie? These were strange titles for this part of the world. If Andrea had been born and raised in Eastridge, she would simply be calling them Aunt Rachel, Grandmama and Granddaddy.

I heard the car and saw the headlights as Troy arrived. I met him at the front door to keep him from disturbing Lucy by ringing the bell or knocking.

"Coffee is brewing, so come on into the kitchen and tell me about your flight. What on earth happened?"

"You aren't going to believe it. Bree, we were hi-jacked."

"Hi-jacked?"

"That's right. And the worst part is, I think I was their target."

"Why would anyone be after you?"

"Because of my investigation into the espionage. I was too close to finding out the truth, so they wanted to stop me."

"Who is 'they'?"

"I don't have all the facts yet, but thanks to some excellent detective work by the FBI and flight marshals, the hijackers' plan was thwarted, and I believe Mitch will soon be proven innocent."

"Good job! But I want details."

"I know you do, but I'm really exhausted." He rubbed his hands over his face, then looked into my pleading eyes. "Okay. I'll tell you what I know at this point. First, pour me some of that coffee."

I poured the coffee and sat down to listen.

"I told you about the cook and Sal's connection. The next day, I found out who Mitch's attorney is, and he was able to get permission for me to talk to Mitch."

"That's great! How is he doing?"

"He's doing better than I would have expected. He has so much faith that things will work out the way they are meant to be."

"Was he able to tell you anything?"

"He said Sal was an undercover agent. He was killed because these thugs found out he was an agent."

"So your theory was all wrong?"

"Not totally. I was right about Sal manipulating Mitch to live with him and work at the restaurant, but it was to protect him."

"So the cook and Sal weren't connected?"

"Yes, they were. Sal was working undercover. He pretended to be working with Luigi and Jacques to obtain government secrets so he could take them down when they actually committed the crime."

My curiosity about the nature of the government secrets nagged at me. "I've been thinking about why Mitch thought I was too inquisitive and might stick my nose in where it didn't belong. The only thing I asked a lot of questions about was the UFO stuff. He got so bothered about the news report on UFOs. Then there was that schematic drawing of a UFO in the conference room where he works. He got really upset when I asked him about that. It seems obvious to me that the top secret project had something to do with flying saucers."

"That wouldn't surprise me. I wonder, though, what they know about them that they're not telling us."

"Tell me about the hi-jacking. Was anyone hurt?"

Troy related to me how the plane went dark and one of the hi-jackers held a knife to his throat.

The realization of how close I'd come to losing him frightened me. "So what happened? How did you get free?"

"Luckily, there were several plain-clothes detectives on board. Since this was a New Year's Eve flight, there were the two flight marshals normally assigned as standard procedure, plus an additional two were added for the holiday flight. Two government agents were also on board because they had a tip that there could be trouble. The six of them were able to overpower the four hi-jackers. The pilot landed in Knoxville, Tennessee, and after I told the officials everything I knew and practically promised them my firstborn, I talked them into allowing me to leave. I took the next flight and drove like a maniac from the airport to get here before midnight."

I looked into his tired eyes and smiled.

"Now can I go to sleep?" he begged.

I chuckled. "Yes, let's both get some sleep. I'll get you a pillow and blanket, unless you want to sleep in Andrea's youth bed?"

"No thanks, I'll take the sofa. I don't think these long legs will fit in her bed. Besides, the sofa is about as far as I can walk." He stood and shuffled across the room.

By the time I returned with the pillow and blanket, he was already asleep.

Chapter 21

The late morning wedding was perfect. Lucy was surprisingly calm, Andrea sprinkled her flower petals like a pro, and Paul behaved himself. I was amazed how smoothly everything fell into place after only one disorganized night of rehearsal. Because of the elaborate festivities the night before, the bride and groom opted for a quiet and relaxing catered luncheon in the church fellowship hall following the wedding ceremony, after which the happy couple left the church in style in a rented carriage pulled by two white horses.

I stood on the church steps watching the carriage depart, the horses' hooves clip-clopping on the paved road. When it disappeared over a hill, I looked to the slightly overcast sky. Two jets had left their vapor trails in the shape of a perfect cross. The sun peeked through white-edged gray clouds at the point where the two vapor lines intersected, causing a glowing halo. It was an amazing sight, and I wondered if there was a message for me in there somewhere. Was God trying to tell me something? I'd heard stories about Jesus returning, but I certainly wasn't ready for that. My life with Troy was finally on track, and I didn't want anything messing that up.

Walking back into the church, I saw Troy sitting on the front pew looking at the stained-glass windows. Each window depicted a scene from the life of Jesus: his birth, his baptism, his teaching, his praying, his crucifixion, and his resurrection.

I sat beside him. "They're beautiful, aren't they?"

"Yes, they are, but that's my favorite." He indicated the image of the resurrection.

"Why is that your favorite?"

"Because even though it represents the resurrection, it could also be interpreted as the Second Coming."

Lucy's ridiculous comment about Jesus returning on a UFO entered my mind. "Maybe he'll arrive on a flying saucer," I quipped to lighten the mood, but only received a half-hearted smile from him. He obviously didn't get my joke, so I changed my tone. "It's a coincidence that you mentioned Jesus coming back. While I was outside, I was thinking about it, but I'm not ready for that. You and I have finally got a life together. I'm not ready to give that up." I thought it was a romantic thing to say, but he looked shocked rather than pleased.

He looked away, then turned back to me and stared into my eyes, his expression much too serious. "Bree, are you a Christian?"

"What kind of a question is that? You know I was raised in the church."

"Yes, but that doesn't make you a Christian."

"If you're asking if I believe in Jesus, then the answer is yes."

"Even Satan believes in Jesus, but have you accepted Christ as your Lord and Savior?"

I stood and walked a few steps, flailing my arms. "Why all these questions? What difference does it make? That's between me and God. It's got nothing to do with you and me." I shook my head at him and marched down the aisle and out of the rear door of the church.

Troy watched Brianna storm from the sanctuary. He looked up at the stained-glass window that illustrated Christ on the cross. *It never crossed my mind before that Bree may not be a Christian. I assumed she was. Now what? I love her so much, but if she's not a Christian—Lord Jesus, I don't know what to do.* A Bible verse suddenly came to mind, as if God was speaking to his heart—"Do not be yoked together with unbelievers" (2 Corinthians 6:14 NIV) *Help me, Lord, to know what to do. Give me the right words when talking to her, and I pray that the Holy Spirit might open her eyes to Your truth. May Your will be done. Amen.*

Troy smiled, knowing His problem was already solved. The prayer had been said, and now it was in God's care. He wasn't sure how yet, but God was handling it now.

Momma and Daddy stood in the parking lot, saying goodbye to the last of the guests. "Thank you for coming. Let's get together soon for dinner." They turned and saw me. Walking toward me with Daddy at her heels, Momma glared at me. "Young lady, we need to talk."

"What about?" I was in no mood for a lecture.

"About that young man you saw fit to invite to this wedding. He had no business here. It's one thing for you to run off to New Mexico with him and quite another to allow him to crash your cousin's wedding. What made you do such a thing?"

This wasn't how I'd planned to tell them, but I was in no mood to tiptoe around the subject. Keeping my voice calm, quiet, and steady, I looked them both in the eye. "Okay, Momma and Daddy. You know I love you both very much, and I respect your opinions, but that 'young man' is going to be your son-in-law. So please try to get past this negative attitude and try to get to know him, okay?" I turned and walked away, leaving them in a state of shock.

Still sitting on the front pew, Troy heard the rear door open and turned to see Brianna walking up the aisle toward him.

"Well, that's over with," she remarked.

"What's that?"

"I spilled the news to Momma and Daddy about our engagement."

"How did they take it?"

"I don't know. I didn't stick around to find out."

Sunday, January 2—

I fidgeted with my ring. Why did I let Troy talk me into this?

Troy sat next to me waiting for the morning church service to begin. He looked down at my hands. "I see you're wearing your ring."

"No need to hide it any longer. I'm ready to tell the world of our engagement."

"Thank you for agreeing to come with me today. I've missed too many services in the past five or six months and way too many communions. I want to start the new year off right."

"I hope you know how much I must love you to do this." I glanced around the congregation to see who else was there. It had been a long time since I'd attended a service, but I knew almost everyone in Eastridge so I wasn't among strangers. I saw my parents standing in the doorway. I watched, waiting for them to look my way. Finally, there it was, the inevitable shocked expressions.

To my astonishment, they proceeded toward us, seating themselves next to Troy.

Momma kept her voice low, her eyes focused on the pulpit as she spoke. "Nice to see you here, Troy. Whose idea was it? Yours or Bree's?"

Ever the diplomat, Troy answered, "It was a joint decision, Mrs. Chavis. It's good to see you both here also." He reached over to shake Daddy's hand.

When Daddy took his hand and acted friendly, I shook my head. *What hypocrites. When we leave here, they probably won't even speak to him.*

After the announcements, singing, offering, and communion, the preacher stood to deliver his sermon. He was still for a moment, looking at his notes. Then he picked them up and threw them over his shoulder. "I prepared what I thought was a terrific sermon for this week. I spent hours getting it right and practicing it, but I'm not going to deliver that message today. Instead, I want to talk to you about answering God's call."

I noticed Troy smile and close his eyes for a moment. *This message must mean something special to him. I wonder why*. My curiosity caused me to listen more intently than I might have otherwise. Something stirred within me, making me question where I stood in God's eyes. If I were to die, where would I go? The thought frightened me, and I began to squirm in the pew, wishing the service was over. The sermon wasn't much different from ones I'd heard in the past, but this time the words made sense. I found myself looking at Troy's Bible and actually understanding the words written there. When the invitation hymn was sung, tears welled up in my eyes and I knew God was calling me. I looked at Troy and he smiled, encouraging me to step out. "I'll go with you, if you want me to."

I nodded. Paying no attention to anyone or anything around me, I followed Troy down the aisle to the front of the church. Troy greeted the preacher, "This is Brianna Chavis," and then he stepped aside.

"Yes, I know this young lady." The preacher spoke with a smile, his voice quiet and welcoming. He looked at me, waiting for me to speak.

"I need Jesus as my Savior." I didn't know how else to say it. I was inundated with emotion and unable to speak further due to the tears. So much joy filled me, more passion than I'd believed possible engulfed my entire being, washing over me like a warm blanket of love.

Affirming that I believed Jesus to be the Son of God who had died for my sins, I was then escorted through the doors that led to the baptismal pool and given a robe to change into.

Minutes later, I stood in the water with the preacher. He explained, "Baptism represents the death, burial, and resurrection of Christ. By being immersed in the water, we are buried with Christ, our sins washed away. When we rise from the water, we are resurrected in Christ Jesus and receive the Holy Spirit. Do you understand this?"

I smiled and nodded.

Then he said, "Romans 6:4 says, 'Therefore we are buried with him by baptism into death, that like as Christ was raised up from the dead by the glory of the Father, even so we too should walk in newness of life' (KJV). I now baptize you in the name of the Father, the Son, and the Holy Spirit." He dunked me under the water and raised me back up again. The congregation began singing. I was so euphoric, I thought my heart would soon burst.

I was led from the pool, and there stood Troy, beaming, his arms ready to receive a bear hug.

I laughed. "I'm dripping wet. You'll get your suit soaked."

"I don't care. Come here." Grabbing and hugging me, tears streaming down his face. "Thank you, Lord."

After changing, I walked back into the sanctuary where my parents stood with Troy. Daddy took me into his arms. "How about you and Troy coming back to the house with us for Sunday dinner?"

Amazed at the transformation in myself and in my parents' attitude, I glanced at Troy, who nodded. "Sure. We'd love to."

"Your momma and I figure we might as well get to know our future son-in-law. Let's go eat."

Everyone filed out of the church, but I held back and stood alone in the sanctuary, looking at the pulpit, the chandeliers, the organ and piano, and the stained-glass windows. This church held a very special place in my heart. It's become a big part in my life. First, Lucy's wedding, then my salvation and baptism, and soon my wedding.

Monday, January 3–Washington, D.C.—

It was late in the day when Mitchell was led by the military police into a conference room. There sat his attorney, his commanding officer, Major Bradford, the federal agents he'd worked with in New Mexico, and Troy. Everyone stood when he entered the room. Mitchell snapped to attention and saluted the Major, who smiled, gave him a return salute, and said, "Son, we have a few questions for you."

Still at attention, Mitch replied, "Yes, Sir. Anything, Sir."

He was told to have a seat and the interrogation began.

First, one of the federal agents related the story of the hi-jacking and Troy's involvement in flushing out the men responsible for the theft of top-secret documents. "We suspected these guys, but couldn't get any hard evidence against them. The countries that were purchasing the information from them were also covering their tracks faster than they could lay them down. Until Mr. Garrison decided to initiate his own amateur sleuthing, we couldn't get them to make a mistake. Somehow he was able to get them riled enough to make the big mistake of hi-jacking an airplane, so we got 'em."

Mitchell spoke up. "Were you able to get Jacques Borgman too?"

Silence filled the room and the officials exchanged looks between them. Mitchell's attorney looked down and shook his head.

One of the federal agents questioned, "Sergeant, why would you ask about Mr. Borgman?"

"I know he was involved. You're not going to sit here and tell me he wasn't, are you?"

"No, he was definitely involved. But how long have you known?"

"Almost as long as I've known the guy."

"You were aware this man was a possible security leak and you didn't inform anyone?"

"I had no real proof."

"You still should have informed your superiors so they could have had him investigated and kept him under surveillance."

Eastridge—

Troy was in D.C. visiting Mitchell and then would be returning to the ranch. Paul and Lucy were still on their honeymoon. The clinic telephone hadn't stopped ringing all day. It was a busy cold and flu season, and our patients didn't care that the doctor had a personal life. They wanted relief from their symptoms.

Finally home and exhausted from the holiday activities and my first day back at work, I curled up on the sofa for a relaxing evening of popcorn and television. Looking through the program listings, I found a movie that looked promising and settled in to enjoy a mindless two hours.

At the precise time the movie was scheduled to begin, the familiar annoying ditty networks use before special reports started to play, and the words "Breaking News" flashed onto the screen.

"We interrupt our regular programming for this special report. For the past month we have been reporting on the arrest of Staff Sergeant Mitchell Sibley with the US Air Force for espionage. ABC news has learned the top-secret information that was sold to China and France, and possibly other countries, concerned classified building and testing of flying saucers. It was released today that these experiments have been conducted since the mid 1950s and the US has been using these highly sophisticated air vessels for surveillance for several years. The DIA has been successful in keeping these flying saucers secret from the world until Sergeant Sibley allegedly began selling highly classified schematic drawings to operatives in France and China.

"The hi-jacking of an East-Air flight last Friday, December 31, proved to be a blessing for Sergeant Sibley."

Pictures of the hi-jackers and Jacques Borgman appeared on the screen.

"Rather than sticking to their flawless plan to procure documents and sell them to other countries, who in turn made sure they were protected, these men developed personal vendettas and decided to take matters into their own hands. They purportedly succeeded in murdering one federal agent, Agent Salvatore Montano, after discovering he was working undercover to expose them. They hi-jacked East-Air Flight 689 when they realized they were being watched by the CIA and would probably not be allowed to leave the country. They chose that particular flight in order to terrorize, and possibly murder, Troy Garrison, who had been engaging in an amateur investigation to prove Sergeant Sibley innocent. The hi-jackers had not counted on there being as many as six air marshals and federal agents on board that New Year's Eve flight.

"Tune in tomorrow night at 7:00 for *The Truth About UFOs.* Our news team will take an in-depth look at how the US government has been able to deceive the American people. We now join our regularly scheduled program already in progress."

I clicked off the television and dialed Troy's cell phone.

"Hi, Bree." He'd recognized my number on his caller ID.

"Hi. Where are you?"

"Leaving the El Paso airport and headed home to the ranch."

"Were you able to see Mitch?"

"Oh, yes. I saw him, along with a room full of officials. I was allowed to sit in on the meeting when they told Mitch about the hi-jacking, among other things."

"Will they be letting him out of prison now?"

"No. Although he is innocent of espionage, he is guilty of not disclosing his knowledge of Jacques and Luigi's involvement. He figured out what they were up to, but kept his mouth shut, hoping to talk them out of doing anything with the information. As an officer in the service, that's dereliction in the performance of duties. They could possibly add 'communicating and aiding the enemy' to his charges, which would be a lot more serious. They haven't determined the extent of his punishment yet, but he could be court-martialed."

My heart ached for Mitchell. Although he'd only joined the military to get his education, a court-martial would still be degrading for him.

Troy continued. "And he might have to serve several years in federal prison."

"Oh no! How long?"

"That hasn't been decided yet. He still has to go to trial, but he sat in that meeting today and confessed. I don't know how the attorney will be able to get him out of that one."

"The news media is all over this. Did you know the secrets that were sold were concerning aircraft the Air Force has been building and testing? Flying saucers?"

"They didn't say anything about it at the meeting, but I've suspected that might be the case. Mitch has made a few comments to me that led me to believe the UFO I saw was actually a military prototype. That's why I didn't get too excited."

"I wondered how you could be so laid back about it."

Our conversation changed to chit chat about my day at work and his uneventful flight home, for which he was grateful.

As soon as I hung up, Lucy called. "Hi, Bree. How are things there?"

It was good to hear her cheerful voice. "Fine. How's the honeymoon?"

"Fabulous! We're having a terrific time, but now we

need to get home so we can find a place to live. His place is too small for the three of us."

"Why don't you live here? I'm going to be moving to New Mexico after the wedding."

"Wedding?"

"That's right." I looked at my ring. "Troy proposed Christmas, but I didn't let anyone know until after your wedding. I knew Momma and Daddy were definitely not going to be happy about it, and I didn't want to spoil your day."

"Oh, Bree, I'm so happy for you! Tell me, how did your parents take the news, or have you told them yet?"

"Believe it or not, they are fine with it now. Since I was baptized, my entire life has fallen into place."

"You were baptized too? I've only been gone two days. You sure work fast, girl."

"Have you heard the news, or have you been too occupied to watch TV?" I teased.

"Yes, I've been a little occupied, and no, I haven't heard any news. What's up?"

"It turns out that the UFOs everyone's been seeing actually belong to the US Air Force. They are experimental aircraft our country has been developing for years. That's the top-secret information Mitch was accused of selling to other countries."

"So you're telling me that UFOs aren't from outer space?"

"No, I'm afraid not."

"Bummer! That sure takes the fun out of things. Let's not tell Andrea just yet. Let her keep believing for a while, just like Santa."

Saturday, February 12–Eastridge—

I stood in the back of the church scanning the guests in the pews. The stained-glass windows caught my eye as the sunlight made them glow, emulating the vision of hope I felt for my future with Troy. Taking a deep breath, I watched my bridesmaids, Sheila and Gina, and Lucy as my matron-of-honor, gliding down the aisle to the front of the church. The music reached a crescendo and the organist began the *Wedding March*. My heart raced.

Daddy stood beside me and smiled. "Are you ready?"

I nodded, and we began the slow procession down the aisle, me clinging to his arm.

In front of me stood the preacher with Troy. When my gaze met Troy's, my nervousness subsided, replaced by peace and calm.

Next to him stood Mitchell, his mischievous grin spreading across his entire face. *Thank you, Lord, for allowing him to be here today.*

Andrea and Manuel, having already completed their duties as flower girl and ring bearer, stood watching me approach. Both children were stiff and scared, aware of all the eyes watching them.

After giving me away, my father joined Momma, Aunt Marty, and Grandpa Raymond in the front pew.

The ceremony was simple, but elegant, and over much too quickly.

In the rear of the church stood two MPs waiting to escort Mitchell back to confinement the minute he'd completed his duties as best man. Although their presence caused whispering and gossip among the guests, it was worth it to me and Troy to have Mitchell attend.

The reception was another Chavis extravaganza, every detail planned by my mother. Since Momma was in her element when planning parties, I'd left that chore to her, thankful she was once again in perfect health and taking on the world in true Rachel Chavis fashion.

Gina sat alone in the corner watching Brianna and Troy dance their first dance as man and wife, but her mind was on Mitchell. He'd been allowed to spend time with her before the wedding in one of the back rooms of the church, under the pretense she was helping him with his tie and cummerbund. He'd assured her of his imminent release in a few days. She should have been ecstatic, but a huge decision had to be made before he arrived home, one that would alter her life forever. *Do I have the courage to do as he asked?*

Riding in the limousine to the airport, Troy looked at me, his eyes filled with love and caring. "I'm sorry we can't have a honeymoon right now. I promise we'll take a cruise or something soon. You do understand, don't you?"

"Of course I do. I don't need a honeymoon. Being at the ranch with you is as perfect as life gets."

Behind us was a procession of cars, honking horns. All but one ceased to follow after a couple of blocks. In the car remaining were Sheila, Joe, Manuel, and Gina, who would be joining us on our flight back to New Mexico.

My thoughts were on Mitchell. "I wish Mitch was coming back with us."

"Me too, but because of his willingness to cooperate with the authorities by telling all he knows, at least they allowed him to attend the wedding."

"I never dreamed when I left here last May for a simple vacation that I'd get entangled in an espionage ring."

"Or a wedding ring." Troy lifted my left hand and kissed my ring finger. "So tell me, Mrs. Garrison, are all your loose ends tied up in Eastridge so you can become my full-time wife and partner?"

"Yes, Mr. Garrison, I believe so. Paul was able to hire a nurse, and I trained Lucy to help in the office, so the clinic is in good hands. Momma is healthy and about to become the sole proprietor of Milliken Fashions, so she's going to have her hands full. Other than visiting Eastridge now and then, I'm all yours."

Wednesday, February 16*–New Mexico—*

There was an entirely new profession for me to learn, managing a ranch. It was a lot more involved than I'd ever imagined, and I swiftly realized I wasn't on vacation anymore. In three days' time, I managed to get acquainted with the filing system, accounts payable and receivable, payroll for the hired hands, and discovered I had a lot to learn about horses and the horse-trade business.

My head buried in research, the quietness of the mid-day siesta time was interrupted by yelling and the constant blaring of a car horn. Everyone roused from their lounging and ran outside to see what the commotion was all about.

Mitchell's old beat-up station wagon came to a halt in the driveway. Gina and Mitchell stepped from the car, their faces aglow with smiles and laughter.

Troy and I ran to greet them with hugs and kisses. "You're out for good?"

Mitchell beamed. "Thanks to the two of you. If you hadn't persisted in proving my innocence, I'd have been dishonorably discharged and possibly imprisoned for a long time."

Troy shook his head. "I couldn't let you take the rap for something I knew you didn't do."

The February air was much too cold for us to be standing outside. I started back into the house. "Come on in and make yourselves comfortable. I'll get the coffee pot going."

We all gathered around the kitchen table as Troy continued the conversation. "What happened to the dereliction of duty charges?"

"The punishment for that charge is forfeiture of two-thirds pay per month for three months and confinement for three months. I served my time. Then they found Sal's reports for his undercover work. In them he noted that he'd told me to remain quiet about my suspicions for the good of the investigation. Since he was a Colonel, he was my superior, so I was following direct orders."

"Unbelievable," said Troy. "What are they doing about the fact that you served time and lost pay for something you didn't do?"

"They're reimbursing me for the pay. There's not much they can do about the time served, but at least they dropped the aiding-the-enemy charges."

There were so many things I still didn't understand. "Mitch, how could they hold you for so long when you hadn't been convicted of anything?"

"The rules of confinement say if they believe an offense triable by a court-martial has been committed, they can apprehend the suspected individual. They can confine him if it is deemed necessary to prevent him from engaging in serious criminal misconduct, or in this case, espionage. It was believed that I posed a serious threat to national security, so they had the legal right to keep me confined."

"What about Jacques?"

"They're sure Jacques murdered Sal and orchestrated the hi-jacking of the East-Air flight, but he's being safe-harbored by the French government. Since our government doesn't have any hard evidence to prove he did it, they can't force the issue. They did capture Luigi though. He'll be behind bars for a long time. It turns out that although he was from Italy, he is a US citizen, so he could get the full penalty for espionage."

I glanced at Troy. His mind was obviously not on the conversation. "Troy, are you okay?"

He frowned. "Mitch, I need to know something. I don't know if you can discuss this or not, but it concerns those flying saucers."

"There's not much secret about them anymore, so what do you want to know?"

"As you know, I've seen two of them. Both times there

was a peaceful, hypnotic trance that came over me. Can you explain that?"

Mitchell's smile faded. "I'm sorry, but that's one of the few things about this that is still classified."

"So it wasn't my imagination?"

"Maybe. Maybe not." There was a twinkle in Mitchell's eye. "I can't be specific, but I will tell you this much. You know about the e-bombs, right?"

"A little."

I knew nothing about them and wasn't about to be left in the dark. "Wait, I don't know anything about e-bombs, so can you bring me up to speed here?"

Mitchell looked around at each person in the room, his gaze finally resting on me. Affection seemed to spill from his eyes as he smiled. "I'll try to explain it as best I can." He stared at the table before beginning his explanation as if getting his thoughts in order. "E-bombs emit electromagnetic pulses. Low-level pulses could temporarily jam electronics systems. More intense pulses could corrupt important computer data, and very powerful bursts could completely fry electric and electronic equipment."

Troy took control of the conversation. "So you can see how this type of weapon could instantly bring modern life to a screeching halt. Although there would be survivors, they would find themselves completely helpless because these e-bombs could neutralize vehicle control systems, targeting systems on missiles and bombs, communication systems, navigation systems, and long and short-range sensor systems, causing a huge psychological impact on an entire nation."

The magnitude of the damage that could be done with these weapons without causing bodily harm was mind-boggling to me. "So is that how these flying saucers work? Do they emit the same kind of electromagnetic pulses?"

Mitch shook his head. "No, but the principal of causing damage without killing is the same. The flying saucers, as you call them, 'kill the enemy with kindness,' so to speak. By mesmerizing everyone, or placing them in a hypnotic state, these aircraft can prevent them from performing their duties. They feel completely at peace, yet are incapable of any motor skills. Once the saucer leaves, they can proceed with their lives as if nothing happened. No innocent people are harmed, yet while they are immobilized, the troops can obliterate the enemy in whatever way they see fit."

"Why aren't the troops hypnotized?"

"There is a sort of antidote that prevents one from being affected."

Gina, who had been quietly listening to everything, now spoke up. "Can we please change the subject now?"

Mitchell looked at Troy, then at me, and shrugged. "I've told you about all I know on this subject."

Troy turned to Gina. "Okay, Gina, what do you want to talk about?"

A smile big as all of Texas spread across her face. "I think it's time to forget about the past few months and begin lookin' forward." She looked at me. "Now that you two have all this weddin' experience, let's put it to good use. Are you up for planning another weddin'?"

Saturday, March 12–Alamogordo—

Mitchell and Gina opted for a small, quaint ceremony in her parents' backyard by the swimming pool, so there wasn't much planning to be done. No one was invited except Troy and me, Gina's parents, and the preacher. There was no reception because their plane was leaving for their honeymoon an hour after the ceremony.

When they walked to the car, Mitchell turned to me with tears in his eyes. "You two have been the best friends a guy could ever have. Take good care of each other."

"We will, but you don't need to be so serious. You make it sound as if you're never coming back." I searched his face for answers.

Mitchell grabbed me and gave me one of his wonderful bear hugs. "I'm being a little overly sentimental. I want you to know how much I love both of you."

Troy slapped him on the back. Mitch released me and turned, giving Troy a hug while I hugged Gina. When I looked into Gina's eyes, I saw the same look I'd seen in Mitchell's, but I couldn't quite read what it meant. As their car pulled away and we waved goodbye, I had the uneasy feeling I may never see them again.

Five hours later…

Mitchell and Gina looked through the airplane window, watching the United States coastline become more and more distant. "Gina, say goodbye to your old life. We're headed for the big time now, baby."

Gina grabbed his hand and grinned. “I can’t believe we’re doing this.” Leaning her head back on the seat, she whispered, “France, here we come.”

Sunday, March 13–Paris—

Entering the magnificent marble foyer of one of the finest hotels in the Left Bank of Paris, Mitchell and Gina began searching for the room number they’d been given. They knocked, their hearts pounding with anticipation.

The door opened, and there stood their partner-in-crime. Mitchell grinned and grabbed the man’s hand. “Jacques, my man, we did it.”

“Shh.” Jacques glanced up and down the hallway. “Come in, my friends, where we can talk more discreetly.”

After closing the door, Jacques reminded them, “Please do not refer to me as Jacques. You must remember my name is now André Sommer.” Handing Mitchell and Gina new passports, he added, “And you are now Francois and Colette Pierpont.”

Gina giggled. “I guess I better lose my southern accent and improve my French.”

“That might be a good idea,” Mitchell agreed, as he placed his arm around her shoulders and gave her a slight squeeze. “We’ll work on that together.”

He turned back to Jacques, now known as André. “I do feel awful about Luigi.”

“You shouldn’t. I did a background check on him. He should have been put away in prison years ago. He only went to America to get away from the law in Italy. He was a mafiosa with the Camorra clan and was also involved with the Ndrangheta, so there's no telling what kinds of crimes he has committed." He reached into a drawer and pulled out official-looking documents. "Your money has already been deposited in your new accounts. Your bank account information is in the pocket of your passports. Our French government is pleased you have decided to become French citizens. Welcome to France."

Mitchell stood looking down at the passports. "Jacques, I mean André, what happened to Sal? I thought no one was supposed to get hurt."

"That was unfortunate but couldn't be helped. He tried to be a hero and pulled a gun on one of my guys. It was either him or us."

Mitchell glanced at Gina and saw the lone tear stream down her cheek. "Are you okay?"

"I'll be fine. It's going to be difficult to never see my family again. This new identity idea is going to be a lot harder than I thought."

"You'll get used to it. I know you haven't had much time to adjust to the situation. I've been planning this for a long time, knowing I'd either end up in prison or a very rich Frenchman, but you had no idea what you were in for until a few weeks ago. I was surprised, but relieved, when you decided to come with me."

"How could I refuse? On the one hand, I could have a restaurant running me ragged, or on the other hand, I could have the love of my life and several million dollars. Some choice!"

God's Plan of Salvation

(All of the following verses are from the NIV translation)

Hear

Romans 10:17 Consequently, faith comes from hearing the message, and the message is heard through the word of Christ.

Believe

Mark 16:16 Whoever believes and is baptized, will be saved, but whoever does not believe will be condemned.

Repent

Luke 13:3 I tell you no! But unless you repent, you too will all perish.

Confess

Romans 10:9 That if you confess with your mouth, "Jesus is Lord," and believe in your heart that God raised him from the dead, you will be saved.

Baptism

Acts 2:38–39 Peter replied, "Repent and be baptized, every one of you, in the name of Jesus Christ for the forgiveness of your sins. And you will receive the gift of the Holy Spirit. The promise is for you and your children and for all who are far off—for all whom the Lord our God will call."

Faithfulness

1 *Corinthians* 15:58 Therefore, my dear brothers, stand firm. Let nothing move you. Always give yourself fully to the work of the Lord, because you know that your labor in the Lord is not in vain.

Be Steadfast

Colossians 1:22–23 But now he has reconciled you by Christ's physical body through death to present you holy in his sight, without blemish and free from accusation—if you continue in your faith, established and firm, not moved from the hope held out in the gospel.

Note from the Author

Dear Reader,

Thank you for reading *Air of Truth.* I hope it lived up to your expectations. If so, I'd like to encourage you to read its forerunner, *Heir of Deception*, if you haven't already done so.

I love hearing from my readers. To contact me or find out more about my world and my books, visit my website at www.liggan.net.

If you know of a writers group, book club, or other organization that would enjoy a presentation, please keep me in mind. I am available for speaking engagements or writing workshops.

Also, if you have any questions concerning the plan of salvation presented within these pages, please feel free to contact me.

Thank you.
May God richly bless you and yours,
Joanne Liggan

www.liggan.net
jliggan@comcast.net

2 *Corinthians* 13:11,14 *(*NIV*)*—

“Finally, brothers, good-by. Aim for perfection, listen to my appeal, be of one mind, live in peace. And the God of love and peace will be with you…May the grace of the Lord Jesus Christ, and the love of God, and the fellowship of the Holy Spirit be with you all.”

Now working on her third novel, Joanne Liggan is a public speaker and member of the the Virginia Writers Club Speakers Bureau and their Board of Governors. In her quest to encourage other writers, she also teaches writing courses and is the founder of the Hanover Writers Club and the annual Hanover Book Festival event. In her other life, Joanne is the office manager for her husband's construction company, a realtor, and the manager and lead vocalist for her classic rock band, *Hearts Afire*. In her spare time, she enjoys spending time at her Mechanicsville, Virginia, home with her husband, three daughters, four grandchildren, her parents, her cat, and three dogs. She praises God for filling her life with so many wonderful blessings.